LOVE IN THE TIME OF BERTIE

Other titles in the *44 Scotland Street* series

ALEXANDER McCALL SMITH

LOVE IN THE TIME OF BERTIE

A 44 Scotland Street Novel

First published in Great Britain in 2021 by
Polygon, an imprint of Birlinn Ltd

West Newington House
10 Newington Road
Edinburgh
EH9 1QS

www.polygonbooks.co.uk

9 8 7 6 5 4 3 2 1

ISBN 978 1 84697 572 1

British Library Cataloguing-in-Publication Data
A catalogue record for this book is available on
request from the British Library.

Typeset by Studio Monachino
Printed and bound by Clays Ltd, Eliograf S.p.A.

This book is for my good friend, Alistair Kerr

1

Belgian Shoes

Angus Lordie, portrait painter, citizen of Edinburgh, husband of Domenica Macdonald and owner (custodian, perhaps, according to modern sensibilities) of Cyril, the only dog in Scotland to have a gold tooth; *that* Angus Lordie stood in a room of his flat at 44 Scotland Street, wondering what to wear.

All the clothing he possessed was either hanging from a number of wooden hangers or was neatly folded and stacked away in a series of drawers within a large wardrobe, called in the second-hand trade, *brown furniture*. Nobody, apparently, wanted brown furniture any longer, as it was considered too cumbersome, not to say too dull, for contemporary tastes. If the Scottish diet had become Mediterranean, then Scottish furniture had become Scandinavian – light and minimalist, consigned to its owners in flat boxes and requiring to be assembled before use – and then reassembled, once the instruction booklet had been read. This was the very opposite of Angus Lordie's wardrobe, as gloriously over-engineered, in its way, as the Forth Railway Bridge, and of similar vintage.

This wardrobe consisted of a series of drawers in which Angus kept what he called his *accoutrements*: his shirts and socks, handkerchiefs, ties, vests and so on, while jackets and trousers were hung from a railing on the opposite side. His kilt, along with his sporran, hose, kilt pin and *sgian dubh*, were also in one of the drawers, protected, ineffectively, by moth-repelling balls of cedar.

He had two suits – a dark one that had been made for him twenty-two years ago and that was described by Domenica as his *kirk* suit, and a three-piece, tweedy outfit that Domenica had disparagingly labelled his *bookie's suit*. Neither of these descriptions was entirely helpful: the kirk suit was well-made and discreet, rather than Calvinist; the bookie's suit was not in the least bit flashy, being made of Harris tweed and designed to withstand Hebridean weather – the horizontal rain and Atlantic gusts that beset the West of Scotland, and the North, South, and East for that matter. There was nothing wrong with these suits, although Angus seldom wore them. Suits, he thought, might be going the way of men's hats and ties – both of which were now seen only infrequently on any man under forty. This was a matter of regret, Angus felt, even if he himself was doing nothing to stem that particular tide of fashion.

Alongside the suits were hung four jackets, all of them in frequent use. Two of these were linen, and formed the core of his summer garb, while the others were of an unidentified fabric that Angus referred to as one hundred per cent unnatural. They were comfortable enough, though, and went with virtually anything, but particularly with the crushed strawberry corduroy trousers by which Angus signalled his status as a resident of the Georgian New Town, as a member of the Scottish Arts Club, and as a man of artistic bent. If these trousers raised eyebrows amongst the ranks of the staid, then Angus did not care in the slightest. There was no fixed ordinance stipulating that men should wear sober trousers: fund managers, lawyers and accountants could dress in grey and black if they wished – he, as an artist, preferred something livelier.

On the floor of the wardrobe was the shoe rack on which Angus kept shoes other than those in regular use. His regular shoes – described by Domenica as his *daily boots* – were a pair of brown brogues made by the Northampton shoemaker, Joseph Cheaney. English shoes, Angus maintained, were second to none. They may not be as elegant as Italian footwear, but Italian shoes would never stand the rigours of Scottish conditions. English shoes were made to last; they were modest, often understated, and they were, above all else, *honest* shoes. That quality of honesty was difficult to define – in shoes at least – but one knew it when one encountered it. That was why English shoes were still sought after when everything else, as far as Angus could see, was being made in distant, unspecified workshops. *Designed in X and made in Y . . .* Angus had never fallen for that particular attempt to sugar the pill of local deindustrialisation and the deskilling that went with it.

The English shoes of which he was proudest were a pair of black brogues, made of soft and supple leather, and bought by his father from the London firm of John Lobb. Lobb made shoes to measure, and while Angus could not afford the expense of bespoke shoes – the price tag ran effortlessly into thousands – his father, a Perthshire sheep farmer, had been able to do so after a particularly good season at the Lanark stock sales. His prize Scottish Blackface tup, Walter of Glenartney, renowned for his noble bearing, his fine Roman nose, and his contempt for lesser sheep, had broken all sales records and had provided him with the funds to order a pair of Lobb shoes.

By great good fortune, Angus and his father had near-identical feet, and when Angus left school, his father passed his shoes on to him. Angus accepted the gift with a degree of concealed embarrassment: at the age of eighteen, when one is busy shaking off parental influence, who wants a pair of bespoke Lobb shoes? At the Edinburgh College of Art at the time, shoes were being worn, of course, but these shoes were *concepts* or *statements*, rather than shoes *simpliciter*. So Angus relegated the Lobb brogues to a cupboard and wore, instead, a pair of Hush Puppies of tobacco-coloured suede, threaded with red laces – a touch that met with the wholehearted approval of his fellow students. "Radical," they said – high praise in those innocent days.

At a crucial stage in life – somewhere in one's mid-thirties – the merits of well-made shoes dawn on one, and that was what happened to Angus. He wore the shoes to his father's funeral, and as he and farming neighbours carried him to his final rest, a tear fell from Angus's eye onto the cap of one of the shoes. Not every man, he thought, will live to see such a thing: his tears falling onto a shoe into which he had, both metaphorically and otherwise, stepped.

Alongside the Lobb shoes, in as complete a contrast as could be imagined, was a pair of Belgian shoes, those light-weight, indoor shoes that are made only in Belgium and are completely unsuitable for active use. Angus had been given these by Domenica, whose eye had been caught by them on a trip to London.

"You can't wear them out of doors," she said, as she presented him with them. "The Belgians, it would seem, don't get out much."

Angus smiled. "How *drôle*," he said.

Domenica accepted the compliment with an inclination of her head. "Belgium is a bit of a mystery to me," she said. "I don't feel I've ever really *grasped* it, if you see what I mean."*

---

*Angus Lordie, it may be remembered, was the author of the hymn *God Looks Down on Belgium*, the first verse of which is: *God's never heard of Belgium/ But loves it just the same;/For God is kind and doesn't mind/ He's not impressed by fame.*

2

Galileo, Orthodoxy, Dinner

Angus was choosing his clothes for a specific purpose – he and Domenica had been invited by Matthew and Elspeth to have dinner at Nine Mile Burn. Matthew had stressed that it would be a casual evening – "kitchen supper", as he put it – but even so, Angus wanted to make an effort in order to show that he appreciated the invitation.

"People like you to dress up a bit," he said. "It shows that you regard them as worth the trouble."

Domenica was in complete agreement. As an anthropologist, she understood the significance of uniform, and of the way in which clothing sent signals. "When I go to my dentist," she had once remarked to Angus, "I expect to find him in one of those natty blue jackets with buttons down the side. Such outfits reassure those facing the drill."

Angus nodded. "And pilots should wear blue uniforms with a bit of gold braid. That, too, is reassuring. I would not feel confident if I boarded a plane to find the pilot wearing jeans with rips in the knees."

Domenica rolled her eyes. "Rips in the knees! Have you ever worked out what's going on there, Angus?"

He shook his head. "It's very fashionable. You buy them with the rips ready-made. It's most peculiar."

"Perhaps it signals indifference to formality," suggested Domenica. "Rips proclaim that you don't care about being smart."

"And that you're not ashamed of your knees," added Angus. "Rips say: I don't mind if you see my knees."

Domenica looked thoughtful. "Are the knees an erogenous zone?"

Angus was not sure. "I've never been attracted to knees myself," he said. "But there may be some who are." He was not sure whether gallantry required him to say something here about the attractiveness of Domenica's knees, but he decided to say nothing. Anybody could tell the difference between sincerity and insincerity when it came to comments about their knees.

Domenica did not seem interested in pursuing the subject of knees, as she now asked, "What about trousers that hang down low, and display the wearer's underpants? I saw a young man at Waverley Station once who was wearing trousers with the crotch roughly level with his knees. He was finding it very difficult to walk. He did a sort of penguin waddle."

"Another statement," said Angus. "But I'm with the prudes on that one, I'm afraid: underpants are definitely private. Exhibitionists may not agree, of course."

Now, as Angus reflected on what he was to wear to Matthew and Elspeth's dinner party, Domenica had already changed into her favourite trouser-suit that she found fitted the bill for just about every occasion except those specifying evening dress. And she had few such invitations, she thought, with a momentary regret. Her full-length dress, with its optional tartan sash, lay folded away, and she had no idea when it would next be needed.

While Angus chose between his two linen jackets, she stood before the window from which, by craning one's neck, one might look up towards Drummond Place Garden, which were touched at that moment – it was six o'clock – by summer evening light. She was not looking in that direction, though, but was gazing, rather, at a patch of empty blue sky. She was contemplating something that she had put off thinking about until that very moment – a request to write a letter that she did not want to write.

Domenica still considered herself to be a practising anthropologist. She held no institutional position – and had not done so for some years – being one of those rare *private scholars* who pursue their subject without the comfortable safety-net of an academic salary. It was not easy being a private scholar: for one thing, you had to overcome a certain scepticism rooted in people's assumption that if you were any good you would have a university post. Why, after all, do research for nothing when there were institutions that would pay you to do the exact same work, give you grants to attend conferences in exotic places, and, if you stayed the course, dignify you with a professorial title?

The private scholar also had to put up with the condescension of those holding academic positions. When applying for research grants from public bodies, he or she had to write *none* in that part of the form that demanded disclosure of institutional affiliation. It was a statement of independence, but one that had long borne considerable risks. And yet the private scholar was now being recognised as being of increasing importance, for all this marginality. In an age of intellectual conformity, the private scholar could ask questions that probed received ideas. That was what Galileo had done, and yet there was no room for contemporary Galileos, it seemed. If those who called the tune, which now meant those who could shout loudest, said that the sun revolved around the earth, then the sun really *did* behave in that way, and it was no use echoing Galileo's *eppur si muove* – *and yet it moves*.

She sighed. It was precisely because she was a private scholar that they had written to her and asked for a letter. She would have to respond, although not just yet. She would do that tomorrow, for now they were about to go out to dinner and there were other things to think about.

And one of these was what Bertie was up to, because there was the small boy from the flat below, leaving the front door of No. 44, accompanied by his grandmother, Nicola, and that spindly-legged little friend of his, Ranald Braveheart Macpherson. They paused briefly, as Nicola bent down to say something to the two boys, and then continued their way up the sharply sloping street.

Angus came into the room and stood behind her.

"I've decided not to wear a tie," he said. "Matthew won't be wearing one – not in his kitchen. But I'm going to wear this jacket, I think."

She did not look round. She knew his clothes off by heart. One day she would replace them, lock, stock, and barrel. She would buy him an entirely new wardrobe and throw out those two dreadful suits and those threadbare jackets. Wives had to do that sort of thing from time to time, as that was the only way husbands could be kept looking vaguely presentable.

Then Angus said, "I'm going to take Cyril for a quick walk around the Garden. Then I think we should think of setting off for Nine Mile Burn."

Domenica nodded, without turning round. "I see that Nicola has had the same idea with the boys," she said. "Boys are just like dogs, don't you think, Angus? They need to be exercised."

Angus laughed. "Possibly," he said.

3

The Terraces of Purgatory

With Cyril straining at the leash, Angus made his way up Scotland Street towards Drummond Place.

"You don't have to be quite so impatient," Angus said to Cyril. "*Festina lente*, remember . . ."

Cyril looked up briefly, but then leaned forward with renewed enthusiasm. He was aware that Angus had addressed him, but there were none of the words that he recognised, his vocabulary being a poor bag of words such as *wall* and *biscuits* and *sit*; and, of course, he had no Latin to speak of. The limited range of canine understanding, though, does not stop people from talking at considerable length to their dogs – a fact which had always amused Angus, even if he himself did exactly that with Cyril. The day before he had overheard a woman in the Garden berating her West Highland terrier at length for his over-exuberant behaviour.

"You really need to bark less, Douglas," she admonished. "There's no point in barking at chimeras, is there? Don't you understand that?"

Angus, who was walking past her at the time, almost stopped to answer that question for her. "He doesn't, I'm afraid," he might have said. "Or perhaps try him in Gaelic."

And yet dog owners persisted in these long one-sided conversations as if the dog really did grasp what they were saying, some even enunciating their words particularly carefully in order to give the animal every chance to get what was being said.

But here he was doing it himself, as he unselfconsciously

remarked to Cyril, "It's a very nice evening, don't you think, Cyril?"

Cyril looked up at him again, and then continued to pull on his leash. His world was one of smells, delectable and tantalising, rather than sounds, and he was picking up intriguing hints of what lay ahead. There was something dead somewhere – a rat probably – and a discarded, half-eaten ham sandwich further up wind. And seagulls – an acrid, annoying scent he did not like at all. And car fumes. And squirrels somewhere or other – an infuriating scent because they always got away. And what was that? Cat? That was an outrage, pure and simple, a challenge that could not be ignored. He would get that cat one day. He would teach it to be superior. He would teach it about arrogance. There was no place for cats in the new Scotland, thought Cyril . . .

They reached the gate to the garden and here Angus extracted the key from his pocket. A key to Drummond Place Garden was highly sought-after in the area, as the garden was private, and access to it was a constantly contested matter. Those with a Drummond Place address had a clear right to a key, as long as they paid their share of the upkeep charge, but the occupants of flats just a few doors away, in Dundonald Street or Scotland Street, were ineligible. That had been long settled, after lengthy internecine struggles, but what about those who lived in one of the surrounding streets, but who had a window overlooking Drummond Place? Dante, contemplating the terraces of Purgatory, might have addressed just such a question of boundaries, but even he – or Solomon, perhaps – might not have reached a decision that was acceptable to all, and there were many who were disappointed at not being able to avail themselves of the garden.

Angus had a key by the application of the overlooking window rule, and the same applied to Bertie's parents. So Angus and Cyril frequently came across Bertie in the garden, just as he met other local residents, such as the Italian socialite nun, Sister Maria-Fiore dei Fiori di Montagna, and her friend and flatmate, Antonia Collie. The two women had garden access on the strength of their occupation of a flat on the north side of Drummond Place, and in fine weather they were often to be seen sharing a picnic served from a large wicker hamper and laughing at some *recherché* witticism from Antonia or aphorism from Sister Maria-Fiore dei Fiori di Montagna's seemingly limitless store of such observations.

Once inside the gate, with Cyril's extending leash played out to its maximum length, allowing him to investigate the undergrowth, Angus made his way slowly round the perimeter pathway. He soon met Nicola, who was standing underneath a tree, gazing up at a couple of wood pigeons that had alighted on a branch above her.

"Such lovely birds," she remarked. "Altogether more engaging than those troublesome feral pigeons."

Angus nodded. "I see that you have young Bertie's friend with you."

Nicola smiled. "Ranald Braveheart Macpherson? Yes, he is funny wee boy, isn't he? He and Bertie are the greatest of friends. Do you remember how important those childhood friendships were? They meant the world, didn't they?"

Angus did remember. "And we never find them again, do we?"

Nicola thought about that. Angus was probably right; we never recovered the things of childhood – we were never readmitted to that lost Eden.

From behind some bushes came the sound of children's voices raised in what sounded like a dispute.

"That's Olive," said Nicola. "Olive and Pansy. Bertie doesn't quite see eye to eye with those two."

"Olive and Pansy?"

"Olive is Pansy's great friend," said Nicola. "Pansy's family has just moved into Drummond Place. Olive lives on the South Side but comes over to see Pansy. Bertie was dismayed when he realised they had descended on his turf, so to speak."

Angus felt sorry for Bertie. He had had his mother to contend with, and now this. He looked at Nicola, trying to gauge whether he could speak directly about Irene. She was Nicola's daughter-in-law, of course, and he would have to be careful, but he had heard that there was no love lost between the two of them.

"How is Irene?" he asked. "Any news from Aberdeen?"

"She's busy with her PhD," Nicola said. "And long may that continue. A PhD should not be rushed – particularly that one."

Angus smiled. "Scotland Street isn't the same without her," he said.

"It's vastly improved," muttered Nicola, and then, looking contrite, added, "Not that we should be uncharitable."

"Of course not," said Angus.

"She's impossible," said Nicola.

Angus said nothing.

"Although I'm sure she has her good points," Nicola added.

"Of course." Angus was relieved at this sign of charity. Irene was difficult, but, like the rest of us, she was probably just doing her best.

But then she said, "Not that I ever noticed them."

Angus looked at Nicola. There was something worrying her, and he wanted to ask her what it was. But how to put it? "Are you troubled?" Could one say that to somebody one did not know very well – in Drummond Place Garden, out of the blue?

4

Debtors and Creditors

In another part of Drummond Place Garden, separated from Nicola and Angus by a yew hedge and a cluster of rhododendrons, Olive and Pansy presided over a game they were trying to inveigle Bertie and Ranald Braveheart Macpherson into playing. They were unwilling victims: the two boys had been dismayed to discover Olive and Pansy in the Garden, and would have scurried off had they not been spotted by Olive and prevented from escaping.

"We can see you, Bertie Pollock," Olive shouted when she first spotted them. "Stay where you are – it's no good trying to run away."

"You're surrounded," cried Pansy. "And don't pretend you can't see us, because you can, and we know you can, don't we Olive?"

"Yes, we do," Olive confirmed. "You must come over here and play with us. We need two more people for our game, don't we, Pansy?"

"Yes," said Pansy. "And if you don't do as we say I'll report you to the Gardens Committee." She paused, and then uttered a final shot, "You're history, Bertie."

Ranald looked at Bertie, who lowered his eyes. "We'll have to do as they say, Bertie," he said, adding, "I hope Olive gets struck by lightning."

Unfortunately, Olive heard this, and uttered a cry of outrage. "I heard that, Ranald Braveheart Macpherson! You're in trouble now!"

"Big time," said Pansy.

Ranald looked flustered.

"You mustn't pick on Ranald," said Bertie. "He didn't mean it."

"It sounded like he meant it," countered Olive. "But I'll let him off this time, Bertie, as long as you both come and join in our game."

Bertie walked slowly over towards the bench on which Olive and Pansy were sitting. Ranald Braveheart Macpherson followed him reluctantly.

"What is this game?" asked Bertie.

"Debtors and Creditors," Olive replied. "This bench is the Abbey at Holyrood, and where you're standing now is the Cowgate."

Bertie waited for further explanation. "And so?" he said.

"You must be patient," said Olive. "I was about to tell you, Bertie, before you interrupted me."

"I didn't interrupt you, Olive," protested Bertie.

"Don't argue with her," snapped Pansy. "You think that just because you're boys, you can argue with people who know better than you do."

Olive gave him a scornful look. "I'll tell you the rules," she said. "And you should listen to them carefully, because I won't repeat them." She paused. "Are you listening, Bertie?"

Bertie nodded.

"Right," Olive continued. "Did you know that in the old days – that's over twenty years ago – the Abbey of Holyrood was a place where you could go and be safe if you owed people money? They couldn't get you there, Bertie, and send you to debtors' prison. They called it a sanctuary."

"That's right," said Pansy. "A debtors' sanctuary. For people like you."

"But you had to stay there all week," Olive went on. "The only day you were allowed to go out was on a Sunday. Your creditors weren't allowed to get you on a Sunday."

"So you could go swimming if you liked," interjected Pansy. "Tell him about how one of the debtors went swimming, Olive."

"He went swimming on a Sunday," said Olive. "He went down to Cramond. But his creditor came and took his clothes while he was in the water."

Bertie was intrigued. "So what happened, Olive?"

"The poor debtor had to stay in the water until people took pity on him and gave him some clothes to get back to Holyrood."

Bertie and Ranald looked at one another.

"You're going to be the debtors," said Olive. "Pansy and I are going to be the creditors. You have to stay on the bench and then try to get out. If we catch you, you're in trouble."

"Why can't we be the creditors?" asked Bertie. "Why do we have to be the debtors?"

"Because you have to," said Pansy. "So just shut up and play."

"I'm not going to play," said Ranald. "I don't see why we should always be the debtors."

"I don't care," Olive retorted. She had lost interest in the game and wanted to talk about something else.

"You know that you're going to have to marry me, Bertie Pollock," she said. "You promised. I've got it in writing. You're going to have to marry me when we're twenty."

"That's right," said Pansy. "And I'm going to be a bridesmaid. It's the bridesmaid's job to make sure that the groom doesn't run away. You know that, Bertie?"

Olive wagged a finger at Bertie. "I've been looking at venues for the reception, Bertie. I've been considering Dundas Castle. That's just outside town, and it has a marquee for dancing. I've been looking at that. And then there's the Signet Library. Do you know the Signet Library, Bertie?"

Bertie was silent.

"The Signet Library is a very good place for weddings," said Olive. "You can dance afterwards, once they clear the tables away. I've been looking at bands, Bertie."

"And at wedding cakes," Pansy chipped in.

"Pansy's aunt knows somebody who makes those cakes," Olive said. "If we put in our order soon, we'll get a discount."

Now Pansy changed the subject. "I see your granny over there, Bertie," she said. "What a pity. I feel really sorry for her." She paused. "My mummy knows her. She feels sorry for her too. And your granny told my mummy something that you're not going to like one little bit, Bertie. Do you want to know what it is?"

This was the signal for Olive to intervene. "He may not be ready for it yet, Pansy. Not yet."

5

Being Aeneas

At the wheel of their custard-coloured car, Domenica drove herself and Angus through the West End of Edinburgh, through bustling Tollcross, and on towards the polite braes of Morningside. Angus had a driving licence, but he did not particularly like driving and was pleased that Domenica should actually relish it – even to the point of her donning completely unnecessary driving gloves. He had held his licence since the age of nineteen, and it was valid, he assumed, in spite of a misprint. He was described as *Aeneas Lordie* instead of Angus Lordie, and although he had intended to correct this bureaucratic mistake, he had given up after a single unsuccessful attempt.

Angus had written to the driving licence authorities, pointing out that he was Angus rather than Aeneas, and asking for a new licence to be issued under the correct name. He had received a reply two weeks later, which began, "Dear Aeneas Lordie, I have received your recent letter, which is receiving attention. We shall contact you when the matter to which you refer has been resolved." And with that the official had signed off. At the top of the letter, printed in large type above the address, was the mission statement of the government department in question: *Working for You and for the Community.*

No further letter was received, and Angus had decided to leave the matter at that. He knew that in Scotland you could call yourself whatever you liked, provided you did not do so in an attempt to commit fraud. There were no necessary formalities – and all you had to do was to start using your new name. A lawyer friend had confirmed this when Angus had asked him, but had pointed out that you could make a formal declaration, authenticated by a notary, in which you asserted the new name. In Angus's case, though, he had never been Aeneas, and so it seemed that no declaration should be necessary. The lawyer considered this, and suggested a declaration with the simple wording: *I, Angus Lordie, do hereby state and affirm that I am Angus Lordie.*

"That should do the trick," he said.

Angus had smiled. "*I, Franz Kafka, do hereby state and affirm that I am Franz Kafka.*"

The lawyer looked at him blankly. "I don't see what Franz Kafka has to do with this," he said.

Angus had not pursued the matter. He rather liked this alter ego, this shadowy Aeneas Lordie, who led a parallel life in a government computer somewhere. He liked the classical associations of the name, and imagined the complications that Odysseus may have faced in his own documentation when required to linger on Calypso's island for years because his boating licence described him as Aeneas, instead of Odysseus.

Now, sitting in the front passenger seat of the car, he crested the brow of Church Hill and descended into Morningside. He liked Morningside, which was not only a geographical area but a state of being, a state of looking at the world. That could happen to neighbourhoods – their name could become associated with a particular set of attitudes and might stand thereafter for a world view rather than a bounded collection of streets.

"Morningside," he remarked to Domenica.

She smiled. "We should not mock, Angus. It's unseemly for us to come over from the New Town and condescend to Morningside."

"I was not mocking," said Angus. "I was simply muttering

the word . . . as one might say *om*, for example, in incantation. *Om* induces a state of peaceful acceptance."

"*Om*," intoned Domenica, as she drew up at the lights at the Morningside Clock, and then, in much the same register, "*Morningside.*"

Angus looked out of the window. Not far from where they were was the street on which Ramsey Dunbarton had lived. He had been a partner in a firm of lawyers, a man of a certain dryness, with an interest in amateur dramatics and singing, whose great moment of glory had come when he played the part of the Duke of Plaza-Toro in the never-to-be-forgotten Church Hill Theatre production of *The Gondoliers*. Poor Ramsey, thought Angus, as they waited for the lights to change; poor Ramsey . . .

Domenica distracted him. "Are they having anybody else tonight?" she asked.

Angus shook his head. "Not as far as I know. Matthew said that they like having just one couple. I think it will be just us."

Domenica was pleased with that. "We'll have the chance to catch up. I haven't seen Elspeth for ages. Of course, the triplets must take up most of her time."

"It can't be easy," said Angus. "Sometimes Matthew looks exhausted when he comes into Big Lou's for morning coffee. He said to me the other day he'd been up since four in the morning, coping with the boys. By the time he got into work he was already finished."

"They have an au pair, don't they?"

"Yes, so I believe. A young man – James. They share him with Big Lou. He works half the day in the coffee bar and the rest of the time he's the au pair out at Nine Mile Burn."

"It's rather exciting – going out to a dinner party," said Domenica. "Remember how we used to go out to dinner parties almost every weekend? Remember?"

Angus did remember. "And then suddenly people stopped having them."

"Or stopped inviting us."

That was an unsettling possibility. "Do you really think . . . ?" he began.

"No, I don't," said Domenica. "I suspect that the formal dinner party just became too much for most people."

"People became too busy?"

"Yes," said Domenica. "Everybody is busier than they were, say, ten years ago. Our lives have expanded to embrace the increased possibilities of our times. There is more information, to start with. We simply get more messages – all the time. We have more to think about. And we can move about more easily too. Places are cheaper and more accessible."

Angus thought this was probably true. Of course, he went nowhere, but he imagined he could go to all sorts of places if he chose to do so. He could go to Iceland, for instance, which he had never visited, but which he would like to see. There was a line of poetry about Iceland that stuck in his mind . . . *where the ports have names for the sea*. It was a haunting line – a typographical mistake that had been left as it was. The poet – WH Auden – had written *where the poets have names for the sea*, but had liked the typographical error, which gave the line greater poetic impact, and had kept it. It was rather like being called Aeneas by the driving licence authorities and keeping the mistake for its poetic possibilities. It was the same thing, really, Angus decided.

6

Blue Remembered Hills

They parked beside the house. As Angus got out of the car, the sun had just dipped below the top of East Cairn Hill, casting a lengthening shadow over Carlops and the winding road to Biggar. In the distance, across a landscape of wheat and barley, of secret lochs and hidden glens, the Lammermuir Hills were still bathed in evening gold.

Angus turned to Domenica. "This view always makes me feel sad. I don't know why, but it does." He drew in his breath, savouring the freshness of the air. Freshly mown grass was upon it, and the smell of lavender, too, from Elspeth's kitchen garden. "Well, perhaps not sad – more wistful, perhaps, which is one notch below actual sadness."

She followed his gaze over to the hills. "What's the expression? Blue remembered hills? Where does that come from?"

"It's Housman," said Angus. "I happen to know that because I used it as the title of a painting I did once – a long time ago. I painted those very hills we're looking at, as a matter of fact." He had been an admirer of William Gillies, who had visited those hills in watercolour time and time again, in all their seasons and moods.

Domenica gazed at the hills. They were blue, just as watercolour hills should be.

"*What are those blue remembered hills?*" Angus recited. "*That is the land of lost content,/ I see it shining plain.*"

She looked at him; the moment of shared feeling had arisen unexpectedly, as such moments sometimes did. It was the beauty of the country before them that had done it. Scotland was a place of attenuated light, of fragility, of a beauty that broke the heart, as MacDiarmid had said it would, with its little white rose, sharp and sweet. And sometimes she felt this Scotland slipping away, which was why Angus should feel sad, she thought, and why she should feel that too.

She reached out and touched his forearm, gently, without words, to show that she understood what he felt. Then she said, "We should go in."

And as she said that, the front door opened and Elspeth came out to greet them. "Perfect timing," she said. "Matthew has left drinks on the terrace." She made a show of looking relieved. "James is cooking. I'm off-duty."

Domenica smiled. "I'm sure you deserve it."

Elspeth said, "Sometimes the boys can be a bit . . . demanding. Triplets tend to go through the same stages together, and all the challenges are multiplied by three. They're currently going through the biting stage – so Tobermory bit Rognvald, who bit Fergus, who in turn bit Tobermory. They all ended up screaming."

Domenica's eyes widened. "Red in tooth and claw . . ."

"Yes," said Elspeth. "That's exactly what little boys are. It's the way their brains are wired. They are impulsive, violent, endlessly energetic, and prone to bite. That's just the way they are."

"And yet . . ." said Angus. "When you see them, butter wouldn't melt in their mouths. I could use them as models for *putti*, if I were ever to paint something like that. Will we see them this evening?"

Elspeth glanced at her watch. It was eight o'clock. "They'll be dropping off to sleep. Next time, perhaps. Matthew has been upstairs reading to them. He'll be down soon."

She led them into the house and then out through French doors onto the terrace. Four chairs ringed a table on which a tray with glasses had been placed. There was a sparkling wine for Angus and Elspeth, and a soft drink for Domenica. As driver, Domenica was to restrict herself to bitter lemon, which she enjoyed anyway; in general, she was not one for alcohol.

Elspeth raised her glass to her guests.

"*Slàinte mhath*," said Angus.

Domenica touched her glass against Elspeth's. "*God blesim yu*," she said, adding, "That's *cheers* in Melanesian pidgin. In Chinese pidgin, it's *chin chin*, which is what you might have said in Shanghai in 1925."

Elspeth smiled. "Lovely! *God blesim yu, too*. I suppose you used that on your fieldwork."

Domenica nodded. "All anthropologists went to Papua New Guinea in those days – if they could. It was the real thing – the copper-bottomed experience of fieldwork that enabled you to outstare anybody at an anthropological conference. If you were really lucky, you were able to study a cargo cult. Less fortunate people ended up dealing with initiation ceremonies or rain-making rites. Have you read *The Innocent Anthropologist*, by any chance?"

Elspeth shook her head.

"It's by an anthropologist who went as a young man to spend some time with a remote people in Cameroon. It caused a bit of a stir."

"Oh? And why was that?"

"He was too frank. Anthropologists take themselves immensely seriously. He didn't."

Elspeth laughed. "Isn't that a fault of many academics? Don't they think that everybody is hanging on their every word?"

Domenica looked thoughtful. "Some of them are like that, I suppose. And I suppose they never realise that people may actually not pay much attention to what they say and just get on with their business. I think I understood that. I was never under any illusions that my conclusions on the societies I studied were of much interest to anybody – other than fellow anthropologists."

Elspeth looked at her. "But you completed your fieldwork *rite de passage?*"

"Yes. Papua New Guinea – I wrote a book about it – eventually. Nobody read it, as far as I know. At least, I never met anybody who had done so. Except my cousin in Melrose. She read it, I believe."

"And you learned pidgin for that?" asked Elspeth.

"Yes. I haven't used it for rather a long time, of course, but it comes back. Languages don't disappear altogether; once you know them, they tend to become embedded in the mind, like fossils in rock."

Matthew arrived from upstairs. The boys had gone to sleep, he said, and he had called in on the kitchen on his way out to the terrace. "James is rustling up something pretty tempting," he said. "He loves his garlic. Smell it?"

Domenica sniffed at the air. "Delicious," she said.

"It has to be handled carefully," said Matthew. "But you won't be disappointed. He is very creative in the kitchen."

"Will he eat with us?"

Elspeth shook her head, rather firmly, thought Domenica. "He wants to go into town after he's served us," she said. "He's up to something. I have no idea what it is, but he's planning something. That boy has a secret – I'm sure of it."

Angus was curious. "Have you asked him?"

Matthew shook his head. "It's not our place."

"Yes, it is," Elspeth contradicted him.

Matthew sighed. "The point about secrets is that people don't talk about them."

"We could try," said Elspeth.

"What possible secret could a nineteen-year-old have?" asked Angus.

"You'd be surprised," said Elspeth. But she did not answer his question.

7

The Holy Family Boxing Club

James had prepared the menu carefully. He enjoyed cooking, and found that Elspeth needed little persuading to allow him to cook dinner at least three times a week, on top of the cooking that he did for the boys. They, of course, liked nursery food, and James was only too happy to rustle up macaroni cheese with tomato sauce, fish fingers, or pizza, followed by semolina pudding into which he dribbled quantities of strawberry jam. Matthew had never lost his taste for the dishes of his childhood, and often succumbed to that temptation familiar to all parents of raiding the children's plates for the odd morsel. Elspeth disapproved: she fought a battle for healthy food rather than this carbohydrate-rich fare, and served the boys grated carrot, kale purée, and vitamin D-enriched, low-GI oatmeal sausages. All of these were toyed with, and often left uneaten, rather than consumed with any degree of enthusiasm. Between these extremes, though, the boys had a balanced diet, in the sense that they received roughly equal quantities of healthy and unhealthy food, and appeared to be doing well on it.

It was on occasions like this, though, that James's prowess in the kitchen came to the fore. Elspeth had given him free rein on the choice of courses for their dinner party, although she had reminded him that Angus was keen on seafood and Domenica was known to have a soft spot for garlic. James had chosen scallops for their first course, followed by a saddle of lamb into which he had inserted liberal quantities of sliced garlic and sprigs of rosemary. A selection of cheeses from

Valvona & Crolla would follow, each one vouched for by Mary Contini, who could give a full provenance for the cows, the milk, and the manufacture.

As he stirred the scallops, James reflected on the day's events. He had been busy, as he had spent the morning working in Big Lou's coffee bar before assuming responsibility for the boys for several hours after lunch. Fortunately, the weather had been good enough to allow most of the afternoon to be spent out of doors, and the boys had passed their time making a fort underneath the rhododendron bushes, destroying it, and then moving on to an energetic hour of hide-and-seek. That had not been without its incidents, including an alarming ten minutes or so when Rognvald had hidden himself away so successfully that he could not be found at all. Eventually he was located in a dustbin, and was given a strong warning by James on the dangers of such hiding places.

James was happy, and was conscious of his happiness. He had the impression that many of those with whom he had been at school, at James Gillespie's, were discontented for one reason or another. They were anxious about the future or felt that their present was not quite what they would like it to be. Some of them believed that others were having far more fun than they were; some thought that nobody would ever love them; others railed at the world for being unjust or indifferent to the suffering that they could see so clearly all around them. These were all normal feelings for nineteen-year-olds – even if James himself experienced none of these reservations about the world. It never occurred to him that he would be judged unworthy of anything, including the devotion of a suitable girl, or even, *seriatim*, of more than one suitable girl. Nor did he ever doubt that he would be able to pursue whatever career he decided upon, and that doors would open to him when he wanted them to.

This self-confidence could easily have been the result of a

sense of entitlement, but in his case it was not. James felt as he did about the world because the world felt as it did about him. The world liked James because of his youth, and the optimism that went with it. That was how the world responded – there was no justice in that, no question of desert: that was just the way things were.

Now everybody was at the kitchen table, James came over, bearing a large tray. He served the first course with a flourish.

"Hand-dived," he said. "All the way from Mull."

Angus sniffed appreciatively at his plate. "Wonderful," he said. "The fact that they're hand-dived is so important, isn't it, James?"

James nodded. "And they've been nowhere near any fresh water."

"Very wise," said Angus.

"If you wash a scallop, it absorbs water like blotting paper," James explained. "A quarter of the weight of the scallops you buy at the fishmonger's or in the supermarket is just water. Never wash scallops."

"And the sauce?" asked Domenica.

"Cream and brandy," James replied. "With a bit of basil."

"Oh my!" exclaimed Domenica.

"I heard about them from somebody at the boxing gym."

Angus raised an eyebrow. "You box?"

"James belongs to a boxing club," Matthew explained.

"Michty!" said Angus.

"I'm not sure how I feel about boxing," said Domenica.

Elspeth nodded. "I know what you mean," she said. "It's definitely a contact sport . . ."

"And yet," said Angus, "boxing clubs can be a force for good. I happened to read about a book on the sociology of boxing. I came across it by chance and found it fascinating."

"Why?" asked Matthew.

"It provides a way out of hopelessness for some young men,"

said Angus. "It channels their energy. It provides structure."

Elspeth looked doubtful.

"No, I'm serious," Angus continued. "One of the chapters in that book was about a boxing club in West Belfast. It was called The Holy Family Boxing Club."

Domenica laughed. "Surely not?"

"No, that was its name," Angus said. "And during the Troubles in Northern Ireland, it was one of the few places where young Catholics and Protestants could meet."

"And punch one another," said Matthew.

Elspeth turned to Matthew. "Don't be so cynical," she said. "It did a lot for reconciliation."

Matthew shrugged. He sliced into a scallop and put it into his mouth.

"Divine," he said.

"The Holy Family Boxing Club," muttered Elspeth. "How very strange."

"And yet, in the event, how ecumenical," said Domenica. "And what did the rest of us do to make that situation better?"

8

Students Eat Anything

The scallops did not last long.

"I loved that sauce," said Angus. "Delicious."

Elspeth pointed towards the kitchen. "I told you: James is a superb cook. He can do anything, that boy. He could probably get a job at Prestonfield or Gleneagles. Anywhere, really."

"I went to Prestonfield a few months ago," said Matthew. "A client took me for lunch. He wanted to talk about buying a Peploe that had come up at auction. We had a wonderful lunch. There were peacocks strutting around on the lawns, people getting married in the marquee. We didn't finish lunch until four o'clock. We'd paid no attention to the time."

"Sometimes time does that, doesn't it?" said Elspeth. "It forgets to whisper in your ear."

Angus looked down at his plate. "That sauce – it was superb. It makes me want to lick the plate. Just to get the last drop of it."

"Please do," said Elspeth. "We're not formal here."

Angus smiled. "I sometimes do that at home. In fact, I often do."

Domenica gave a look of mock disapproval. "He does, believe it or not. Most people stop doing that when they're about ten." She paused. "I've always assumed that he picked it up from his dog, Cyril."

Angus defended himself. "I don't see what's wrong with it." He gave Domenica a reproachful look. "We all have little things we do when nobody else is looking – harmless little habits that we wouldn't want anybody else to see."

There was a sudden silence at the table, as they each contemplated the truth of what had been said. Matthew blushed. Angus noticed, and wondered what it was that Matthew did, the mere thought of which caused embarrassment. Did he lick the plate too, or was it something worse – not that there was anything *wrong* in licking the plate. It was mere social custom that dictated that you should not do it. But waste not, want not: why not enjoy every last morsel rather than put the scraps in the food-waste bin?

It was as if Elspeth had read Angus's thoughts. "I caught Matthew going through the food-waste bin the other day," she said. "He takes out scraps and eats them. I caught him."

All eyes turned to Matthew, who blushed again. So that was it, thought Angus. It was nothing to be ashamed of – nothing involving something that could not be talked about at the dinner table. Mind you, he thought, was there *anything* that could not be talked about at the dinner table today?

Domenica laughed, perhaps slightly nervously. "I can understand that," she said. "We throw away far too much."

"But it's not the purpose of the food-waste bin," said Elspeth. "The council collects scraps for a purpose."

"I've often wondered what they do with the scraps," said Angus. "You can't feed swill to pigs these days, can you? They don't want the wrong things getting into the animal food chain." He paused. "Somebody said that they took it off somewhere and reprocessed it as food for students."

"I doubt it," said Elspeth. "If you can't feed it to pigs, then should you be able to feed it to students?"

"Students eat anything," said Domenica. "And drink any-thing as well. They are utterly undiscriminating."

James reappeared with the next course – the rolled saddle of lamb. Matthew wanted to carve it at the table, which he now did, observing as he did so the perfection of the meat.

"This comes from just up the road," he said. "From Baddinsgill.

Local produce."

James served the vegetables.

"Will you cook for us forever?" asked Domenica.

James smiled. But Domenica thought: I really would like things to be forever. I would like to be able to sit at this table once a week, perhaps, with these friends. I would like to talk about the things we talk about, the small things, whatever happened in the world. I would like to wake up in the morning and not think that things were getting worse. I would like not to have to listen to the exchange of insults between politicians. I would like to hear of people co-operating with one another and helping others and bringing succour and comfort to the needy and . . . and I would like to think that we were not still in the seventeenth century here in Scotland, as divided amongst ourselves as they were at that time, pitted against each other, with one vision of the good battling another, and people despising others for their opinions. If only we could put that behind us and . . ."

She sighed.

"You sighed," said Elspeth.

"Yes, you did," said Angus, his mouth half-full. "Or were you just breathing?"

"I was thinking of the seventeenth century," said Domenica. "I was thinking of what it was like to live in Scotland in those days."

"Unpleasant," said Matthew. "No antibiotics. No anaesthetics. Unremitting toil. Religious extremism. No midge repellent, if you lived in the Highlands."

"It was the religious extremism that was worst," Angus suggested. "And the plotting of the various factions. Those ghastly nobles."

"Have we changed all that much?" asked Domenica. "I mean, obviously things are better in some respects. People have rights; they have freedoms. We don't have public executions.

We aren't forced to profess a particular religion."

"Oh, that's all infinitely better," Elspeth said. "But I wonder whether there isn't the same tendency to bicker, and whether the moral energy that gave us the religious extremism isn't still there, just the same, but showing itself differently. There are still plenty of people who are keen to tell other people what to do."

Angus agreed. "There certainly are. We may not be lectured from the pulpit any longer, but we're certainly lectured. And we might be every bit as intolerant of dissent as we were back in those days."

The silence that had attended the earlier recollection of social solecism now returned, but only for a few moments. Then Matthew said, "Our history is so violent."

"Isn't everybody's?" asked Domenica. "We're a violent species."

Elspeth looked pained. "There must have been some peaceful societies. Domenica, you're an anthropologist – you must know of some society where . . ." She shrugged. "Where people share and co-operate and look after one another." Sometimes, she thought, such *desiderata* seemed so unlikely as to be impossible.

"Eden?" suggested Angus.

"The Peaceable Kingdom theme," mused Matthew. "Do you know those pictures? There's that famous one in the Phillips Collection in Washington. I've actually seen it. All the animals are together – the lion and the lamb, and so on. All are at peace with one another."

"That's wishful thinking," said Domenica. "Not painted from life."

"Perhaps," said Matthew. "But then don't we have to have some idea like that – somewhere in the back of our minds? An idea of civilisation? An idea of what things might be?"

"Nobody uses the word *civilisation* these days," said Domenica.*

Matthew reached for his glass of wine. "That's the problem," he said. "We don't believe in anything . . . except *things* – the material."

Angus looked at him. He was right. We had forgotten about the spiritual; we had forgotten about the idea of civilisation; we had forgotten about how important it was to be courteous to one another and to love your neighbour. And nobody talked about these things except in a tone of embarrassment or apology, but at least they could do so here, in this kitchen, in the warm embrace of friendship, under the gaze of these gentle hills, this lovely country, this blessed place.

* Not entirely true: see, for example, *In Search of Civilization* by the Scottish philosopher John Armstrong, a profound defence of the tarnished concept.

9

An Orcadian Spell

Discreetly, like a barely visible waiter, James cleared away the plates before returning with a large platter of cheese. Placing the platter in the centre of the table, he recited the names of the cheeses. Angus tried to follow, and to remember which was which, but found himself remembering only an Orcadian cheese and a Mull cheddar. One might forget so many exotic cheeses, he thought, but the memory of cheddar always remained.

"Should one be embarrassed by choosing cheddar every time?" he asked.

Matthew laughed. "There's no need to apologise for simple things."

"But is cheddar simple?" Domenica enquired. "Just because there's a lot of it, does that make it simple?"

Elspeth thought it did not. She, like Angus, preferred cheddar to the other cheeses. She did not like runny cheeses, nor those that smelled too strongly; she did not like cheese that had blue veins running through it. She wondered what exactly was in those blue veins. Bacteria? Of course, there was nothing wrong with bacteria – we were full of bacteria, ourselves – populated by millions, no by billions, of tiny organisms, leading remote, bacterial lives inside us and covering our skin.

She gave an involuntary shudder, and changed the subject. "This Orkney cheese," she said. "Is it nicer than the Mull cheddar?"

"I love Orcadian cheeses," said Angus, realising, as he spoke, that he could name none. But he could broaden his declaration of love. "In fact, I love everything to do with Orkney. The Italian Chapel. Scapa Flow. George Mackay Brown. Peter Maxwell Davies . . . *An Orkney Wedding, with Sunrise* . . ."

Matthew nodded. "I heard that at the Festival last year," he said. "The Scottish National Orchestra played it. That beautiful, swelling music, rising to a climax, and then the piper comes in. It takes the breath away."

"The pipes always do that," agreed Elspeth. "I don't mean just do that to the piper – it's the same thing with the listener. There's nothing more stirring." She paused. "*Mist Covered Mountains* does it for me. There's an extraordinary . . ." She struggled for the right word.

"Gravity," suggested Matthew. "I know what you mean. There's a grave beauty to that tune. All the sorrow of Scotland is somehow distilled in that music."

Angus nodded. There was a deep well of sorrow in Scotland . . . or was it wistfulness? Perhaps wistful longing was what Matthew was talking about: longing for something that had been there in the past, but was no longer.

But Domenica now said: "This Orcadian cheese – why was it so rare?"

Elspeth smiled. "Because the woman who made it had only one cow."

Angus laughed. "A good enough reason."

"I love the idea of that," said Matthew. "Can't you see it? An idyllic scene. A croft house surrounded by green fields. And a woman going out to milk her only cow."

"And not far away," Elspeth said, "cliffs at the end of her field, with the sea moving below, and the sun on the sea, and Norway only a few hundred miles away." She paused. "And the woman with her single cow and her little shed in which she makes the cheese – tiny blocks of it – that are sent off to Edinburgh, where people can eat it and think about Orkney and how beautiful it is and how . . ."

They were silent. Then Matthew pointed at another cheese and said, "That one's a goat's milk cheese."

The Orcadian spell was broken, and as Angus cut off a slice of Mull cheddar, reassuringly yellow, he said, "I'm reading a book about friendship."

Matthew looked at him enquiringly. "About a particular friendship?"

"No. Friendship in general. It's by a Professor Dunbar. He invented something called the Dunbar Number."

They waited.

"It's one hundred and fifty, apparently," Angus said.

Elspeth looked puzzled. "One hundred and fifty?"

Angus explained. "That's the number of people with whom one can maintain stable social relationships. You can have about one hundred and fifty people in your life. After that, it becomes too impossible to relate to them properly."

"You mean close friends?" asked Elspeth.

Angus shook his head. "No. These are just people with whom you can sit down and have a chat. These are the people on your Christmas-card list."

"And how many closer friends can you have?" asked Elspeth.

"I forget exactly what he says," Angus replied. "But I think it's not much more than ten. We just can't cope with more than that."

For a moment, nobody said anything, as each of them discreetly measured themselves again this standard. Angus thought: does Cyril count as one of my ten? A dog could be a very close friend, but maybe that was a separate category. Perhaps Professor Dunbar had a figure for the number of dogs one could have in one's life. Ten would be a bit much. Even two dogs could be emotionally demanding, he thought. And then he started to compile his list: Matthew would be on it, of course, and Elspeth too . . . unless a married couple counted for one in this context. He would count them as one, he decided.

And then there was Domenica. Did one's spouse count? That could be tricky. If you didn't count your spouse or partner, then that implied a lack of friendliness in the relationship. No, a spouse definitely counted.

Elspeth was thinking: Domenica and Angus were friends, but would they be part of her allowance of ten? Did she know them all that well? Probably not. There was Molly, of course, with whom she had been at school, where they had been not only friends but best friends. Good old Molly, with those awful shoes of hers and that irritating way of saying, *You know what I mean?* They had drifted apart, particularly after Molly had married Steve, who made model aeroplanes and talked about Hearts football club all the time – but *all* the time, or at least when he was not talking about model aeroplanes. Poor Molly. She was embarrassed by Steve, Elspeth thought, because her voice always dropped when she mentioned his name. That was a sign; that was definitely a sign.

Then she thought: Big Lou. Elspeth liked Big Lou, but she very rarely saw her. She would like her to be among her ten, but she was not sure whether, realistically, she was. Perhaps one would be allowed two lists: a list of those with whom one was currently a good friend, and then a list of those whom one would like to have as a close friend. There might even be a waiting list, like the waiting list for membership for Glyndebourne or for membership of Muirfield Golf Club, both requiring a wait of some years. Elspeth would have loved to be a member of Glyndebourne, but was indifferent to Muirfield Golf Club.*

But *chacun à son goût*, she thought – in this, as in all matters.

---

*Aka The Honourable Company of Edinburgh Golfers, located just outside Gullane (pronounced Gillin).

10

Scotsmen Can Skip

At the very time at which Elspeth was thinking of Big Lou, Big Lou herself was thinking of Elspeth – an example of the synchronicity that Jung believed meant something, but which may occur simply because there is a limited number of people to think about and things to do, and some of these thoughts and things are destined to occur at the same time. Big Lou, who had been endowed through her upbringing on Snell Mains with a healthy capacity for scepticism, would have agreed with that.

That evening, Big Lou was sitting in her second-floor flat in Canonmills, which had a distant view of the river, the Water of Leith, on its winding progress through the city towards its appointment with the Firth of Forth and eventually the sea. At her feet, on the floor of her living room, her adopted son, Finlay, was struggling to complete a large jigsaw puzzle. The theme was the Massacre of Glencoe, an unfortunate incident in Scottish history, portrayed here in a nineteenth-century painting entitled *How Not to Behave Towards Your Guests*. Finlay was now attempting, without much success, to find a place for a piece that looked as if it came from a Campbell kilt. It was a 500-piece puzzle, and Big Lou had already had to speak to him on the need for patience in tackling jigsaw puzzles.

"It's not simple, Finlay," she said. "And it's no good trying to force a piece to fit. That never works."

As she said this, she reflected on the fact that this was advice that held for most things, not least for our personal lives. Forcing yourself to be something you were not was never entirely satisfactory, and was likely to lead to at least some degree of unhappiness. Very rarely, people got away with it – they acted a part, and then, at length, discovered that the created persona had put down deep enough roots to become the authentic person. But for the most part, the result was more likely to be inauthenticity or bad faith. Big Lou had read Sartre, whose works were amongst the collection of books she had inherited when she bought the bookshop that became her café. She knew about existentialism, but was not convinced by the arguments around authenticity. These left so many questions unanswered, and in particular she wondered what existentialists had to say about those who felt authentic only when being cruel or exploitative. In other words, what was the essential merit in authenticity, if the self to which one was being honest was flawed in some way? Would it not be better overall to pursue an aspirational, pro-social ideal, even if that was something that you felt was not authentic to you? Was there a moral distinction between the authentically bad, on the one hand, and those on the other hand who were authentically bad but behaved in an inauthentically good way?

She thought of this as she gazed down at the spread-out puzzle. Finlay had finished a corner in which a sheepdog belonging to the unfortunate Macdonalds was cowering in a corner watching its owner being put to the sword. The artist had been particularly skilful in revealing the dog's expression, which was one of abject terror.

"Poor dog," she muttered.

Finlay looked up. "I wonder if the Campbells killed the Macdonald dogs too. Do you think they did, Lou?"

Finlay had called Lou by her first name from the beginning, when she had first fostered him. Now and then he had called her Mum, and her heart had leapt with delight when he did so, but he had always corrected himself, and she thought it best not to ask him to address her thus. If, in due course, he chose to make that change, she would quietly accept it, and rejoice in the bond that it created, but until then she would not raise the subject.

She addressed his question. "I doubt it, Finlay. The Campbells were certainly a ruthless bunch, but I don't think they would have slaughtered the Macdonald dogs. Stolen them, perhaps, but not massacred."

"There's a boy at school who's called Campbell," said Finlay. "He says it's not true. He says that the Massacre of Glencoe never happened. He said that the Macdonalds had stolen the Campbells' cattle and they were just trying to get them back."

Big Lou shook her head. "I'm afraid it did happen," she said. "But I don't think we should make too much of it, you know. A lot happened in history."

She looked at her watch. It was time for Finlay to have his bath and then be tucked up in bed. He would have a story, of course – she was currently reading him *The Wind in the Willows,* and they were at a crucial moment for Toad. Justice was about to be done, with reckless driving getting its comeuppance, and Big Lou found herself looking forward to each night's chapter every bit as much as Finlay was.

"Ten minutes more with the jigsaw," said Big Lou, "and then it'll be time for your bath."

But Finlay had had enough. "I'll never finish this," he said, tossing the problematic piece down on the ground. Then, getting to his feet, he suddenly leapt into the air, brought his toes together, separated then in a scissor movement of the legs, and landed back on his feet. Finlay studied ballet.

"Very neat," said Big Lou, with a smile.

"And then there's this," said Finlay, quickly managing a further *échappé* and *cabriole.*

Big Lou smiled. "You're making such good progress," she said.

Finlay inclined his head in acceptance of the compliment.

She watched him, and thought about how difficult it would have been for a boy like him in the time of her own childhood. She could not imagine any of the boys with whom she had been at school in Arbroath all those years ago being able to do what Finlay was doing and profess an interest in ballet. That would have been greeted by cries of derision, by ruthless teasing from the other boys, and by smirking looks of disapproval from the girls. Insults would have been hurled, each with a barb and a not-so-subtle innuendo, and the boy would have gone home each day with those hurtful words ringing in his ears.

How things had changed. Scotland was now simply a kinder place. And that was true of just about everywhere, except for those few countries, redoubts of old-fashioned machismo and reaction, where men strutted, where cruelty still reigned. And that kindness – how had it been brought into existence? The answer, Big Lou thought, was easily discerned: feminisation. Scotsmen, previously encouraged to be strong and silent, afraid to cry, afraid to be seen to be weak, afraid to *feel* . . . Now released from the tyranny of their gender straitjacket, men had been allowed to be something different. *Scotsmen can skip*, Big Lou had read on a poster somewhere. Absurd, embarrassing; but it was true. They could.

She stopped herself. Men had become liberated by a side-wind to the liberation of women. Or *some* men had been transformed: she was not sure just how far this applied to her new boyfriend, Fat Bob. If there were indeed new Scotsmen, then Fat Bob was definitely not one.

11

Fat Bob

Big Lou had met Fat Bob outside her café one morning. She
had arrived at seven-thirty, as she usually did, in order to be
open by eight, and had found him standing at the railings,
peering down the stone steps that led to the café entrance,
slightly below street level. At first, she wondered whether
he was up to no good – there had been an attempt to force
the door a few weeks ago, and Big Lou had arranged for the
installation of a more secure lock. But that sort of thing, she
imagined, would hardly happen in broad daylight, when there
was a regular stream of people walking up Dundas Street on
their way to work.

He turned to her, as if surprised that anybody should come
to open up the café.

"This your place?" He spoke in an accent that was familiar
to her – Dundee perhaps.

She nodded. "Aye, it's my place."

"You Big Lou then?"

Again, she nodded. "That's what they call me."

He looked at her and smiled. She saw that he had a tooth
missing to one side, in the upper row. The effect was not
unpleasant – giving him a slightly raffish, almost piratical
look. But just as she noticed this, her gaze fell to the broad
shoulders and the powerful, stocky build. This was a man who
would be more at home on a building site, or the docks, rather
than a New Town coffee bar. He was the size – and shape – of
a large industrial fridge, and she found herself thinking that
one could probably attach fridge magnets to him.

"They call me Fat Bob."

Big Lou raised an eyebrow. Her inspection had continued, and had picked up the tattoo on his right forearm, just below his rolled-up sleeve. It was a large thistle, under the legend, SCOTLAND FOREVER. "Your friends?" she said. "That's what your friends call you?"

Fat Bob shrugged. "Everybody. I don't mind." He grinned. "And it's muscle, not fat."

"Well," said Big Lou, extracting her keys from the bag she was carrying. "Folk often get it wrong, don't they?" She paused. "We're not open yet, you'll have seen. Eight o'clock."

Fat Bob looked at his watch. Big Lou noticed that it was a large, round watch of the sort that sportsmen – or the slightly showy sort of sportsmen – liked to wear. She had heard Matthew describe such watches as Dubai Airport watches, and she had been struck by the description. Yet there was something unusual about this watch: it was a Mickey Mouse watch, with Mickey's rotating arms being the hands.

Fat Bob intercepted her glance. "Aye, Mickey Mouse," he said, a note of apology in his voice. "But I've always liked him."

"Nothing wrong with Mickey Mouse," said Lou. She hesitated for a moment. Then she said, "You can come in, if you like. I'll get the coffee going – if that's what you want."

"I've heard about your bacon rolls," said Fat Bob. "I'd like one of those. But no hurry, of course."

Big Lou was pleased by the mention of her bacon rolls. Since James had come to work for her, their food menu had improved greatly, but the most popular item continued to be their bacon rolls. These were carbohydrate-rich rolls that made no concession to whole-grains, in which two rashers of bacon were inserted, curling crisply at the edge, untrimmed of surplus fat, dripping in grease. When they were cooked, the smell permeated the coffee bar, pushing that of freshly ground coffee into the background. And like the distant sound of the sirens on Scylla, this olfactory lure enticed people off the street and into the café. Some of this passing trade felt guilty, and would explain, as they placed their orders, that it was years since they had treated themselves to a bacon roll; that they otherwise had a perfectly healthy diet, consuming a lot of roughage and *plenty* of Omega-3 oil; and anyway, wasn't there research somewhere that showed that one bacon roll a week was positively beneficial, in the same way as two glasses of red wine *per diem* (and, of course, *per os*) were – or was it that the two glasses of red wine would cancel the cholesterol-raising effect of the occasional bacon roll – something like that? And anyway, could I have my bacon quite crisp, if you don't mind, and is that tomato sauce I see: I haven't had that for years – for years! – or not since I was at school and we used to cover our chips with it – you should have seen us. We had such an unhealthy diet in those days, with all those E numbers that went into everything. Mind you, nobody had allergies in those days, did they? It's only now that people are developing all sorts of allergies because their food is so pure and their immune system is not getting the challenge it needs to build up a memory.

Big Lou unlocked the door and pushed it open. It occurred to her that it was perhaps slightly unwise to be letting this stranger into the coffee bar when there was nobody else around. What if he suddenly pushed past her, slammed the door behind them, and demanded money from the till? That sort of thing happened, she knew, because she had read about it recently in the *Sunday Post*, the newspaper on which she had been brought up, and still read each weekend, cover to cover, along with *Scotland on Sunday* and the *Sunday Herald*. A shopkeeper in Oban, of all places, had let a customer into his shop before normal opening hours and had been rewarded for his consideration with the theft of the entire contents of his safe.

She looked over her shoulder. Fat Bob was immediately
behind her, but there was nothing in his demeanour that
suggested malicious intention, and she relaxed. There was
something about him that Big Lou liked. She did not like
thin men – at least she did not like thin men in *that* way.
Nor did she like men who took too much trouble with their
grooming: men simply did not do that in Angus, where she
had been brought up. There had been a man in the coffee bar
recently who quite clearly plucked his eyebrows, and Big Lou
had been unable to keep her eyes off them. What sort of man
plucked his eyebrows? She was not sure how to answer her
own question, but she was certain that Fat Bob would not do
something like that: some men might be in touch with their
eyebrows, she thought, but not him.

Fat Bob was looking around the coffee bar appreciatively.
"Braw," he said.

Big Lou smiled. Yes, it was braw. Of course, it was braw,
and the fact that he used the Scots word to describe what he
saw further endeared him to her.

"I'll heat up a bacon roll for you," she said, as she went
behind the counter, adding, "Two maybe."

He thanked her. "You're a great lass, Big Lou," he said.

"Thank you, Bob . . . er, Fat Bob."

The compliment was completely sincere. Fat Bob himself
was completely sincere. He was authentic – in a way that
only those who have never heard of Jean-Paul Sartre can be.
Here was no hesitant aesthete; here was a man who could
manage two bacon rolls, and who had SCOTLAND FOREVER,
not SCOTLAND PRO TEM, tattooed on his forearm.

12

The Story of Mags

Fat Bob, having eaten his bacon rolls, paid the six-pound bill entirely with fifty-pence coins. These were extracted from a wallet that he produced from his back pocket. The wallet was tartan, and had been engraved with *Bob*, and, beneath that, with a lover's heart symbol, complete with Cupid's arrow. Big Lou's eye was caught by this, and Fat Bob noticed.

"Nae doot about who that wallet belongs to," he said, winking at Lou. "That's my tartan, you see. Macgregor, of course."

Big Lou nodded. She pretended to busy herself with wiping the coffee bar counter. "It's bonny." And then she added, rather absently, "Macgregor. Of course. Macgregor."

She had been dismayed to see the heart. That suggested that somebody had given the wallet to Bob – somebody who loved him sufficiently to have his name engraved, along with a heart. That meant a girlfriend or wife, and Big Lou suddenly felt that she did not want this man to have a wife or girlfriend. She did not stop to ask herself why; she just did not want him to have somebody else.

"And the . . . the heart?" she stumbled on the word. All the men I meet are *taken*, she thought. There are no men left. None.

Bob laughed. "Oh that. That was a long time ago." He paused. "It doesn't mean anything."

She saw a faint glimmer of hope. "You were married?"

Bob shook his head. "Never quite married. Almost."

"Engaged?"

This brought a similar shaking of the head. "Never quite."

She looked away. She did not want Bob to see that this disclosure had pleased her.

"She was a great girl," he said, in a voice tinged with regret. "Mags, she was called. We had something going – we really did. And then . . ." He shrugged. Now he was wistful. "Her career got in the way."

Big Lou sighed. "A familiar story." She wondered what Mags had done.

"She was doing so well," Bob continued. "She had to make a choice, I suppose. And I can't blame her, to be honest. If I had been in her position, I would probably have done the same." He fixed Big Lou with an intense look. "You never know what you're going to do until the chips are down. Then . . ." He shrugged. "Who knows how they'll react?"

Big Lou made an understanding noise. Then she said, "Of course, it depends on what the career is, doesn't it? Some things you can shelve for a few years and then take them up again – others you can't. What do they say: there's a tide in the affairs of men?"

"Aye," said Fat Bob. "You can say that again. You have to make a choice or you may lose a once-in-a-lifetime opportunity. That's what happened to Mags."

Big Lou waited, but it seemed that further information was not going to be vouchsafed.

"What was it?" she asked.

Bob's tone was matter-of-fact; it was as if Mags had pursued the most mundane of occupations. "Weight-lifter," he said.

Big Lou's eyes widened. "Weight-lifter?"

"Aye. She was the Scottish champion – female, of course. And she would have been European champion if it weren't for the fact that one of the Russians cheated. She was entered as a woman, but she was really a man – people heard her

being called Ivan. That's a man's name in Russia, you know.
A dead giveaway. In fact, Mags inadvertently came across her
in the showers at one competition, and she saw that he was
definitely a man. She said you don't get things like that wrong
– usually."

"Did she complain?"

Fat Bob nodded. "She went to the organisers of the competition and told them what she had seen. They made enquiries
but were met with a blank denial. They said it was bad
sportsmanship on Mags' part. So nothing was done."

"That must have been hard for Mags."

Fat Bob agreed. "She was pretty cut up. But then she got this
offer, you see, and she accepted. It was a weightlifting scholarship to a university somewhere near Boston. That's in America.
You heard of the place?"

Big Lou nodded.

"It has a great reputation, they say. And they offered Mags
full tuition fees and living expenses. How could she say no?"

"I don't think she could," said Big Lou. She wondered
what Mags had studied. "And her degree?"

"Oh, that's nae bother with these scholarships. You register
for whatever you like – either that, or they allocate you to
some programme where they don't have enough students.
That's not the important part."

"So what was it?"

"Philosophy," said Fat Bob. "Mags liked it. She had always
been an ideas sort of person, and philosophy was just right for
her."

"Very fortunate."

"Yes, and Mags found that they didn't mind too much if
she didn't go to any lectures – they said they would tell her
what they were about later on. What they really wanted her to
do was to lift weights and, in particular, to win against a place
called Yale. Have you heard of that place?"

"Aye," said Big Lou. "Yale."

"She spent a lot of time practising. She went to some classes, she said, but she used to sit at the back and lift those small portable weights while the professor was talking. Nobody minded, she said, because they all knew that she was their big hope to beat Yale, and they were in on it – the professors, the works."

Big Lou said nothing. She had a deep respect for education, and she would have leapt at the opportunity to go to university, although she would much prefer Aberdeen to this Boston place. Had she been in Mags' position, she would have made use of the academic opportunity and immersed herself in her studies. But nobody would ever offer her a scholarship to anywhere, and so all that was hypothetical.

"What happened to her?" she asked. "Did she come back to Scotland?"

Fat Bob shook his head. "No," he said. "She stayed in the US. She took a job teaching at Princeton. She runs a course called *Intellectual Heavy Lifting*. It's very popular, I'm told. There's always a waiting list."

"Will she ever come back to Scotland?" asked Big Lou.

Fat Bob looked doubtful, perhaps rather regretful. But then he brightened. "I don't think so. But she was a great woman," he said. "One of the very best – and I miss her an awful lot. Right here." He placed a hand across his chest. "A man needs a woman, you know, Big Lou. He needs somebody to go through life with – know what I mean? Just to share things with. Have a laugh with – that sort of thing."

Me, thought Big Lou. *Me.*

13

Great Lass, Big Quads

"But what about you, Bob?" asked Big Lou.

He seemed taken aback by the question – as if he were surprised that anybody should take any interest in him.

"Me?"

Big Lou smiled encouragingly. "Yes, Bob. You've told me about Mags, but what about you?"

He still seemed surprised. "You want to know about me, Lou?"

She was taken by his modesty. "Unless you're in a hurry to get away." She glanced at her watch. There were still fifteen minutes before her normal opening time.

"There's not much to tell," he said. "I'm not one of those people who've done very much. Not really."

Lou pointed to his empty plate. "Could you manage another bacon roll? On the house?"

Bob grinned. "Now I know why they're legendary," he said.

Big Lou took a container of bacon out of the fridge and put two generous rashers into the grill. From the high-stool on which he had seated himself, Fat Bob watched Big Lou at work.

"I tell myself that eating bacon rolls is part of my job," he said. "That makes me feel a bit better. Somebody said I could claim them against tax."

Big Lou smiled. "I doubt that, Bob. The tax people don't like you claiming things that you need anyway, if you see what I mean. You need food whatever you do. They don't treat food as a business expense."

Bob frowned. "But I was told that I could claim *extra* food. There's the stuff I need to keep alive – that's not an expense as far as the tax people are concerned. All right. But the food that you need to build up strength for the job, so to speak – that's different."

Big Lou waited for an explanation.

"You see," continued Fat Bob, "I need to have extra energy for my job. I'm a professional strongman."

Big Lou could not conceal her astonishment. "Professional . . ." She did not complete the sentence. She had not anticipated the effect that his announcement had on her. Had Fat Bob said that he was a builder, or a driving instructor, or a pastry chef – or anything of that sort – she would have not thought much about it. But a professional strongman was quite different, and considerably more interesting than any of those other, unexceptional occupations.

"You mean you . . . you tear up telephone directories? That sort of thing?"

Fat Bob laughed. "Oh, Jeez, Lou – there's more to it than that. I go to Highland Games." He reeled off a list of Highland events. "Strathmore. Deeside. The Braemar Gathering. Inverary. Mull. The whole circuit."

Big Lou put a hand to her forehead in a gesture of realisation. "Of course," she said. "Of course. I should have guessed. You're one of those fellows who goes around winning prizes for tossing the caber and so on."

"Hoping to win prizes," Fat Bob corrected her. "But that's not guaranteed. There are quite a few of us who are professional. I don't always win. Sometimes it's Wee Eric or Billy Mactaggart – people like that. Then there's a young guy from Lochearnhead who's doing rather well these days. He works for the South of Scotland Electricity Board. That's how he discovered his talent."

Big Lou did not see the connection.

"Electricity poles," explained Bob. "He was working with those big poles they use for electricity wires. You know the sort? Telephone poles, they used to call them."

Big Lou nodded. "And he . . . ?"

"Yes. They found that he was good at moving these things. If they wanted a pole moved from one place to the other, this guy just picked it up and threw it. Amazing. He's called Jimmy Wilson. Not a particularly large fellow, and still in his early twenties. But pure muscle. Built like a tractor."

"And the hammer?" asked Big Lou. "You throw that too?"

"Yes," said Bob. "I do caber and hammer. I actually prefer the caber, but I won several big hammer events last year." He paused. "You don't think I'm boasting, Lou? You did ask me."

She reassured him. "Of course not. I'm interested – that's all. How much does that hammer weigh, by the way?"

"Twenty-two pounds," said Bob. "These things are all strictly controlled. It's sixteen pounds for the women's events. There's Lilly Mackay at the moment – she's from Inverness. Great lass. Big quads. She's the one to watch when it comes to the hammer. I wouldn't get on the wrong side of her."

The bacon roll was ready, and Lou passed it over to Fat Bob. He leaned over the plate and sniffed. "This is the first thing you get when you get to heaven," he said. "A bacon roll."

Lou laughed. She had been right, she thought. Fat Bob was fun.

"Yes," said Bob, as he took his first bite out of the roll. "It's a very well-regulated sport. And there's no cheating. Most sports these days are full of cheats – aren't they? And people who are too competitive. Look at Formula One racing. Look at it, Lou. They do their team-mates down all the time. Cut corners. All that stuff. It's not a sport for gentlemen."

Lou noted his use of the word *gentlemen*. It was an unfashionable word, and only used apologetically, in most cases. But she knew what he meant, and she was pleased that he was not embarrassed to use a word that was widely sneered at. Big Lou believed that it was still a good thing to be a gentleman, which involved treating other people with courtesy and consideration. That was all that it entailed.

She looked at Far Bob. He was a gentleman. That was perfectly apparent.

"The caber weighs even more," Fat Bob was saying. "It's between one hundred and one hundred and eighty pounds. And there are regulations about its length."

"How long is it?" she asked.

"Between sixteen and twenty-two feet," said Bob, as he swallowed the last of the bacon roll. "That was terrific, Lou. And are you sure I can't pay?"

Big Lou politely refused his offer.

"In that case," said Fat Bob. "Would you let me buy you dinner? This evening? No notice, of course, but . . ."

Big Lou hesitated. "I have a wee boy," she said. "I can't."

Fat Bob stared at her directly. "Have you got a man, Lou? I'm sorry if . . ."

"No," she said quickly. "I'm single. But there's Finlay, you see."

"Bring him along," said Fat Bob. "We can eat early. Six o'clock. Seven. There's an Indian restaurant down in Leith that I like. Does he like Indian food?"

"He loves it," said Big Lou.

She turned round, so that he should not see the emotions within her. That she had been sent a man like this, and that he should be prepared to include Finlay in their date, was more than she could ever have dared hope for. Big Lou had been unlucky in matters of the heart, but runs of bad luck came to an end – statistically, that was more likely than not – and now, perhaps, her own turn for happiness had at last arrived.

14

The Wolf Man Again

After their brief sojourn in Drummond Place Garden, Bertie and his friend, Ranald Braveheart Macpherson, were taken back to the flat in Scotland Street by Bertie's grandmother, Nicola Tamares de Lumares, *née*, and once again, Nicola Pollock. She had reverted to her earlier married name after her second husband, a Portuguese wine producer, had gone off with his housekeeper. Most men who go off with somebody else will have some justification: *my wife doesn't understand me* is said to be the typical excuse, although, in fact, few men actually say that. Men are now far more subtle, and will use explanations, such as *we drifted apart,* that provide a good smokescreen for the avoidance of blame. Very rarely does a man give the real explanation for his conduct, which might be something like *I wanted somebody younger.*

In the case of Nicola's husband, his excuse was disarming in its effrontery. He had, he said, been instructed by the Virgin Mary, no less, to go off with his young housekeeper. It is difficult to argue with such an explanation, other than to suggest, perhaps rather lamely, that the Virgin Mary can hardly be expected to get everything right, and that her advice should not always be followed to the letter, well-intentioned though it undoubtedly might be.

Nicola returned to Scotland from Portugal. She was pleased to be back, although during her marriage she had immersed herself in Portuguese culture, spoke the language fluently, and had even begun writing a critical biography of Fernando Pessoa. She was financially secure from two sources: the generous settlement that the Virgin Mary instructed her former husband to make, and from an inheritance that Nicola had received in Scotland. This included ownership of a Glasgow pie factory, formerly known as Pies for Protestants, but now called, more appropriately, Inclusive Pies. Nicola did not have the time to adopt a hands-on approach to the pie factory, and had proposed a scheme in which the firm's management and employees were given a major stake in the enterprise. It was just the right solution: the staff in Glasgow now shared in the profits and participated in management decisions. From Nicola's point of view, she was happy to involve herself in certain aspects of the company's affairs while leaving the day-to-day running of the business to those who knew about Scotch pies and the people who ate them.

The life she had planned for herself in Edinburgh was to have been one in which she enjoyed the cultural offerings of the city while re-establishing contact with old friends with whom she had lost touch on leaving for Portugal. It was to have been an unhurried existence: morning coffee with friends, followed by a visit to a gallery. Then lunch with further friends and, after that, something she had become accustomed to in Portugal – a siesta. In the evening, there might be a visit to the Lyceum Theatre, or a concert, perhaps even a dinner party with entertaining guests. It would have been a comfortable, fulfilling existence – not particularly strenuous, but also not markedly sybaritic. It would have been what is sometimes called *me time* – the time so appreciated by those whose lot it has been to look after others – by exhausted mothers, in particular, who have had to juggle child-care with work and the running of a household. Such persons richly deserve *me time* but often do not have the chance to claim it because those they are looking after are enjoying *me time* themselves.

That had been the plan, but then everything changed when Bertie's mother decided that the time had come for

her to move to Aberdeen to begin a PhD with Dr Hugo
Fairbairn, recently appointed to a chair at the university
there. Dr Fairbairn had been Bertie's psychotherapist, and
Irene had discovered they both shared an interest in the work
of Melanie Klein. This gave an added point to the weekly
visits they made to Dr Fairbairn's Queen Street consulting
rooms. While Bertie sat in the waiting room, paging through
the old copies of *Scottish Field* provided for patients to
peruse while awaiting their appointment, Irene would
sequester herself with Dr Fairbairn and discuss matters of
interest. This suited Bertie, who did not enjoy his sessions
with Dr Fairbairn, whom he thought to be certifiably insane.
Bertie had read about the State Hospital at Carstairs, and
thought it only a matter of time before attendants in white
coats arrived to take Dr Fairbairn away for much-needed
attention. That this never happened was put down by Bertie
to inadequate resources.

And now, of course, Dr Fairbairn was safely in Aberdeen,
where Bertie had read hypothermia was a real issue. Cold shock
therapy might help him, he imagined, but in the meantime he
was pleased to be spared those weekly sessions in which Dr
Fairbairn invited him to tell him about his dreams, and Bertie,
obliging as ever, made up enough dreams to keep Dr Fairbairn
scribbling away in his notebook. Bertie had discovered a book
about Freud's cases on his mother's bookshelf, and had read
with great interest about the famous Wolf Man, who had
described a dream in which he had been observed by wolves
sitting in the trees. This had intrigued Bertie, who thought that
the Wolf Man was probably just fibbing: wolves did not sit in
trees – everybody knew that, even Larch, a boy in his class
at school who was famous for knowing nothing at all about
anything, but who, on request, could burp the melody of *La
Marseillaise*, perfectly in tune and with surprising attention to
the dynamics of the music.

Bertie had told Dr Fairbairn about a dream he had had in which wolves had stolen his underpants and had hung them in a tree. The narration of this dream had been received with rapt attention by Dr Fairbairn, who twice broke the lead in his propelling pencil in his eagerness to write down the details. He was pleased that he had been able to satisfy Dr Fairbairn so easily – he did not bear the psychotherapist any ill-will; Bertie bore ill-will towards nobody – but if a few tall stories needed to be invented in order to keep Dr Fairbairn from becoming too unstable, then he saw no particular harm in that. Everyone made things up, Bertie had concluded – especially adults – and a few helpful stories of this sort would do no harm, particularly since they appeared to give such inexplicable pleasure to Dr Fairbairn. Adults, Bertie thought, are often desperate for something to do, and psychotherapists, it seemed, were no exception.

15

Dear Little Argonaut

Nicola might have been expected to feel disappointed when she heard of Irene's departure for Aberdeen. She might have been expected to regret the dashing of her plans for a relaxed, even if slightly self-indulgent, existence in Edinburgh, but, as it happened, she felt quite buoyed by the news, and lost no time in volunteering to fill the child-care gap that Irene had so selfishly created.

Stuart was reluctant to take advantage of his mother. "I could always employ somebody," he said. "I gather that there are plenty of qualified people searching for jobs looking after children. I heard of somebody who received thirty-two applications for a job they advertised. Thirty-two!"

"It doesn't exactly surprise me," said Nicola. "People like working with children."

"But thirty-two, mother!" exclaimed Stuart. "Thirty-two – and apparently they were all pretty impressive. One had a master's degree in early education."

Nicola made a dismissive gesture. "Everybody has a master's these days."

"Another was a qualified music teacher," Stuart continued.

This did not impress Nicola. "Frankly, I don't think you need any formal qualifications to look after children. You don't need them to be a parent – and I don't see why you should need them to be *in loco parentis*." She paused. "No, Stuart, you don't need to get anybody in. I shall be only too happy to do my grandparental duty. I shall make myself available and, with any luck, we can start undoing the damage that . . ."

She stopped herself, but Stuart had heard. "Go on, mother," he muttered, tight-lipped. "Say it."

"Well, I thought that perhaps a small corrective might help to deal with the influence of the last little while . . ."

Stuart interrupted her. "Irene's influence?"

Nicola lowered her eyes. "One might say that."

Stuart bit his lip. He knew what his mother felt about Irene, and it made him feel uncomfortable, even if he also knew that her animosity had every justification. Irene was intolerable – at least from most people's perspective, and it was only loyalty, and a certain embarrassment, that prevented him from acknowledging that fact.

He fixed his gaze on his mother. "You never liked her – right from the start, you never liked her, did you?"

Nicola hesitated. Then she said, "No, I didn't. I couldn't stand her. But I did try, you know. I made an effort."

He granted her that. "Yes," he said. "I noticed. I don't think anybody would fault you on that. You did your best."

She looked relieved. "I'm glad that you saw that," she said. "It's an odd thing – having to like somebody as a matter of duty. We all know that we have a duty to the people we have to live with, but sometimes . . . Well, sometimes, it's an awful effort."

Stuart thought about this. "Like, or tolerate? I'm not sure that anybody says to us that we have to *like* others. They do say, though, that we have to tolerate them."

"I think that Christianity has something to say about that," said Nicola. "Love your neighbour as yourself. Isn't that the second great commandment?"

Stuart said, "If you're talking about religion, yes. But not otherwise. Not in ordinary morality. That's less . . ."

"Less strenuous?"

"Yes, that's what I meant. We're not meant to be unpleasant to others, but we're not told to *like* them." Stuart paused.

"Well, you did your best. You tried – I know you tried."

"And so did you," said Nicola. "You worked at your marriage."

Stuart was silent.

"I saw how you bit your tongue," Nicola continued. "I saw how you struggled when she was going on and on about Melanie Klein and Bertie's psychotherapy. And his yoga and his saxophone lessons, and his Italian. All of that. You bit your tongue when another might have exploded and said that enough was enough and all that Bertie needed was to be left alone and allowed to be a little boy. To have a Swiss Army penknife and join the Wolf Cubs or whatever they call them these days. To do all of the things that little boys like to do and that people like Irene try to stop them doing."

Nicola stopped. She understood that there were limits to what she could say about Irene because everything that she said – the entire catalogue of Irene's failings – could be taken as an indictment of Stuart's bad judgement in choosing to marry her, and, after that event, of his weakness in not standing up to her barrage of criticism. Bullies got away with what they got away with because people allowed them to do their work of bullying without standing up to them. Stuart should have put his foot down a long time ago. He should have told Irene that she could not expect him to share all of her attitudes, and that a civilised marriage involves acceptance by each party of the fact that two people might have different views of certain subjects. Jack Spratt could eat no fat, and his wife could eat no lean. They got on all right in spite of these different tastes. People could do that – at least they could in the past. It was different now, of course, and today the Spratts might well be expected to be searching for more personal space.

Nicola moved into 44 Scotland Street, taking over a room that Irene had previously used as a study. Her days became busy, as Ulysses was getting bigger and was requiring more attention. That kept her busy all morning until it was time to set off to collect Bertie from the Steiner School. She did that by bus, taking Ulysses with her. As often as not, Ulysses would be dressed in a neat sailor suit, on the sleeves of which Nicola had embroidered the name *Argo*.

"Dear little Argonaut," she muttered, kissing him on the top of his head, as the bus wended its way up the Mound.

Ulysses beamed. He had been in a much better frame of mind since Irene had gone off to Aberdeen, and was sick far less often. Prior to Irene's departure, he had manifested the trying habit of being sick whenever Irene picked him up or addressed him directly. That behaviour seemed to have been completely corrected, and now nobody could remember when Ulysses had last brought anything up. That was not to say that he was completely without vices. He still made somewhat embarrassing bodily noises whenever a friendly adult face beamed at him, and it was generally impossible to take him into any form of human society, owing to the somewhat overpowering smell that tended to emanate from him. Apart from that, though, he was an ideal baby and a little brother of whom Bertie was quite proud.

It had not always been thus. Until recently, Bertie had been rather too ready to speculate in public about what might happen if Ulysses were to be left somewhere – inadvertently – and never recovered. Could they sell his toys, he asked, and if he did the selling, could he get commission on his brother's estate?

"I'm not saying that I want Ulysses to go away, Daddy," he told his father. "I'm not saying that we should get rid of him. All I'm saying is that I don't really see the point of him. I've tried, but I just can't."

Bertie looked miserable. He was a kind boy. So he concluded, "I'll carry on trying, though. I promise. Scout's honour."

He was not a scout. Irene had always forbidden it. But a moral profession is often aspirational, and all the more forceful for that.

16

Aberdeen Beckons (or Threatens)

Now, while Bertie and Ranald Braveheart Macpherson started a game of *Jacobites and Hanoverians* in Bertie's room – a popular game among Edinburgh children, and almost as frequently played as *Accountants and Clients* – Nicola prepared a cup of tea for Stuart.

"I'm ready for that," said Stuart, glancing at his watch. It was not quite yet a respectable time to pour a gin and tonic, but tea would always do. He had been looking after Ulysses and had eventually managed to settle him for a much-needed nap.

"Dear little Ulysses," said Nicola. "He can be a touch exhausting." And then added, quickly, "Not that I mind in the slightest. He is, after all, my grandson."

"I wish we still had old-fashioned gripe-water," mused Stuart. "Did you give it to me when I was a baby?"

Nicola smiled. "It was a great tragedy when they changed the formula. You can still get it, but it's a pale imitation of the original thing."

"Everybody says it settled babies miraculously," said Stuart.

"Yes, it did. It worked a treat."

"What was the magic ingredient?"

"Gin," said Nicola. "Babies love gin. It stops them girning."

Stuart laughed. "I can see why they stopped it."

"Perhaps," said Nicola. "There used to be all sorts of questionable things in popular products. Coca-Cola used to contain cocaine, I'm told – right up to the nineteen-twenties. And then there was a wonderful mixture that my mother swore by for upset stomachs, until it disappeared from the pharmacies. It was invented by one Dr John Collis Browne, and he called it Dr Collis Browne's Chlorodyne. It was a horrible brown liquid and you put a few drops in water and drank it. It worked because it contained chloroform and opiates into the bargain. It put your stomach to sleep, so to speak."

Stuart thought that a rather good idea. "What was that stuff in *Brave New World*? Soma, wasn't it?"

"It's a long time since I read that," said Nicola. "But I think you're right. The whole population was dosed with soma to keep them happy."

"Huxley may have been more prescient than we thought," said Stuart. He paused and looked morosely into his teacup before continuing. "We need to talk, Mother."

Nicola knew what was coming. She had been dreading this conversation, which she and Stuart had been having on and off for more than a week, but which had yet to be concluded. Now she took a sip of tea and put down her cup with a clatter.

"You're right, Stuart. We need to talk. I've been dreading it, but we can't pretend that Irene does not exist. She may be up in Aberdeen, but it's as if she's in the room with us here. Pachydermatically, so to speak."

Stuart nodded glumly. "Denial never works," he said.

Nicola was not sure about that. "Oh, I don't know. I think denial has its place. There's no point in fretting unnecessarily. People who deny things often strike me as being quite cheerful."

"But there's a difference between denial and that sort of attitude. You might accept that something exists but don't worry too much about it. I'm not sure if that's denial. You might call it optimism, or putting on a brave face, or whatever."

Nicola sighed. "Possibly. But here we go again. We're talking about something else when we know that we should be talking about . . ."

"About Irene's plan."

Stuart nodded again. He looked up at the ceiling, but then realised that looking up at the ceiling was a form of denial. He looked down at the floor, and thought the same. He closed his eyes. That was pure denial. "All right," he said. "She phoned me this morning."

"And?"

"She hasn't changed her mind."

For a few moments, neither spoke. Then Nicola said, "So she's insisting that Bertie go to Aberdeen?"

"Yes. For three months."

Nicola pursed her lips.

"I told her that we all thought it was a ridiculous idea," Stuart continued. "I told her that Bertie's teacher said that it would set him back if he had to go to a new school up there and then, just when he would be settling in, to bring him back to Edinburgh."

"Of course, it would," Nicola exploded. "Anybody can see that. Children need routine. They need security. They don't need to be carted off to Aberdeen for three months."

Stuart said that he had argued along those lines when Irene first raised the issue, but had got nowhere. "The thing about Irene," he said, "is that she thinks she is always right. Most of us experience the occasional moment of self-doubt, but I'm afraid she doesn't."

"No," agreed Nicola. "It must be marvellous to have such complete confidence in oneself."

Stuart continued with further details of the morning's conversation. Irene had hinted that if Stuart were to contest her decision to have Bertie with her in Aberdeen for three months, she would review their entire agreement as to custody. "It might be simpler for me to come back to Edinburgh," she said. "There's a strong case, I think, for my returning to Scotland Street full-time."

Stuart had been aghast. "But your PhD? What about your

PhD and Dr Fairbairn . . . ?"

"*Professor Fairbairn*," Irene corrected.

"Yes. What about Professor Fairbairn?"

She did not reply immediately. Then she said, "I'm not proposing to return. All that I'm asking is for Bertie to come and live with me for three months in Aberdeen and do a term at a school up here. It's all arranged. It'll broaden his horizons."

And end his world, thought Stuart.

Stuart had noticed that nothing had been said about Ulysses. "But what about Ulysses?" he said. "What about your baby?"

Irene snapped back, "*Your* baby too, may I remind you. It takes two people to produce a baby, Stuart, as I have pointed out to you before on numerous occasions. It's only because of the patriarchy that people refer to *mother and child* and so on."

Stuart gritted his teeth. "I think that perhaps you should take both of them for three months. Poor little Ulysses will wonder where his brother has gone. Wouldn't it be better for him to be up there with you?"

"Certainly not," replied Irene. "I have my PhD. I'm extremely busy. You have your mother living with you. I'm sure she's looking after Ulysses in a very satisfactory way, thank you."

After that, there was little to be said, and now Stuart explained to Nicola that the rest of the conversation had been about details, rather than the principle that Bertie should go. Irene would come to collect him, she said, the following week. Could Stuart please pack a suitcase of Bertie's clothes?

"Do I have to tell him now?" Stuart had asked.

"Of course," said Irene. "He has to be involved in this decision. He has to take his share of the ownership of it."

"You won't be here to see his tears when I tell him," Stuart muttered.

"Did you say something?" asked Irene.

Stuart put down the telephone. Now, remembering that conversation, he stared at Nicola. She was resourceful. She was constant. She was what a real mother should be – everything that Irene was not. But in this particular matter, she was powerless.

17

The Coolest Boy by Far

Amongst those who particularly enjoyed Big Lou's bacon rolls was Bruce Anderson, an alumnus of Morrison's Academy in Crieff – where he was voted, amongst other things, *Coolest Boy by Far* by the girls in the two top forms of the school; a qualified surveyor with a particular eye for undervalued property; a one-time wine dealer (not very successful); a member of the Merchants Golf Club, with a handicap of twelve; a devotee of a particular brand of clove-scented hair gel, not used by many (in fact, by virtually none); and now contemplating a new business venture, the details of which would shortly be revealed.

Bruce had gone into Big Lou's coffee bar shortly after Fat Bob had left but before Matthew was due to arrive for the cup of coffee that started his working day at the gallery.

"The usual, Lou," Bruce said, tossing his newspaper down on the table he habitually occupied.

Normally Lou said, "Right you are, Bruce," and started to prepare the double-strength cappuccino that she knew Bruce enjoyed before preparing the roll that served as his breakfast. On this particular morning, Bruce noticed that she merely nodded.

"You all right, Lou?" Bruce asked.

Big Lou looked up. "Aye, I'm just fine. And yourself?"

"It's just that . . . well, you seem a bit preoccupied."

Big Lou shrugged. "Thinking," she said.

Bruce grinned. "A dangerous thing to do, you know."

"You should try it sometime," said Big Lou.

"Hah!" Bruce paused. "Who was that guy I saw coming out just before I arrived?"

Big Lou busied herself with the coffee machine. "Guy? What guy?"

"That big chap."

Lou pressed the button that produced the steamed milk. "A customer."

"I've not seen him before," said Bruce. "And he's not a type you'd miss."

Big Lou remained silent. Bruce glanced at her. "Just asking, Lou."

He took the cup of coffee she slid across the counter and returned to his table. He glanced at his watch. Ed had said nine-fifteen, and it was now five-past. He would have time to flick through the paper before then, and at least make a start on the easy Sudoku. Bruce had only recently started doing Sudokus after reading an article in a magazine that suggested that the brain started its decline at about eighteen years of age and it was downhill all the way from there. Bruce was, in his view, exactly the right age – not yet having experienced any of the significant birthdays about which people became nervous or concerned, although his last birthday, he reflected, was one that some people regarded as significant. But whatever view one took of that, the fact remained that if your brain cells were dying off at a rate of thousands every day – and some people could really ill afford to lose that number – then at least you should do what you could to make sure that those that remained were capable of firing correctly. It was all a question of neural networks, the article explained, and these could be kept in good order by doing things like crosswords and Sudokus.

Simple, thought Bruce, and had turned to the crossword on page two of his newspaper. He had never done crosswords before, but he imagined that the clues would be simple enough if you had his intelligence. He had achieved an A grade in every one of his Higher subjects at school – every single one! And then he had waltzed through his university examinations doing virtually no work because . . . and here Bruce felt that he simply had to recognise reality without any false modesty – *simply because I am exceptionally bright*, he thought. That was all there was to it. Some people were dim, and others were so-so, not exactly *dim*, in so many words, but what Bruce liked to call 2.5 amp types. Like that fellow Steve, who was married to Molly What's-Her-Face, who was friendly with Elspeth because they had been at school together. Like him. Poor Steve. That stupid Hearts supporter. Molly was all right, if you liked that sort of girl, Bruce thought. She had been interested in him at one point, he remembered, but then most girls were. They couldn't help themselves. Poor Molly. It would have been so easy to throw her a crumb of attention – perhaps to have asked her out when they were both nineteen, something like that – but one had one's *standards*, and there was never enough time to spend with every single girl who showed an interest. Well, Bruce knew what they wanted, these poor girls. That was not their fault – of course it wasn't. You can't help biology, thought Bruce, and thought: *I am biology.*

Yes, *I am biology.* And then he looked at the crossword, at 1 across, which would probably be the best place to start, he decided, before he progressed to 2 down, and so on. He might time himself. Fifteen minutes? He was already doing the Level One Sudoku in eighteen minutes, and a crossword would not be much more difficult than that. It would probably be easier, in fact. So, here goes, he said to himself. And then, as an afterthought, *I am biology.* Yes, he liked that. *L'état, c'est moi.* Who had said that? President de Gaulle? That tall chap with the large conk? That was good as well, but *I am biology* had a certain ring to it.

1 across: *Did a former girlfriend sit for an artist to bring things to light?*

Bruce reached for the pen he carried in an inside pocket. What? Old flame? Bring things to light? *Lighten?* No, this was meant to be six letters. *Lighten* was seven.

He looked at 2 down. *Was the first clever girl in the form.* Five letters.

What? This was stupid.

Bruce looked up and saw that Big Lou was looking at him, "Having difficulty with your Sudoku, Bruce?"

There was something in her tone that irked him. Big Lou had left school with no Highers, he said to himself. Zilch. None. She made great bacon rolls, but that was about it.

"The crossword, actually, Lou."

Big Lou smiled. "What's the problem?"

"You won't get it, Lou. It's the cryptic one."

"Probably not. But what's the clue?"

"Did a former girlfriend sit for an artist to bring things to light?" Then he added. "See?"

Lou began to butter the bacon roll she was preparing for Bruce. "*Expose*," she said.

18

An Incident in Crieff

"Bruce Anderson, no less!"

Bruce looked up. He had become absorbed in the crossword, and the fifteen minutes had passed without being noticed. He had not solved any of the clues, which irritated him, particularly since Big Lou had so effortlessly come up with the answer to 1 across. *Expose.* What a stupid clue, thought Bruce. Perhaps that was the problem – the clues were just too basic, and that if he were to tackle one of those more complex crosswords – like the ones in the heavier Sunday papers, composed by people with impressive, classical *noms de plume* – then the solutions would come to him.

Bruce had not seen Ed Macdonald for almost a year, and he noticed that he had grown a small moustache. It did not suit him, thought Bruce, but then nothing suited Ed. He looked as dim without a moustache as with one. And he always wore those excessively heavy brogues in that strange-coloured leather. Ed called it *light tan*, but it was really pale yellow; and those socks with pictures of dogs on them. A serious lack of taste, thought Bruce. Poor Ed, but perhaps what you should expect from . . . where did Ed come from originally? Somewhere near Falkirk. He claimed to be from Crieff, but he wasn't really. It was somewhere nobody had ever heard of. Poor Ed.

Bruce and Ed had been at school together at Morrison's Academy, where Ed, Bruce recalled, had come last in just about everything. Not that anybody believed in ranking any more, but if they did, Ed would certainly be at the bottom. What had they voted him – those girls, Priscilla and her friends? *Worst-dressed Boy*, wasn't it? Or was it *Creepiest Guy*? Or did that go to Ed's friend Vince Treadmill? What happened to Vince, Bruce wondered. Poor Vince. Poor Ed. How tragic. Both of them. Tragic.

Ed sat down. "Doing the crossword, I see," he said. And then, sniffing at the air, "This place stinks of bacon."

Bruce looked anxiously in Big Lou's direction, but decided she had not heard.

"Keep your voice down, Ed," he said. "It's because of the bacon rolls. You should try them."

"I'm a vegetarian," said Ed. "I don't eat dead animals."

Bruce was surprised. "You used to eat hamburgers. I remember it. The grease used to run down your chin and cover your pimples. I have a very clear memory of it."

Ed smiled. "Used to, Bruce. Used to. You used to . . . No, I won't say it. Not here."

Bruce blushed.

Ed glanced again at the crossword. "You don't seem to have made much progress."

Bruce waved a careless hand. "I've been doing it mentally. I haven't written anything in."

Ed reached for the paper and looked at the crossword. "What's this?" he said. "*Interdict girl, lacking small number, fruity!*"

He looked at Bruce. "Did you get that one?"

Bruce shrugged. "Not yet."

"Banana," said Ed.

Bruce looked at him. "Banana?"

"Yes," said Ed, tossing the paper aside. "Interdict Anna? Ban her. Take one *n* out of Anna, and you're left with *banana*."

Bruce pursed his lips. "Yes, I see. I would probably have reached the same conclusion. No, I definitely would have." He paused. "You said you were going to bring somebody."

Ed nodded. "Gregor? Yes, he said he's going to be a bit late. He'll be here in ten, fifteen minutes. Don't worry. You read his e-mail I sent on to you? The one with the details of that house in the Grange?"

"We call them *particulars*," said Bruce. "In the business, details are called particulars."

Ed shrugged. "Same difference. You read it anyway?"

Bruce said that he had. "It's interesting. Just off Dick Place. Near the cricket ground."

"That's the place," said Ed.

"I played cricket there a few times," Bruce remembered. "Scored sixty-two runs once. Then I was bowled by that guy MacQueen. I wasn't ready, but the umpire was looking the wrong way."

"They often do," said Ed.

"I could have made a century. I was in with Rob Houlihan. Remember him?"

"The guy with one leg?"

"No, Rob had two."

Ed nodded vaguely. "Maybe. I get them mixed up. There was Rob Robson. You'll remember him. He stayed in Crieff. He was run over last year, you know. Outside Valentine's. Remember the outfitters – T. Palmer Valentine?"

Bruce looked down at Ed's shoes. "You got those shoes there?"

Ed nodded. "They always stock them. Anyway, Rob – Rob Robson, that is – was there with his new wife. I don't know her name – Gemma, or something like that – but she worked at the Hydro, I think. She was quite a stunner – how Rob got her is anybody's guess. He's a real minger. Anyway, he was there walking along the street, and this guy in an Alfa Romeo came round the corner and ran Rob over. Broad daylight. Bang. *Buonanotte, Roberto.*"

Bruce winced. "Poor Rob. What with his dandruff and

now . . . now being run over."

"But don't worry," Ed said quickly. "You know what? Rob picked himself up from under the car. Just like that. Picked himself up. He was unharmed – completely unharmed. Can you believe it?"

"Rugby," mused Bruce. "He was in the scrum, remember? Those guys can take anything."

"Yes, well, you know what Rob did next? This Alfa Romeo chap had got out of the car and was rabbiting on about how the sun had been in his eyes or whatever, and Rob just socked him in the jaw. Right there and then. Knocked him down."

Bruce laughed. "Rob never hung around."

"No. Not this time either. He had a lot of anger in him, I think. Years of it. All pent up. Maybe because of having his head crushed in the scrum. You know how it affects them. So this anger all came out and this guy hits the deck. Knocked out."

"No!"

"Yes. And somebody had called an ambulance for Rob, but when it arrived Rob didn't need it, so it just picked up the Alfa Romeo chap and took him off to Perth Royal Infirmary. He was okay, but the Alfa Romeo got a parking ticket."

Bruce sipped the last of his coffee. "I'm still hungry. What about you, Ed? Carrot roll?"

Ed smiled. "Very funny, Bruce."

Bruce became serious. "This place in the Grange – you want to buy it?"

"No," said Ed. "We're going to sell it. It belongs to Gregor, you see."

"The Gregor who's coming here?"

"Yes. He's an interior decorator. Paint, wallpaper, presentation. All that. He can transform anything. Saughton Prison? No problem. That old gasworks down near Trinity? Bijou flats. No question. Flair, you see. You need flair, and Gregor has serious flair." He paused. "He comes from Glasgow."

Bruce looked thoughtful. "And this place in the Grange – you say that it could be converted into flats?"

Ed nodded. "It could be. But not by us."

Bruce waited for an explanation.

"No, we'll be working on another place down the road. This one is different. We're the sellers. Or Gregor is, but we're involved. He acquired it six months ago."

Bruce asked why, if it had only recently been acquired, it should now be sold.

Ed touched the side of his nose. "Wait until Gregor comes. Then I'll tell you."

He looked at Bruce. "I hope you're discreet."

"Of course I am."

Ed hesitated. "Because what I have in mind is . . . how shall we put it? Creative. Have you got the guts for that? If not, end of story."

Bruce stared at Ed. He would not let Ed Macdonald, of all people, think he was scared of a challenge.

"Who do you think I am?" he answered scornfully.

"Good," said Ed.

19

The Money Rolls In

Gregor arrived ten minutes later.

"That's him," said Ed, half-turning in his chair. "See what I mean? A bit of style. You can't *create* that, Bruce – you've either got it or you haven't. You and I can simply look on."

Bruce bristled with resentment. What was Ed thinking of – lumping him in with himself? He began to say something, but Gregor had spotted them and was making his way towards their table.

Gregor looked at his watch. "I'm sorry to be late," he said. "My car wouldn't start." He sighed. "For the *nth* time. It's got a new starter motor, but no luck."

Ed reassured him that he understood, and then explained to Bruce, "Gregor has a Morgan – an old one."

"1953," said Gregor, smiling at Bruce. "A very good year for Bordeaux, but not necessarily for Morgans. Or not for *all* Morgans."

"That was the year they introduced the new Plus 4 with the Triumph TR2 engine," said Ed. "You probably didn't know that, Bruce."

"Yes," said Gregor. "They already had the one with the 2088cc Standard Vanguard, of course."

Ed nodded. "Sure. You heard of Vanguard, Bruce?"

Bruce smarted. "Of course."

Gregor sat down and looked in Big Lou's direction. "Does the girl come over? Or do I go to the counter?"

Bruce caught his breath. "Girl? That's Big Lou," he whispered.

Gregor smiled. Bruce noticed his perfect teeth, white against the tanned complexion. He noticed the green eyes, the confidence.

Ed offered to order coffee, and when he got up, Gregor looked at Bruce and smiled again. "I like your hair," he said.

Bruce looked down at the floor, and blushed. You did not say that sort of thing. You did not.

"What do you put on it?" asked Gregor.

Bruce cleared his throat. He felt strangely embarrassed. "Gel," he said. "Same as everybody. A lot of people use gel these days."

Gregor was still staring at him. "Oh, I know that. I use a lot of products myself. But yours has an odd smell. Is it cloves?"

Bruce drew a deep breath. He was used to being in command of social situations, but now he felt at a distinct disadvantage.

"Might be," he said.

"I think it is," said Gregor. "I rather like cloves. I've never encountered them in hair gel, though." He paused. "Ed said you're a surveyor."

"I am. And you?"

Gregor adjusted the cuff of his shirt. Linen, thought Bruce: green linen. "I do interior work," said Gregor. "Hotels, offices, private houses. I source things."

"Interior decoration?" asked Bruce.

"It's a bit more than that," said Gregor. "I source furniture. Say you have an office suite and you need twenty desks. You come to me. I get you what you need. Or flooring. You're renting an office that needs new flooring. You phone me. You get a floor."

"I see."

"Or you have a house, right? You think: I could do with some new stuff, e.g. a couple of sofas. Where do you go? You come to me, and I get you sofas that aren't going to *argue* with one another. Most furniture, Bruce, is argumentative. Give it a chance, and it'll argue with what's around it."

Bruce smiled. He thought the remark a bit arch, but it was funny.

"So," continued Gregor, "I facilitate. You could call me a facilitator."

"Or an interior decorator," said Bruce.

Gregor's manner changed. There was a coldness in the green eyes. "Let's get one thing clear, Bruce. I don't need any of that, see. E.g. implications, right?"

"I wasn't . . ." Bruce stuttered.

"You were, actually," said Gregor. "I'm not naïve." His eyes narrowed. "There are some people who are anxious about where they stand, e.g. in relation to sexuality. They make remarks that tell you more about them than the person they're making remarks about. See? Freud, e.g., opened our eyes to that one, I can tell you."

"I didn't . . ." Bruce began.

Gregor cut him off. "I'm not saying you did. I'm just saying: don't."

Any further developments in this conversation were stopped by the return of Ed, carrying Gregor's cup of coffee. "All right," he said as he sat down. "I'm going to explain to Bruce." He glanced at Gregor, who nodded.

"Bruce can keep his mouth shut," Ed went on.

Gregor glanced at Bruce. The hostility that had crept into his manner seemed not to have dissipated. He smiled. "Good."

"So this is the story," Ed began. "Let's say you're selling a property in Scotland. The standard method is to put it on the market and ask for offers. Right?"

"I know all that," said Bruce. "Remember I worked for a property company."

"All right. But there's nothing wrong with a bit of back-ground. So the house or whatever goes on the market and the lawyer gets the offers – all sealed. Then they look at them after the closing date and see who's put in the largest. That person gets the place – subject to whatever conditions they may have put in."

"It works," said Bruce. "The system works."

"Yes, I know," said Ed. "But what if you have somebody working in the solicitor's office who sees the offers and tells a potential bidder what the highest one so far is? What then? I'll tell you. That person then knows that he only has to offer one hundred pounds more – or even one pound – and he gets it."

Bruce was silent.

Ed lowered his voice. "So the idea is this. Gregor has this place in the Grange. He bought it six months ago. Now the market has moved – upwards. If he sold it now he would make . . ."

"Sixty thousand quid," said Gregor. "I.e. sixty thousand above what I paid. Sixty grand profit."

"But," Ed said, now descending to a whisper. "If we have somebody . . ."

"E.g. you," said Gregor.

"Yes, somebody e.g. you who puts in a really high offer. But then we have someone who works in the lawyer's office – big friend of Gregor here – who goes to the person putting in the next highest offer and says the highest offer so far is . . ."

"What you . . . i.e. you, Bruce, have put in," supplied Gregor.

"Then the under-bidder puts in a slightly higher offer than the figure he's been told, and *bingo!* Gregor makes one hundred thousand rather than sixty thousand. Maybe more."

Bruce thought about this. "That depends on the under-bidder doing what you expect him to do."

"Under-bidders always will," said Gregor. "In today's market they are often desperate to be the one who makes the best offer. Some of these people have lost three, four, maybe more auctions. They are at the end of their tether."

Ed sat back. "We pull it off in this one," he said. "Then we do it again. Discreetly. Carefully. And the money rolls in."

"You in, Bruce?" asked Gregor. "Some of it will roll in your direction. Percentage to be agreed."

20

Torquil at the Door

Domenica Macdonald was seated at her desk when the doorbell rang. She was struggling with the composition of a letter that she did not wish to write, because she knew the power of words – even just one or two – to end a world. She had always been in awe of the ability of a document – perhaps no more than a few lines of print on paper – to bring down a whole edifice of human arrangements, even to turn upside down the lives of million. The protocol to the Molotov–Ribbentrop Pact had been such a document – a few lines on a piece of paper, once revealed, many decades later, precipitated Estonia's departure from the Soviet Union and the events that eventually brought down the entire empire. And, in a more domestic setting, the uttering of a few words could do the same – could change the whole landscape of a life. *I love another*, for instance: three words that could bring an ocean of tears in their wake. Or a monosyllabic *no* might do the same thing: the sound of *no* was tiny, but its echoes could be huge.

Domenica sighed. Did she have an alternative but to do what was asked of her? She thought not. If she failed to respond to the request for an opinion, she herself could be accused of indifference to presuppositions and values that lay at the heart of anthropology. It would be easier to decline the request that had been made of her – there were numerous excuses to which she could resort: being overcommitted, being out of touch, being on holiday or sabbatical. Eyebrows might be raised, but eyebrows held no terrors for her. Yet she could not do that; she could not dissemble or lie outright. Not to do something was impossible – she would have to act.

She sighed again, and reached for her pen. And at that moment, as if scripted by a dramatist careless of implausibility, the doorbell rang. Domenica's next sigh was one of relief. Angus was out, and she would have to answer the door. The letter could be put off in good conscience.

She opened the door and saw before her on the landing her neighbour, Torquil. Torquil was one of a group of students who had moved into the ground-floor flat a few months earlier. There were five of them: three young men – Torquil, Dave and Alistair; and two young women, Phoebe and Rose – all of an age, all barely twenty, Domenica thought. Domenica had met Torquil on several occasions before this – he seemed to be the spokesman and was the only one who bothered to sweep their shared stair according to the rota agreed by all the flats. He was a student of classics, he had told her, while Alistair was a mathematician. Or was it Dave who was studying mathematics? No, Dave had been described by Torquil as being "too thick to study anything but environmental science" – an extraordinary assessment. Domenica did not think that environmental science was an easy or intellectually unchallenging option. Surely that was media studies – or so people said, perhaps unfairly. And if Dave was at university in Edinburgh, then he would have had to have satisfied high entry standards, otherwise he would have gone elsewhere – and enrolled in a course on media studies.

Dave had come to the party that she and Angus had thrown, and although on that occasion she had not had the chance to speak to him at length, their conversation had been enjoyable. She had found him good company, in fact, with a wry sense of humour of the sort she appreciated. Torquil had mentioned that one of the young women, Rose, had been keen on Dave and that they had been, as he put it, an *item*. It was not an expression she liked, as it had her think of shopping trollies, and she imagined Dave sitting in a shopping trolley being pushed by a triumphant Rose. Alongside him would be other household necessities obtained from the supermarket: washing-up liquid, kitchen towel, detergent, and so on, all gathered from shelves so labelled, until one came across the shelf that said *Men*, with some, perhaps, being advertised as *On Offer.*

She could understand what Rose saw in him. Like Torquil, Dave was good-looking in a way favoured by the compilers of men's clothing catalogues or advertisements for expensive watches. No thin or ungainly men are ever featured in such publicity – only those with decisive jaws, who gaze, into the middle- or far-distance, from the teak deck of a yacht or from the driver's seat of a desirable sports car. Such men not only have impeccable taste in clothing, which they wear with insouciant elegance, but they also display a penchant for Swiss watches that tell the time only incidentally to the information they provide on such matters as barometric pressure and its concomitant, height above sea-level. Domenica had never needed to know her altitude, and although she had once toyed with the idea of buying Angus a watch with elaborate functions, she had decided not to, as Angus, too, was indifferent to altitude, and indeed to the hour. As far as she could make out, he relied on the sun to tell him what time it was, and seemed unconcerned by the margin of error that such a method of time-keeping involved.

"As long as I know what day it is," he once said, "and as long as I know roughly what the month is, then do I really need to burden myself with more information?"

Now, as she stood in her doorway, she saw that Torquil was holding a parcel – what Angus called a *Maria parcel* ("brown paper packages tied up with string").

"They left this with us yesterday," he said. "You were out and it didn't fit through your letter box."

"Very little fits through there," said Domenica. "I think people used to get very thin letters in Georgian times."

"And no junk mail," said Torquil, grinning.

"Junk mail is a recent curse," said Domenica, reaching out for the parcel he was offering her.

"It feels like books," said Torquil, and then immediately qualified what he had just said. "Not that I actually felt it – not deliberately, if you see what I mean."

Domenica laughed. "I don't mind. I think one is entitled to feel a neighbour's parcels if they are left with one. That is entirely understandable human curiosity."

"But you're not entitled to hold their envelopes up to the light?" asked Torquil, in a tone of mock disappointment.

"Only *in extremis*," answered Domenica. "For a *very* good reason, that is."

She smiled at Torquil. She liked this young man – so much so that she would offer him coffee. There were people to whom one offered coffee, and people to whom one did not offer coffee. She felt in the mood for conversation. So she said, "Can I tempt you with a cup of coffee?"

And he replied, "Yes, you can tempt me." Adding, "With coffee."

They were getting on extremely well. And why not? she asked herself. Many twenty-year-olds were rather dull company because they knew so little about anything. Torquil, she decided, was different.

21

Aunts and Spies

Torquil said to Domenica, "Arabica?"

Domenica shrugged. "Possibly. I must confess, I never look at the provenance. Life is complicated enough without having to find out what sort of coffee one's drinking."

Torquil sniffed at the cup of freshly percolated coffee that Domenica had passed him. "I'd say so," he said. "There's a hint of caramel there."

Domenica shrugged again. "Coffee is coffee, as far as I'm concerned. As long as it isn't instant coffee, which isn't really coffee at all. I don't think I would be able to tell the difference between the various types."

Torquil took a sip, as a wine connoisseur might interrogate a Médoc. "You probably think it a bit showy of me," he said. "But I'm interested in the various types of coffee and what they taste like. It's not coffee snobbery."

"Of course not," said Domenica. "People should not have to apologise for knowing a lot about something." She paused. "And yet there is a certain anti intellectualism in some quarters that makes fun of expert knowledge – that regards it as pretentious."

"I wasn't accusing you of that," Torquil reassured her. He took another sip of his coffee before continuing, "I love this stuff, but it makes me feel so guilty."

Domenica looked at him. "Because you feel you should be doing something else – rather than sitting around drinking coffee?"

"Maybe," said Torquil.

"Or guilt over the origins of what you have?"

She waited.

"Each cup of coffee," Torquil said, "takes a hundred and forty litres of water to make. That's a hundred and forty litres of the world's finite supplies of fresh water."

Domenica looked up at the ceiling. "A water-print?" she said. "Is that what we should call it?"

"I like that. A water-print. A liquid footprint. Everything will have one. We get through a lot of water."

"Don't we just?" agreed Domenica. "So, should I cancel the coffee?"

"*Da mihi castitatem et continentiam, sed noli modo,*" said Torquil, smiling. "Oh Lord make me chaste, but not just yet, as St Augustine said."

Domenica remembered that Torquil was a student of classics. She topped up his cup. "In that case, here you are." She racked her brains. She wanted to keep up with this clever young man. "*Carpe calicem* . . . if that's correct."

Torquil laughed. "Seize the chalice? Why not?"

"I'm not sure if my Blue Spode should be described as a chalice," said Domenica. "But *faute de mieux.*"

"Precisely," said Torquil, and smiled, revealing the dimples she had observed when first she met him. Their placing was perfect, she thought.

Torquil was looking at her too. "You remind me of somebody," he said.

Domenica looked away. She had not intended to flirt nor to provoke flirtation on his part: her interest in this young man was not of that nature. And she was too well aware of the absurd to engage in such a fantasy, even if she had been inclined to do so. She had Angus, and was content with him, and he, she believed, with her. There was no call for any dalliance outside that – no call at all. And she was *not*, to the slightest extent – even in thought – a . . . what did they call such women? A *cougar*. She was not that. And yet, subject to all those qualifications, it was flattering to be *noticed* by a young man, and she felt, slightly, and, she hoped, imperceptibly, a blush on her cheeks.

"Yes," said Torquil, taking a further sip of his coffee, and looking at her again, as if trying to dredge an answer from memory. "You remind me of . . ." And then it came to him. "Of my aunt," he concluded.

Domenica came down to earth – so quickly that she felt the bump might even have been detectable through the floorboards.

"Oh," she said, adding, lamely, "I see. Your aunt. How . . ." How what? She decided: "How evocative."

There was no sign that Torquil had noticed her dismay. "She has the same high cheekbones," he said. "And the same lines around the side of her mouth." He indicated on the side of his own mouth where the aunt's – and Domenica's – lines were. "Here. There's one in particular that goes up at an angle of about seventy degrees, like this."

"Erosion happens," said Domenica reflectively. And thought: except to the young. For them, the ravages that afflict the skin are theoretical – things that happen to other people – like death itself. Of course, when it came to any discussion of the ageing of the skin it was best to be disarming in one's frankness – to own, in a courageous way, the ravines and gullies to which the flesh was heir. How was WH Auden's famously cracked face described? As looking like a wedding cake left out in the rain. And of course Auden himself had referred to his face as having experienced a geological catastrophe. That was the way to refer to oneself. *I am falling to bits.* If you said that before anybody else said it, then the process of disintegration was far less painful.

Torquil frowned. "I hope I'm not being tactless," he said. "You don't mind, do you?"

"Mind?" exclaimed Domenica. She waved an insouciant hand. "Why on earth should I mind? This aunt of yours . . . tell me about her. No, let me guess. Where does she live? Helensburgh? That's a very suitable place for an aunt to live. Helensburgh and Rhu are stuffed full of aunts. I know somebody who has *three* aunts in Rhu. Can you believe that? Or North Berwick? Once again, aunts haunt North Berwick, I'm led to believe."

"She lived in Broughty Ferry," Torquil began. "*Lived.* I'm afraid she's no longer with us. She's dead."

"Oh, I'm sorry." So, she had invoked memories not only of an aunt, but an aunt who had expired. Oh well . . .

Torquil was philosophical. "Old age. She was pretty ancient, and nobody was all that surprised when she died."

Domenica sighed. "It doesn't do to surprise people. If one is going to die, then ideally one should try to give some indication in advance – like a character in an opera who sings *I am dying* for a number of bars before expiring. Poor Mimi in *La Bohème* is a case in point."

"I was very fond of her," Torquil reminisced. "She worked for British intelligence. She knew Anthony Blunt. You know about him?"

"Of course I do. The art historian spy. The authority on Poussin. The Soviet agent who was a cousin of the Queen Mother."

"She told me a lot about him," said Torquil. "They got on rather well, although she knew him well after he had retired from espionage. He was at the Courtauld Institute then. She understood why he did what he did, she said, even if it was the wrong thing to do. At the time, he believed that that was what was morally required of him. He later regretted it bitterly."

"I can see that," said Domenica. "I don't think that he saw Stalin for what he was. Quite a few people made that mistake."

"She told me that Blunt went to the cinema after he had been outed as a spy," Torquil went on. "It was in Notting Hill. People recognised him and slow-clapped him out of the auditorium."

Domenica winced. People loved to shame and humiliate others. It was universal. *The fact that you are so bad makes me feel a whole lot better about myself . . .*

22

Oedipus, the Minotaur, Guilt

"We were talking about guilt," said Torquil.

"Yes," said Domenica. "*Inter alia*. We also touched on aunts and Soviet agents."

Torquil smiled. "But you're the one who brought up guilt."

"I think you did. Or did I? Anyway, the topic did come up. I think it was in the context of drinking coffee and how getting coffee beans to market used so much precious water. That sort of guilt."

"That's right. I find that interesting."

Domenica agreed that it was. "Guilt is definitely one of the great subjects. It's pervasive, ubiquitous, and profoundly unsettling."

"I'm doing a course in classical mythology as part of my degree," said Torquil. "Guilt figures prominently."

"I'm sure it does," said Domenica. "Oedipus springs to mind. He certainly felt guilty once he discovered that Jocasta was his mother. It made him put his eyes out in expiation."

"I felt sorry for him, but then, who wouldn't? I also felt sorry for the Minotaur. Did you? The pain of being a genetic freak."

"I haven't given much thought to the Minotaur," said Domenica. "I suppose I never really related to him. But I definitely felt sorry for Oedipus." She paused. "I can think of very few societies where incest fails to give rise to a particular horror. Did you know that in Scots law, until not all that long ago, the offence of incest was simply defined by reference to Leviticus, chapter 18?"

Torquil raised an eyebrow. He was not sure about Leviticus.

"Yes," said Domenica. "It was convenient, I suppose, and it expressed a repugnance that would have been widely shared."

Torquil thought of something. "Could you base an entire system of criminal law on the Ten Commandments?"

"No," said Domenica. "Coveting one's neighbour's ox is hardly criminal. Nor are most forms of lying. Nor adultery, come to think of it." She paused. "Criminal law requires clear definition – the lines we're not meant to cross should never be vague ones. Mind you, we have some pretty odd corners in Scots criminal law. There's an offence known as *lewd and libidinous conduct*. A vivid description."

"How do you know all this?" asked Torquil.

"I'm an anthropologist," Domenica replied. "*Homo sum, humani nihil a me alienum puto*, as you – or Terence – might say."

"Ah, Terence," mused Torquil. "You know he was a slave? He was freed and went on to write six comedies."

"His sense of humour obviously survived."

Torquil returned to guilt. "We go in a lot for guilt, don't we? I mean, by comparison."

"By comparison with whom?"

Torquil looked out of the window. "Oh, just about anybody, I think. Mediterranean cultures don't seem to me to be very concerned with it. The Italians rarely mention Mussolini. It's almost bad form to do so, I believe."

Domenica agreed. "It's not exactly a guilt-ridden culture," she said. "You have to go further north for that. It's to do with the Protestant conscience, of course." She paused. "Look at Germany. Look at how they have been burdened with guilt for what happened. By and large, they then faced up to it. They berated themselves. Others perhaps less so . . . The Poles have suffered so much, and there are those who might consider apologising to them. Not that I'm thinking of anybody in particular."

"Whereas we . . ."

"We don't have a conspicuous record of apology. We haven't been keen to see ourselves as wrongdoers," said Domenica. "We've brushed a lot under the carpet, even if we have occasionally felt the odd twinge of guilt. Not enough, some people say."

"Didn't Tony Blair apologise to Ireland – for failing to help during the famine?"

Domenica smiled. "I remember him with a certain nostalgia – along with all the others. Yes, he apologised, as did Mr Clinton – for various wrongs previous American governments had committed. All governments, it seems, have acted shabbily on occasions. As have we all."

Torquil looked momentarily uncomfortable, and Domenica wondered what this young man could have done. But he was not about to confess, moving instead to a general observation on apology. "Of course, there's a lot for which nobody has apologised, isn't there?" he said. "Child labour? Land grabs? Opium wars? Slavery? Highland Clearances? It's a long list, once one starts it."

"We've begun to be more aware of just how awful all that was," said Domenica. "We preferred to put it out of our mind in the past, but now . . . Well, we're looking in the mirror a bit more."

"And?"

"Everything we have is tarnished," Domenica continued. "Once you start to follow the money, so to speak, that becomes clearer and clearer. And yet . . ."

"And yet what? Are you saying we should forget about it?"

Domenica shook her head. "No, I wouldn't say that. All that I'd say, I suppose, is that there must be a limit to the extent to which one shoulders a burden of guilt. You can make out a cogent case for saying that any financial advantage a society like ours enjoys is ill-gotten and that if we were being morally scrupulous, we would rid ourselves of all our assets – absolutely everything. But what would that do? It would lead to immense suffering – in the here and now, amongst ordinary people who may not share the sense of guilt of those with a more developed historical awareness."

"So you're saying that excessive guilt is impractical?"

"Yes, I suppose it is, because you don't really help anybody living today – any actual people – if you destroy yourself through guilt. That's pathological guilt – it would be crippling – and crippling oneself hardly makes sense if you want to change the way the world is."

She watched his expression as she spoke. Sometimes it was hard to argue with somebody of his age. Everything was so clear-cut to the student mind; the truth was passionately proclaimed, rather than half-believed in, which was how more experienced people thought of things. The more experienced had generally discovered that there were no longer any privileged, exclusive truths – there were just the various shades of possibility.

But Torquil appeared to understand. "Do you know Luc Ferry's book, *The Wisdom of the Myths*?" he asked.

Domenica did not.

"He deals with the world-view of Greek mythology," Torquil said. "And the whole point about their myths was that they set out to illustrate how humans fitted into a world that was governed by elemental forces – certain givens that just *were*."

"I see." He understands, thought Domenica: this young man *understands*.

Torquil continued with his observation. "The Greeks wanted to show how a balanced, good life could be led by somebody who accepted his limitations and the arbitrary nature of the world in which he lived. That was at the heart of the good life – acceptance. They thought that you shouldn't go around feeling miserable because of what had already happened, about what happened in the past."

He's very good-looking, thought Domenica, even when talking about ancient Greek cosmology. But then she remembered that she reminded him of his late aunt, and within herself she sighed – a sigh that was like the movement of the most imperceptible of breezes on a still day, when the air lay heavy over Scotland and nothing moved.

23

Torquil and Domenica Converse

Like all good conversations, that between Domenica and her student neighbour, Torquil, moved easily, as if borne on a slow-flowing river – a broad waterway that knows where it is going, is confident that it will get there, and is in no particular hurry to reach its destination. They sat and talked in Domenica's kitchen, watching a shaft of light inch gradually across the floorboards, past the place where Angus had once stood on a tube of paint, spreading a Rorschach blot of vermilion across the wood, inadequately lifted by paint stripper; past signs of ancient woodworm; past the tip of the nail hammered in squint over a hundred years ago by the hand of a disgruntled apprentice.

Torquil shared Domenica's interest in the neighbours – unusual for one still at an age when solipsism is standard. "I've met a lot of them," he said, "including people round the corner in Drummond Place. There's a nun . . ."

Domenica smiled as she interrupted him. "Sister Maria-Fiore dei Fiori di Montagna?" she said. "A slight figure with a rather sharp nose?"

She realised, of course, that the description was otiose: there were fewer and fewer nuns about, and none, she thought, in the immediate vicinity.

Torquil nodded. "That must be her. And that's a name-and-a-half. She didn't introduce herself when we met. She just said she was Antonia's friend. That's all."

"Antonia Collie," said Domenica. "My former neighbour through the wall. We go back some time."

Torquil picked up a note of reservation in Domenica's voice. "You're close to her?" he asked.

Domenica took a sip of her coffee. "I must be charitable," she said. "What are we without charity?"

Torquil laughed. "Charity should not prevent one from saying what one thinks."

Domenica thought about this. It was quite wrong: that was exactly what charity should do. She said, "Do you really think so? I'm afraid I must disagree. It's charity, surely, that stops us giving voice to our thoughts. If I took exception to your appearance for some reason, I should not tell you what I was thinking. If you did something really badly, charity might prevent me saying anything about your lack of skill. *Und so weiter*, Torquil."

"What?"

"And so on. It's German. One might say *etcetera etcetera*."

"Or *And so on and so forth?*"

"Yes. It just sounds a little less . . . how shall I put it? Dismissive?"

"Tell me about Antonia," asked Torquil. "I think she must be the woman I saw walking down Great King Street with Sister Maria-Fiore dei . . ."

". . . *Fiori d'etcetera etcetera*," supplied Domenica. "*Schwester und so weiter*, indeed."

"Yes, her. I saw the two of them walking along Great King Street, deep in conversation."

"Plotting," said Domenica. "Those two do plot a great deal."

"About?"

"I have no hard evidence," said Domenica. "But I think a lot of it is about strategy for Sister Maria-Fiore dei Fiori di Montagna's social advancement. She's a ruthless social climber, positively Alpine in her ambitions. In fact . . ." Domenica paused to grin, "In fact, I said to Angus the other day that we might expect her at any moment to appear in the street hooked up to oxygen cylinders – you know, of the sort that climbers use when they get above a certain altitude on Everest. She'd need those for her high-altitude social climbing."

Torquil burst out laughing. "It would be a dead giveaway for the really serious social climber, wouldn't it?"

Domenica nodded. They were having such fun. "She's scaled unimaginable heights since she arrived. Remember that she came from conditions of great obscurity – she was an unpromoted nun from the Little Sisters of the Bourgeoisie, or whatever her order was called. They kept a house outside Florence where they looked after people who had been afflicted with Stendhal syndrome while visiting the Uffizi. Poor Antonia was one of those."

"That's where you're overcome by great art?" asked Torquil.

"The very condition. Shortness of breath caused by looking at *Primavera*. Raised temperature caused by exposure to Ghirlandaio and Raphael. That sort of thing. It's a very refined syndrome. Antonia got it and was looked after in Florence before they sent her out into the country to this place run by these rural nuns. They kept bees and had a lettuce farm, I believe, but I gather their life was not quite the simple affair that we expect nuns to be content with. No, they looked after themselves quite well, I gather. Not only did they make gin, which they had the bad taste to call *Communion Gin*, but they also made tonic water. And grew lemons. That gives the overall picture, I think."

"Well, why not?" said Torquil. "People talk about a broad church."

"Indeed, they do. And the Catholic Church has always been quite happy to allow sybarites to flourish. Cardinals traditionally kept a good table. And they had a place for all sorts of intellect – from simple brothers whose job it was to pick carrots and scrub floors to calculating Jesuits who could twist on the head of a pin. It has always been broad."

"I'm Episcopalian myself," said Torquil. "In a sort of way. I like a high service. Music by Byrd. Incense and so on."

"Nothing wrong with incense," said Domenica. "I love the sight of wafting smoke. It reminds us that not everything is linear and purposeful. It drifts. Suffuses. I most definitely do not approve of the habit of spraying incense from aerosol cans."

"No! Nobody does that, surely?"

Domenica smiled. "It's conceivable. A convinced modernist might."

Torquil brought the conversation back to reality. "So Antonia met her there? In the convent?"

"It was more of a villa than a convent," said Domenica. "But yes, that's where they met. And she brought her over to Scotland out of gratitude for what they had done for her. She actually joined them in some capacity or other – a lay sister or a member of the supporters' club, or whatever they call it."

"Did she take on a name?" asked Torquil. "Something like Sister Maria-Fiore's?"

Domenica thought for a moment. They were not only having fun – they were having *great* fun.

"Sister Antonia of the Blue Spode," she suggested.

Torquil's eyes shone. Blue Spode? Life in Edinburgh was so intriguing – who would have thought? But Domenica, by contrast, now reproached herself. She had overstepped the mark: it was only easy to make fun of somebody like Antonia. She should not.

"Antonia has many good points," she said. "And I wouldn't want to be dismissive of her. We all have our faults – some, of course, having rather more than others." That qualification was somewhat self-defeating: charity, she reminded herself, *charity*, and was ashamed.

24

Agrippina and Nero

"But then," said Torquil, "what about downstairs? Stuart, is it? And his two boys? And his mother, who seems to have moved in permanently? Somebody said that Stuart's wife has gone off to Aberdeen with a lover. Is that true?"

Domenica poured both of them a fresh cup of coffee. She was enjoying this conversation with her neighbour, even if it was . . . well, if one were to be honest with oneself, it was gossip. But then what was wrong with that? A life devoid of at least the occasional gossip would surely be a bit bland – like an endless stock-market report, or some such recitation of simple fact, or a meal without salt, pepper, or any other seasoning. Gossip allowed one to be amused by the human comedy, involved irony and other shadings of the palette, and was permissible, surely, as long as it refrained from cruelty. Gossip cemented our links with one another, reminded us of community. In the foibles of others, after all, we saw ourselves – or should do.

"Yes," said Domenica. "Irene – Stuart's wife, and mother of Bertie and Ulysses – is now doing a PhD in Aberdeen. She comes down here from time to time – I saw her a few weeks ago, briefly – but it's Nicola – Stuart's mother – who is looking after the boys. Stuart himself, of course, is a conscientious, hands-on father, but he struggles a bit." She paused. "In fact, he has struggled for years, that man. Irene was a touch on the dominant side. In fact, she was completely appalling. A termagant. The day she left was liberation day as far as Stuart was concerned. And the boys. And the rest of us too.

There was dancing in the street. Fireworks." She looked at Torquil, who was listening wide-eyed. "I exaggerate a touch. But we were certainly pleased."

"I see," said Torquil.

"I suppose she meant well," said Domenica, slightly reluct-antly. "But she was devoid of tolerance of other people's views. She hectored. And that poor little boy, poor wee Bertie. How he suffered! He's composed of pure goodness, and he never complained about that mother of his – he bore it all with fortitude. Italian lessons from the age of four – yes, four! He's seven now, and, if anything, the pressure is worse – or at least it was until Aberdeen beckoned Irene. Psychotherapy every week – every week! Yoga sessions down at Stockbridge. It was relentless. And all the time he just wanted to be an ordinary little boy, doing the things that ordinary little boys do."

Torquil shook his head. "It's rather hard to be a boy these days, I think."

"Virtually impossible," Domenica agreed. "There may be a place where boys roam free – but it's not here."

Torquil looked thoughtful. "She sounds a bit like Agrippina."

Domenica tried to remember who Agrippina was. A Roman clearly, but beyond that . . .

"She was Nero's mother," Torquil explained. "I've been writing an essay on Nero in my ancient history course. You have to do ancient history if you do classics – you can't do just the languages and literature, you have to do the Caesars and the corn supply and the decline of the Republic and all that. Nero's rather interesting. He's being rehabilitated at the moment, believe it or not. There's been a big exhibition in London of Nero-related material, and the line is: Nero wasn't as bad as he's been portrayed."

"Revisionism," said Domenica. "People can't resist the temptation to change the way we see figures of the past.

They've been doing that with the Vikings. There are quite a few historians now who argue that the Vikings meant well."

"That they weren't just about burning and pillaging?"

"Exactly. Apparently, that was not the whole point of Viking raids. The real point was to spread Scandinavian culture. The Vikings were very keen on art and music, according to this view."

Torquil shook his head. "I doubt it."

"So do I."

"Nero, of course, was interested in the arts."

"All I remember learning of him at school," Domenica said, "was that he played the fiddle . . ."

"While Rome burned. Yes, that was his metaphor, so to speak. But he was actually rather interesting."

"And Agrippina was his mother?"

"She was married to Claudius. You may have read . . ."

"Robert Graves? Yes, I did." It was a long time ago, though, and she remembered nothing about the book except its title, and the fact that Claudius stammered.

"She was a great poisoner. They murdered Claudius by feeding him a poisoned mushroom. Of course, he had a food-taster, who sampled the mushrooms and pronounced them fine, but they slipped in a large, choice one that he knew Claudius would go for. And he did. And that was the end of him."

"She was ruthlessly ambitious," Torquil continued. "She loved power, and her sole objective in life was to acquire more of it for herself and her son, Nero. That was the agenda. So, once Claudius was out of the way, Nero took over with Agrippina standing behind him, so to speak. He was just a teenage boy when he found himself ruler of a vast empire. He was a bit wild. I read that he used to disguise himself in ordinary clothes and go out at night with the boys, and get into all sorts of fights."

"Others have gone out in disguise," Domenica mused. "The Gudeman of Ballengeich? James V? He used to dress in humble clothes and go out among the people."

"Of course. And the Duke of Edinburgh used to drive himself round London in a taxi cab."

"Agrippina?" Domenica reminded him.

"She tried to control Nero. She was the ultimate interfering mother. Unfortunately, Nero murdered her. He had a special boat built that was designed to break in two and tip her into the sea. He saw her off on this after inviting her for dinner at his seaside villa. Halfway across the Bay of Naples, the boat performed as intended. Agrippina found herself in the water, but managed to get herself picked up by some obliging fishermen. Nero sent men round to her house to finish her off. It was very unpleasant. One should not treat one's mother like that."

"Definitely not," said Domenica. "One should appreciate one's mother. One should not tip her into the sea."

"And ye cannae shove your granny aff a bus," added Torquil.

Domenica laughed. "That goes without saying," she said.

25

Bertie's Fate

As the conversation between Domenica and Torquil was taking place, downstairs in the Pollock flat Stuart and Nicola were breaking to Bertie the news of his forthcoming exile to Aberdeen. Both adults were putting on a brave face and trying to present the uncomfortable news in as positive a manner as possible.

"Just think," Stuart gushed. "Aberdeen! You're a very fortunate boy, Bertie. There are lots of boys who would give anything to go to Aberdeen for three months."

"Yes," said Nicola. "Lots."

Bertie had his eyes fixed firmly on the floor. "Name one," he said.

Nicola glanced at Stuart. "Well, we weren't thinking of anybody in particular. But that doesn't mean that there aren't lots of boys who would give their eye teeth to have the chance to spend three whole months at a different school."

"Yes," enthused Stuart. "Three months at another school will mean a whole lot of new friends. Just think of that."

"I don't want new friends, Daddy," Bertie pleaded. "I've got Ranald Braveheart Macpherson. He's my friend. He's the best friend anybody could ever have."

Stuart assured Bertie that he was second to none in his admiration for Ranald. "But it's always good to have a bit of a change, you know, Bertie. Meeting new people broadens the horizons. New people are exciting. You'll have a lot of fun with your new friends in Aberdeen."

"I have a lot of fun with Ranald," said Bertie.

"Of course, you do," said Nicola. "But Daddy has a point, you know, Bertie. New friends are always interesting." She paused. "Aberdeen is a very friendly place, you know. It's a bit like Glasgow. I know how much you admire Glasgow, Bertie – well, Aberdeen is very similar to Glasgow, I think."

Bertie looked at his grandmother. Did she really believe that? Did she really think that Glasgow and Aberdeen were in the slightest bit similar? Was there something wrong with his grandmother? Was this the cognitive decline he had read about in one of Irene's psychology books?

"I don't think they are, Granny," Bertie said politely. "You don't find people like Mr O'Connor in Aberdeen, I think."

Stuart forced himself to laugh. "Oh, Mr O'Connor – my goodness me – I'd forgotten all about him." Bertie had met the late Lard O'Connor (RIP) in Glasgow when Stuart had mislaid their car there, and the meeting had made a deep impression on him.

Nicola took over. "Places have different merits, Bertie," she said. "You wouldn't want everywhere to be the same, would you?"

Bertie considered this. "But you're the one who said Glasgow and Aberdeen were the same," he pointed out. "You said that, Granny."

Nicola sighed. "I was just trying to reassure you, Bertie. And what I said is a bit true, even if not completely true. Glasgow and Aberdeen have some things in common – and other things that are a bit different. What I'm saying is that you will find the equivalent in Aberdeen of things you might expect to find in Glasgow."

Bertie looked unconvinced. "Are there polar bears in Aberdeen?" he asked.

Stuart laughed. "Good heavens, Bertie. Where on earth did you get that idea? No, there are no polar bears in Aberdeen. It's in the north, but not that far north."

Something else was bothering Bertie. "Will I get enough to eat?" he asked.

Stuart and Nicola exchanged glances. Poor little boy – how prey were children to the most extraordinary insecurities.

"Of course you will," said Stuart. "Mummy will be looking after you. You know what a good cook she is."

This was quite untrue, and all of them knew it, including Bertie; Irene was completely incompetent in the kitchen. But it was not his mother's lack of cooking prowess that was worrying him – it was the general question of what would be available.

"Ranald said that everybody thinks they're mean," Bertie explained. "Ranald said that people in Aberdeen can survive for a whole month on three plates of porridge. He said that there has been research on this. He said that it's because they don't like spending money. They save on food."

"That's absolute nonsense, Bertie," exclaimed Stuart. "People in Aberdeen are *not* mean, Bertie. They are the most generous, warm-hearted, joyful people you could possibly hope to meet."

Nicola gave Stuart a sideways look.

"And Ranald says it's very cold," Bertie continued. "He said that they won't spend money on heating their houses."

"Nonsense," said Stuart.

"Ranald says that people in Aberdeen don't need to buy fridges," Bertie continued. "He said that food keeps for ages in Aberdeen."

"Pure nonsense," said Stuart. "Ranald clearly doesn't know what he's talking about."

Bertie became silent. Then he said, "I don't want to go, Daddy. I don't want to upset Mummy, but I think it's best if I didn't go. I'm very happy here with you and Granny, and even with Ulysses. I don't see why I have to go to Aberdeen."

Stuart tried to explain. "Mummy loves having you with

her, Bertie," he said. "She's keen that you go and spend some time with her. She thinks you'll love Aberdeen and you'll have great fun together."

Bertie shook his head. "I won't, Daddy. I really won't. I like being here with you – and with Granny. I like going to Valvona & Crolla. I like having my own room and all the things in it. I'm really very happy, Daddy."

"I'm sure you are, Bertie," said Stuart. "And let me tell you this: if it were up to me, you'd stay. But it isn't entirely up to me, Bertie. Mummy is allowed to have her turn. That's only fair, isn't it?"

"Couldn't she take Ulysses instead? Wouldn't she be happy with that, Daddy?" It was, Bertie knew, a vain hope. Ulysses, with his regurgitation and his smells, was not everybody's cup of tea, and certainly not his mother's.

"But . . ." Bertie stopped. It was hard for him to go on. He knew that there was nothing that he could do to stop his being sent to Aberdeen. He had never – not once in his life – been able to stop the things that happened to him. They simply happened, as if ordained by some cosmic force, some destiny, that was beyond him to influence. In that respect, he felt as any small child feels. He knew he would not like Aberdeen, even if it was only for three months, and three months, people said, could go quite quickly.

He was content in Edinburgh. He was happy at school, in spite of the terrible people in his class – Olive and Pansy, whose delight, it seemed, was to taunt him at all points; Tofu, whose criminality in all matters lay just below the surface, and who put pressure on Bertie to bring sausages to school so that he might purloin them; Larch, who was generally unpredictable; Luigi, who had recently joined the school from a Montessori School in Palermo, who had set up a small protection racket in the playground, and who spoke, darkly, of his cousins upon whom he could call if thwarted. There were others, of course, of whom the adult world, in its innocence, was quite unaware. In spite of all that, Bertie was happy, and he saw no reason why his life should be turned upside down simply so that his mother could show him off to her new friends. He was not a Pinocchio, an animated toy on strings. He was a boy, and he wanted to stay with his dad, of whom he was so proud.

He looked at his father, willing him to declare that there was a change of plan and Bertie could stay where he was, in Scotland Street. But Stuart came up with no such statement.

26

Stuart Goes Out

Stuart felt exhausted. The attempt that he and Nicola had made to persuade Bertie that three months in Aberdeen was something to which he should look forward had failed, as he feared it would. At length, after they had said all they possibly could about the attractions of life in the northern city, resorting even to reference to the delights of Aberdonian bread rolls – *butteries* – silence descended, capped with Nicola's comment, "Well, Bertie, you're old enough to know that there are some things that we just have to do. We may not like them, but we have to do them." That remark, true enough in its way, had nonetheless undone the entire official line presented to that point that Aberdeen, like Glasgow, was a shining city on a hill, and that Bertie should look forward to three months there in the company of his mother.

Nicola was in charge of bedtime that day. Ulysses was already asleep, snoring loudly in the way in which, atypically for a young child, he had always done. Medical advice had been sought, and his nose had been closely examined by a paediatric ear, nose and throat specialist at the Sick Kids. It had been pronounced to have slightly unusual properties but nonetheless to be within the range of normality and would not require any medical attention.

"It's very large," Bertie had observed. "That's why he snores, I think. Could they not cut a bit off at the hospital? Just a bit?"

Stuart had smiled, but his smile had faded with Bertie's next comment, innocently made, but nonetheless not the sort of remark that Stuart wished to hear.

"It's funny, isn't it, Daddy," Bertie had continued, "that Ulysses' nose is so like Dr Fairbairn's. It's the same shape, I think, particularly if you look at it from the side." He paused. "I wonder if Dr Fairbairn snores. Mummy probably knows that. I could ask her, I suppose."

This had been said in the hearing of Nicola, who was setting up the bread-maker at the time, and who, distracted by what had been said, spilled a large quantity of flour on the floor. She did not know Dr Fairbairn well, but had met him on a couple of occasions and knew that what Bertie said about the similarity was quite true. She also suspected that any resemblance between Ulysses and the psychotherapist was not merely coincidence, although she had not voiced her doubts in this respect to Stuart. But now that was exactly what Bertie was doing, and Nicola waited anxiously to see how Stuart might respond.

Stuart had looked up at the ceiling. He had always done that, Nicola reminded herself. Even when he had been a small boy and had been found to have committed some minor transgression, he had looked up at the ceiling while being reprimanded. And Nicola remembered how at his wedding, when vows were exchanged, she had glanced at her son from her position in the front pew of the church and had seen that he was looking up at the ceiling. That had struck her as a bad sign, and for a moment she had reflected that perhaps her instinct to wear black to that particular wedding had been a sound one. But one did not wear black to a wedding, however strong the temptation.

Stuart had stared at the ceiling and had then said to Bertie, "I don't think we should talk about other people's noses, Bertie – I really don't."

That was typical of Stuart, thought Nicola. Much as she loved her son, she was not blind to his faults, and one of them was an unwillingness to address painful issues. It was that failing that had led, she thought, to his putting up with Irene and her ways as long as he had. If he had only had the courage to stand up to her at an early stage – their honeymoon would have been a good time to start – then he might not have been relegated to the subsidiary role that had then been his lot for the remainder of the marriage. And even now, when the two of them were leading separate lives, it seemed to be Irene who was calling all the shots.

Of course, it was difficult to see what he could possibly do about this tricky issue of paternity. Even if it were the case that Ulysses *was* Dr Fairbairn's son, as she suspected was the case, it was not at all clear how the admission of that fact would change anything. Parentage could never be a child's fault: none of us, after all, chose the bed in which we were born, and nor did that have any bearing on the immediate needs of a child. It was unthinkable that she or Stuart could ever claim that Ulysses was nothing to do with them: he was their son and grandchild whatever his provenance, and it would be quite wrong to open that issue.

Now, with Ulysses' snores reverberating from his small bedroom at the back of the flat, Bertie had been tucked up in his own bed and left to read for half an hour or so before lights out. When Stuart next checked up on him, he found Bertie was fast asleep, having dropped the book that now lay on the rug beside his bed. Stuart picked it up, glancing at the title. Bertie was a prodigious reader, picking up anything he came across, and devouring books well beyond anything one would normally expect a seven-year-old to read. That evening it was Eric Linklater's *The Prince in the Heather*, a book that Bertie had discovered in the help-yourself library box at the end of Scotland Street and in which he had quickly immersed himself, giving regular précised accounts of the contents to Ranald Braveheart Macpherson, who had yet to learn how to read.

Stuart looked down at Bertie's tousled hair upon the pillow. He looked at the space-rocket motif of the pillowcase: little astronauts in bubble-helmets, floating in space alongside their space dogs, similarly clad in shiny inflated space-dog suits. He looked at the lobe of his son's right ear, with its tiny indentation, a genetic peculiarity of the Pollock family, passed down from generation to generation like a family badge, from the earliest ancestor they had identified, a Covenanting minister from the south-west of Scotland. The minister had been captured in a pencil sketch by his wife, who had drawn his ear with its characteristic mark. In these little ways, we were bound up in the notion of family and continuity, of identity – the things which we held so tenuously against all the confusion of this world. We had to believe in something, thought Stuart; we had to think that something was important, that something counted, because otherwise what were our lives but tiny events of no significance at all?

He reached down and switched off Bertie's light before returning to the kitchen.

"I'm going out," he said to Nicola.

She looked at him. She did not ask him why, or where, but he told her nonetheless.

"I'm going to walk round Drummond Place Garden. I need some air."

She sighed. She knew what was going to happen. He was going to get in touch with Irene and go back on everything that had so far been agreed. Irene would resume control of their lives, running them from Aberdeen, returning to Edinburgh from time to time to exert her control. He would never leave that woman – never. She sighed again. Even an anticyclone of sighs would not be sufficient to express the regret engendered by this situation; Irene was permanent; Irene was immutable; Irene was omnipotent.

27

Sister Maria-Fiore dei Fiori's Secret

Stuart was pleased to find that he was alone in Drummond Place Garden, where the late evening light, slanting in from the west, was still touching the highest branches of the sycamores. The sky above the city was empty of clouds and marked only by the high vapour-trail of a passenger jet bound for America. The jet itself could just be made out, a tiny arrow of steel slicing through the attenuated blue, and Stuart thought of what it would be like to be unencumbered in this life, to be free, to be able to step aboard a plane like that and leave everything behind you. The manacles we forge for ourselves might be comfortable ones, may not chafe too much, and yet they are manacles nonetheless – bonds of family, of profession, of debt, of personal obligation. Or they may be woven of the simple and only too familiar lassitude that prevents us from doing anything to disturb the established patterns of our life.

He began his walk round the perimeter of the Garden, following the path widdershins, as he usually did, enjoying the crunch of gravel underfoot. Somewhere off to his left, a bird called out a greeting – or was it a challenge? It was as difficult, he thought, for us to interpret what birds were saying as it was for them to make sense of our human babble. He hoped it was a thrush, because he loved thrushes and believed that a pair of these birds had taken up residence somewhere nearby, possibly in the Garden itself.

Irene was in his mind, her disapproving gaze fixed resolutely upon him, even here, in the solitude of the Garden. He now suspected that the three months that Bertie was to spend in

Aberdeen would be the beginning of a longer sojourn there –
one that would soon become, if he were insufficiently vigilant,
six months, and then a year, and ultimately an indeterminate
time. He feared that he might lose Bertie altogether; Irene
had never been one to share, in spite of her communitarian
rhetoric, and she would not hesitate to unpick their carefully
negotiated custody agreement. And the mere thought of
losing Bertie was too awful to contemplate, because Bertie,
he realised, was his world. Yes, he had his career as a statis-
tician; yes, he had a few friends whom he saw from time
to time; yes, he had the constant and unstinting support of
his mother, Nicola; yes, he had interests that diverted and
sustained him, but none of these things was as central to him,
as important, as his son. Without Bertie, he would be bereft, at
a complete loss, devoid of any real reason to continue with life.

His eyes fixed on the ground beneath his feet, Stuart only
saw Sister Maria-Fiore dei Fiori di Montagna when he was
more or less upon her. She had been walking deosil, in the
opposite direction to him, and he almost bumped into her as
he turned a corner in the path.

The nun smiled. "I had thought myself alone," she said.
"And now, here you are."

Stuart felt a slight irritation at her presence. The Garden,
although privately owned, was open to anybody who was
fortunate enough to possess a key, as both he and Sister Maria-
Fiore did. And yet there were times at which the presence of
others seemed like an intrusion, and that was how he now felt.

"Yes," he said. "Here I am."

Sister Maria-Fiore dei Fiori di Montagna clasped her
hands together, as if about to pray. But it was not into words
of prayer that she now launched, but rather an aphorism.
"Those we find before us are often those who we have been
seeking," she said, adding, "Even if we did not know that we
were seeking them."

Stuart stared at her. "Possibly," he said. "Although you and I disprove the proposition, I would have thought: neither of us has been seeking the other."

This might have deflated the nun, but it did not. "*A contrario*," she said, unclasping her hands to make the point. "We may have been seeking one another because we know – even if we do not know – that the other is the one we need to find." She paused, and then, in a lower, more matter-of-fact register, continued, "You look upset, Stuart. Is there something wrong?"

Stuart was about to say that nothing was wrong, but found that he lacked the energy to dissemble. "I feel awful," he said, and then, without waiting for further encouragement told her about Irene's demand that Bertie go to her in Aberdeen for three months. Sister Maria-Fiore listened sympathetically, and then said, "She's punishing you, of course."

Stuart's eyes narrowed. What did this nun know of the history of their troubled marriage?

"I don't know . . ."

"No, she is," insisted Sister Maria-Fiore. "She is making you and Bertie suffer because she is unhappy – and you do not share her unhappiness. You never will – nor will Bertie. And so she is determined to make you unhappy in the way in which she herself is unhappy. It's fairly basic psychology. I've seen it time and time again."

For a while Stuart was silent. Then he said, "What should I do?"

"Do not fight her," said Sister Maria-Fiore. "When we fight others, we are simply fighting ourselves."

"I see."

"Allow her to make her point. Do not harbour resentment in your heart. Allow healing to take place."

Stuart looked doubtful.

"That is the only way," said Sister Maria-Fiore.

She looked at her watch. "The sun's over the chapel tower," she said.

Stuart looked confused. "The chapel tower . . ."

"Do you not say *the sun's over the yardarm* when it's time to have a drink?"

Stuart laughed. "Oh, that. Yes, some do. It's a naval expression, I believe. Rather old-fashioned."

"I wonder whether you would care to come and have a gin and tonic with me," said Sister Maria-Fiore. "Antonia is in Broughty Ferry, visiting her aunt – such a needful lady, bless her – and so it's just me, I'm afraid."

Stuart hesitated. He felt at ease coping with most social situations, but this one was rather unexpected. To be invited to have a gin and tonic with an Italian nun *à deux* was a new experience, and he was not quite sure how to respond.

"Please say you will," implored Sister Maria-Fiore dei Fiori di Montagna.

There was something in her voice that made Stuart hesitate even more, but it seemed that time for hesitation was over, as the nun now seized his elbow in a surprisingly firm grip and began to guide him back down the path towards the gate.

"I have a little secret to impart," said Sister Maria-Fiore dei Fiori di Montagna.

Stuart said nothing.

"Antonia and I are thinking of moving," she continued. "We've found a delightful double-upper flat in the Grange. It's just come on the market. I can't wait to tell you about it."

Stuart smiled. He was relieved that Sister Mari-Fiore's agenda was so innocent. A move to the Grange? What could be less controversial, less unsettling than that?

28

Bruce Prepares

Mr Murthwaite, who had once almost played rugby for Scotland, and would have done so had a slight knee injury not interfered with his summer training, had been Bruce Anderson's physical education teacher at Morrison's Academy. He liked Bruce, although he occasionally berated him for failing to maximise his potential. "You could perform far better, Anderson," he said, "if you spent less time preening yourself in front of the mirror and more time in the gym." This reproach, publicly delivered, caused giggles amongst those girls present and smirks of *Schadenfreude* amongst the boys. It was entirely deserved criticism, though, and Bruce took it in the spirit in which it was offered. But it nonetheless failed to spur him to the efforts that might have led to greater sporting distinction, even if he still maintained not only his membership of a gym but also, as a non-playing winger, of a small and not very successful rugby club, The North Edinburgh Stalwarts.

On that Monday morning, Bruce set his Apple Watch to wake him an hour earlier than normal, as he wanted to fit in a visit to the gym before his planned on-site meeting with his new business partners, Ed Macdonald and his friend, Gregor. The Apple Watch, obedient to its electronic vows, awoke him at exactly the right time, invoking, via a Bluetooth link, an mp3 file of the Red Army Choir singing the Russian folk song, *Kalinka*. This had been recorded on that remarkable occasion when the famous military singers had met, and sung with, the Mormon Tabernacle Choir at a choir festival in Seville. The resultant musical energy was significant, and the volume and enthusiasm of *Kalinka* was such that it would have been impossible for even the drowsiest sleeper to remain in bed once the choir reached the first full-blooded chorus.

Little more than an hour later, Bruce returned to his flat in Abercromby Place, having successfully completed the four demanding circuits that his personal trainer had prescribed for him. Now he was ready for his shower, which usually took at least fifteen minutes, and which involved the application of a special garlic-and-rosemary pre-shower toner, followed by shower treatment, shower gel, and an olive-oil based post-shower skin conditioner. Drying with a high-GSM ring-spun cotton defoliant bath towel was next and then a careful self-examination before the full-length mirror Bruce had installed in what he called the post-shower room, a large, walk-in cupboard directly off the bathroom.

Bruce liked what he saw. A combination of diet and exercise meant that he carried not an ounce of spare flesh, unlike so many of his fellow members of the rugby club who had allowed muscle once exercised in the scrum to turn to flab. These were people, Bruce thought, who had no inner Mr Murthwaite to reproach them over their various shortcomings – their failure to walk to work rather than take a bus, their refusal to eschew fattening carbohydrates, their disinclination to use the stairs at the office rather than the lift. These people ended up with the bodies they deserved, Bruce told himself, with some satisfaction. I, by contrast, end up like this . . . And here he tensed his muscles, delighting in the rippling effect that he had come to realise so entranced women. Women, he said to himself, simply couldn't *ripple* in the way in which men could – if they looked after themselves.

The toilette performed at Versailles in its heyday was but as nothing compared to that witnessed each morning in Abercromby Place. The last stage of this elaborate process was the application of hair gel (clove-scented, by tradition), the smoothing down of the hair (it always sprung up, *en brosse*, whatever Bruce did), and then, with the regret that must be felt whenever any masterpiece is concealed from public view, the selection of clothes and the act of dressing.

That morning, Bruce wore a pair of charcoal chinos, red-striped bamboo socks, polo-brown calf-suede Crockett & Jones loafers, a sky-blue shirt from a Jermyn Street mail-order catalogue, and a mustard-coloured casual linen jacket that he had first seen in the window display of Stewart Christie in Queen Street and that he had known, with utter certainty and at first sighting, was destined to be his.

Fully dressed, he took a final appreciative glance at him-self in the mirror, while his coffee percolator gurgled promisingly in the kitchen. He found it hard to imagine any way in which the image that he presented to the world might be improved upon. Nothing was overstated, and yet everything spoke of his assuredness, of his confidence that he might be regarded from whatever angle and the admiration would always be the same.

Breakfast was a brief affair – a boiled egg, a small portion of smoked Argyll salmon, and a large cup of black coffee. Then Bruce set off for the Grange, where, at the address given him in Ed's earlier email, he joined Ed Macdonald and Gregor in front of a large South Edinburgh villa. The house, set back from the road, was partly concealed from view by a yew hedge and two well-established copper beech trees.

Ed, who was busy with his mobile phone, greeted Bruce perfunctorily; Gregor was more attentive. "Like your chinos," he said.

Bruce acknowledged the compliment with a smile.

"And your jacket," Gregor added. "Mustard suits you."

Bruce inclined his head. He was not quite sure what to make of Gregor. "Some people can't wear it," he said, and glanced briefly at Ed.

Gregor grinned. "Ed can't wear anything," he said. "Poor guy. He looks sad in everything. Even beige." He laughed. "Those shoes? Is that the colour they call snuff? Or is it tobacco?"

"Polo-brown," Bruce said.

Gregor gave a sigh that might have been envy or simple admiration. "Cool," he said.

Ed finished his telephone call. He turned to Bruce. "Like what you see?"

Bruce gazed at the house. "Private," he said.

Ed looked pleased. "Privacy easily adds an extra hundred grand to the price – sometimes more."

"A rare commodity these days," said Gregor.

Gesturing for the other two to follow him, Ed led them up the paved path to the front door. "Greg divided it," he explained to Bruce.

"Yup," said Gregor. "Me."

"There's a double-upper and a ground-floor flat," Ed continued. "We're going to hold on to the ground-floor flat until the market moves up a bit. Aren't we, Greg?"

"Yup," said Gregor. "A rising market. Helped on its way a bit. Cool."

"Oldies love ground-floor flats," Ed went on. "No stairs, you see. Oldies hate stairs. But the double-upper will go in a week – and at a pretty hefty price." He winked at Bruce. "All the ducks, so to speak, are lined up."

Bruce was gazing up at the front of the house. His surveyor's eye caught a small section where the mortar had flaked out of the join between blocks of stone.

"Pointing needed," he said. "There. Over there, too. And there."

Ed followed his gaze. "Yes. We have that on our list for this week. There's still a bit to do here and there, cosmetic stuff, that's all. But let's not waste time. Let's go in and take a look round."

29

The Merits of the Double-Upper

Ed explained that with the conversion of the house into two separate flats, the entrance to the top flat – the double-upper, as such flats are called in Edinburgh – was round the side of the house.

"Gregor has done it fantastically well," he said to Bruce. "Sometimes it can be hard to convert these places and you end up with an outside staircase climbing up the side of the house."

"Not at all attractive," said Gregor. "Ugly, even. To be avoided, if poss."

"And it was poss here," Ed continued. "Gregor got the builder to knock a hole in a side wall and make a new entrance hall on the ground floor, just to the side of the main staircase. Then he separated the staircase from the ground-floor flat by building an internal wall, and there you have it – two flats. Brilliant."

"Not rocket science," said Gregor, modestly.

"Still, pretty smart work," Ed insisted. "Give credit where credit is due. You've got a great eye, Greg, for this sort of stuff."

Gregor smiled. "That's what I do. I love doing this stuff. It floats my boat."

Bruce glanced at him. People had said that he had a good eye too, but he did not think he should mention it. Clearly Gregor thought that his eye was better. "Are you an architect, Gregor?" he asked.

He asked this question while Ed was fumbling with the

front-door key. Gregor turned round and fixed Bruce with a glassy stare.

"What do you mean?"

"I was just wondering whether you were an architect. That's all."

Gregor gave a toss of the head. "Architects!" he said. His tone was dismissive.

Ed managed to get the key into the door. "Architects aren't always what they crack themselves up to be. They get things wrong."

Gregor addressed Bruce. "I told you: I do interior decoration."

Bruce laughed uneasily. "I wasn't accusing you of architecture."

Gregor stared at him. "What's that meant to mean? Have you got a problem with interior decoration, Bruce?"

Bruce shrugged. "No. Of course not. It's just that architects know about load-bearing walls and things like that. You have to be a bit careful if you start knocking holes." He paused. "Just saying."

Ed raised a hand. "Gregor knows what he's doing, don't you, Gregor?" And then he answered his own question. "He does, you see. And he has this builder out at Penicuik who knows about that stuff, doesn't he, Gregor? Bill knows all about load-bearing walls." And then he added, "He's an Orangeman."

Gregor was reassuring. "Of course he does. He deals with load-bearing walls every day. That's what he does."

"And he would have got the building warrant," said Bruce. "He'd know about that, of course."

Gregor said nothing.

"This is the hall," Ed announced. "You see, Bruce? The hall. Look what Gregor's done to the floor. See it? You like it?"

Bruce looked down at the floor. "Encaustic tiles."

"Yes," said Gregor. "I designed the pattern myself. You get these designs in a lot of houses on this side of town. The Victorians loved these floors. They thought of them as mosaics – which in a sense they are."

"Seriously brilliant," said Ed. "Now let me show you the staircase."

They climbed the stairs, which had already been carpeted. Gregor pointed out the brass stair rods. "Those are not repro. Those are the real thing – Victorian stair rods."

"Dead gen," said Ed. "We had them in our house in Crieff. They'd been there since the house was built. Way back. 1875."

"I remember your place," said Bruce. "I remember going there after school every Friday. Remember? You had those tartan carpets. All the way through the house."

Gregor made a face.

"You've got unresolved issues with tartan carpets, Gregor?" Ed challenged.

Gregor shook his head. "If that's what you like, they're fine. *Chacun à son goût.*"

"But you personally?" Ed pressed. "You think that people who have tartan carpets . . ."

Gregor looked away. "I wasn't saying anything about the sort of people who have tartan carpets. You're too sensitive, Eddie. Not that people who have tartan carpets are known for their sensitivity . . ."

Ed spun round. "What exactly are you saying?"

Gregor sighed. "It's nothing personal. It's just that I don't do tartan carpets. Some people do. I don't. I don't do flying ducks on the wall or . . ."

Suddenly Ed reached out and grabbed the lapels of Gregor's jacket. Bruce, who was in the way of this attack, pushed the two of them apart. "No need to fight, boys," he said. "We've got a house to look at."

"I'm sorry," said Gregor. "I didn't mean to offend you, Ed."

Ed glowered briefly, and then assumed a business-like manner. "We should go upstairs," he said, and began to lead the way up the broad, now-enclosed staircase with its Victorian stair rods and its mahogany balustrade. At the top of the staircase was a spacious hall giving access to the rooms on that level – a drawing room, a dining room, a kitchen, a bathroom, and two rooms of unspecified usage.

"You could live perfectly comfortably on this floor alone," said Ed. "But there are three further bedrooms up that small stair over there. Three, Bruce. And another bathroom. If you have kids, you could put them there and close the door. Or guests, if you like. There's serious room in this flat."

Gregor took them into the drawing room. "The *pièce de résistance*," he said. "Typical Victorian high ceilings. Lots of room to breathe. And the light. That's what I like about a double-upper – you get this gorgeous light. Really gorgeous." He paused. "This is south-facing, of course. So you get the southern light. It's great if you're facing north and you're an artist. Different light. Slightly blue, like a nineteenth-century Danish painting. This light makes me think of . . . of Tuscany. The warm south. Sun-tanned bodies completely at ease with themselves. Vine leaves rattling like dice. Warm evenings."

Bruce looked about him. He noted the elaborate cornice, undisturbed by any nineteen-sixties or 'seventies experience. "Nice," he said.

"More than nice," said Gregor. "That's the original marble – at least the mantelpiece is. The hearth has a Thomas Bogie metal surround. All intact."

He pointed to a small brass fixture beside the fireplace. "See that?" he said. "That's a speaking tube. It connected to the kitchen down below – just like the system you found on ships. They spoke into a tube that ended up in the engine room."

Bruce smiled. He crossed the floor to pick up the small mouthpiece. "Hello," he said. "Bridge here. Anybody down below?"

From somewhere in the depths of the house, faint from distance, came the reply. "It's me."

Bruce turned and stared speechlessly at Ed and Gregor.

30

What Tam Didn't Do

On that very first dinner with Fat Bob, Big Lou felt that she had done the right thing in accepting his invitation to join him for dinner at an Indian restaurant in Leith. He had invited Finlay as well, and she had been touched by that. There were few men, she thought, whose face might not fall, even slightly, on finding out that the person whom they were inviting out was encumbered by a young child; Fat Bob's insistence that Finlay should join them on this outing had been as sincere as it was spontaneous. "Of course he must come," he said. "I imagine he likes Indian food – poppadoms and so on. He can have as many of those as he likes."

Big Lou had smiled. "He loves poppadoms. Of course, he goes for the milder curries – most youngsters do. But Indian restaurants understand that. They usually have a children's curry somewhere on the menu – one of those dishes with plenty of yoghurt."

Fat Bob agreed. "A strong curry is an acquired taste, isn't it? You have to get used to it. I go for the milder curries myself, although my friend Tam can't get enough of those really hot ones . . ."

"Vindaloos?"

"Yes, that's the stuff. The ones with the government health warnings. He loves those. You see the smoke coming out of his mouth."

The meal had been a success. Fat Bob had been kind to Finlay, and the young boy had responded accordingly. Children, Big Lou knew, had an innate ability to understand when an adult was condescending to them and when they were addressing them as equals. Finlay had told Bob about his ballet lessons, and Bob had revealed that he had gone to see Scottish Ballet perform *Swan Lake* in Glasgow and had enjoyed every moment of it. "Those people can dance," he had said with admiration. "Boy, can they dance!"

Finlay had asked about his career in the Highland Games, and he had told him about his first big win – a fifty-pound prize purse in the Mull Highland Games, when he had first competed against the same Tam Macgregor who so enjoyed strong curries.

"I won the caber event," Fat Bob said. "Tam was expected to win, as he had won at Mull the previous year, but do you know something? When I threw my winning throw, he came up to me and shook my hand. Straight away. Straight away he came up to me, and he said, 'Fat Bob, that was a great toss. I'll no be able to match that, and that's the truth.'"

"A true sportsman," Big Lou observed. "Do you hear that, Finlay? That's how a gentleman behaves when he loses. He congratulates the winner – and he means it."

"True," said Fat Bob. "That's the way to do it. Tam's a good man. One of the best."

There was something in the way he said this that gave Big Lou the impression that he was harbouring a reservation. And that was revealed on their second date – this time without Finlay, for whom Big Lou had been able to arrange a babysitter. On this occasion, they went to a bar at the west end of Princes Street before going to another Indian restaurant near Haymarket Station.

"Your friend, Tam Macgregor," Big Lou began. "When you were telling Finlay about him the other day . . ."

"Aye?"

"I wondered if . . ."

He interrupted her. "You picked it up. Yes, there's something."

She waited. It seemed to her that he was uncertain as to whether to reveal whatever it was. But he did.

"Tam was up in Perth Sheriff Court. Three years ago."

Big Lou frowned. She was not sure what to say.

"He was charged with an offence he didn't commit," said Fat Bob. "He was innocent."

Big Lou said nothing. Fat Bob was obviously being loyal to his friend.

"I'm not just being loyal," he said.

She felt that he had read her thoughts. "I wasn't going to say anything," she said quickly.

"His brother did it," explained Fat Bob. "His brother, Stuart, pinched a police motorbike. It was a stupid thing to do, as the police don't like it if you pinch their motorbikes."

"I can imagine that," said Big Lou.

Fat Bob nodded. "They found the motorbike at their mother's house. It was hidden in the shed, under some sacking. It was Tam, though, who confessed. He was fined three hundred pounds and given one of these payback orders. He had to wash police cars for six months."

"But why did he confess – if his brother did it?"

"Because of their mother," Fat Bob said. "She has Parkinson's and relies on the brother, you see. He's the carer. If anything happened to him it would be really hard for the mother. Tam said they couldn't risk the brother being sent to prison. The police were really cheesed off, you'll understand, about their motorbike, and they may have pressed to make an example of him. Tam took the blame. Now he has the criminal record. But he's really a good man – an honest, good man."

Big Lou thought about this. He should not have confessed to something he did not do – that was called perverting the course of justice, she thought – but she could understand why he did it.

"Did their mother know about this?"

Fat Bob shook his head. "They managed to keep it from her. She's never found out."

"And the brother?"

"Stuart said he felt really bad about it. He didn't want Tam to do it, but by then it was too late. Tam had made a statement to the police, and if he withdrew it, then they would be even crosser with the brother."

Big Lou saw that. She remained puzzled, though, as to why the brother should have done something so ill-advised as to steal a police motorbike. Was it not clearly marked?

"Yes, it was," answered Fat Bob. "But it was in Gaelic. You know how all police vehicles now have *police* written in Gaelic on them? They had done that with this motorbike, but had run out of space, and so they just had *police* in Gaelic on it – there wasn't the space for the English translation. The brother said he didn't know what it meant."

Big Lou raised an eyebrow. "I find that hard to believe," she said.

Fat Bob agreed. "So do I. I think the brother's lying."

"Could be," said Big Lou. She gave the matter further thought. "It's an odd way to make a statement," she said. "Bringing motorbikes into cultural politics. A bit odd, don't you think?"

"It's making up for the wrongs of the past," said Fat Bob. "It's all to do with what happened after the Forty-five. The attempt to obliterate Gaelic culture. Remember?"

"Yes," said Big Lou. "I suppose points have to be made."

They looked at one another, each aware, at that particular moment, that they were at an historical crossroads, when the past came back and met the present. Such a realisation can come to any of us, at any time, and in any place – including in an Indian restaurant when we are looking at the menu and trying to decide which of the curries are unpalatably hot and which are not.

31

Garlic Naan

Over a kadai paneer with a side-dish of onion bhajis, Big Lou tactfully set out to discover more about Fat Bob. She realised that she knew virtually nothing about him – other than that he liked Indian food, that he came from a small town in Perthshire, and that during the summer he did the circuit of Highland Games, tossing the caber and throwing the hammer throughout Scotland. Was that enough to know about somebody before you allowed yourself to fall in love with him? Lou was not sure.

"Do you have brothers or sisters, Bob?" she asked as the waiter produced a bowl of Indian breads.

Bob nodded. "Four sisters," he said. "Amelia, Annie, Maddy, and Ginger. All of them, apart from Ginger, are younger than I am. Ginger is two years older. Maddy is the baby of the family."

"Where does Ginger get her name?" asked Big Lou. "Is she a redhead?"

"Very slightly," said Bob. "Just a touch. Her hair's lovely – a bit like a fox's coat, you know – that sort of red." His voice was filled with pride. *This is a man talking about his sister*, thought Big Lou.

"Pretty."

Bob offered the bread basket to Lou before helping himself to a piece of garlic naan. "Yes," he said. "Just like you."

Big Lou caught her breath. Had he said that Ginger was pretty – just like her? Had he really said that?

She blushed in her embarrassment.

Bob reached out to put his hand upon hers. His touch only lasted for a moment, and was gentle. *The strongest of men are the gentlest of men,* she thought.

"I mean it," he said. "You're a very beautiful woman, Lou."

Big Lou knew neither what to say nor where to look. She was unused to compliments, and indeed could not recall when last she had received one. She was accustomed, of course, to hearing her bacon rolls commended – and her cups of coffee, too, on the milky surface of which she often traced a trademark thistle – but a personal remark of this sort was quite different. She was not one for flattery, and would never have sought plaudits of any sort, least of all ones pertaining to her appearance. And yet to hear Bob say this was intensely pleasing, and she felt a sudden welling of affection for this well-set man with his fresh, open face and his rather old-fashioned manner; with his gentleness and his regard for his sister. She could certainly fall in love with this man, she decided – and indeed perhaps she already had.

"You're very kind," she said. "But you don't have to say things like that to me."

She realised immediately that this sounded ridiculous. Of course, he did not have to say things like that – and to draw attention to the fact made her sound ungracious.

Bob was undeterred. "I know I don't. But I want to. I want you to know what I think."

She seized the opportunity to show her appreciation. "It was really kind. And thank you." Then she added, "You're not so bad yourself."

He smiled. "Och, away with you. Not me. I'm . . ." He hesitated. Then he went on, "I'm nothing. Not me. I'm just nothing."

Big Lou was adamant. "You're not nothing, Bob. You're strong."

Once again, it was not what she intended to say. Of course he was strong. He was, after all, a professional strongman – or semi-professional – and that was what such people were: they were strong.

"I do my best," said Bob, taking a bite of garlic naan. "But there are guys who are stronger than I am, you know. There's this fellow in Glasgow who can pull a train. I never thought I'd see it, but I did. It was for charity – for the lifeboats, I think. He pulled a railway carriage along the length of a platform at Queen Street Station. It was in all the papers."

Big Lou shook her head in wonderment. "You'd think that would be impossible."

"You would," agreed Bob. "But he did it. And then there's Neil Ainslie. You heard of him, Lou?"

She shook her head. "I don't know much about these things."

"Well, Neil could tear a telephone directory in two. I saw him do it many times. He ripped them up."

Big Lou took a sip from the glass of mango juice the waiter had brought her. "Amazing," she said.

She wanted to move the conversation on, and so she asked him about Aberfeldy. Had they lived in the village itself? He explained that they had lived just outside town, on a large farm, where his father was the stockman. "My dad never had his own farm," he said. "He would have loved that. Nothing big – just enough to keep some cattle and maybe grow a bit of hay, some neeps, maybe; that sort of thing. But he never had the money. Nor the land. So he worked as a stockman on this farm owned by a woman who had inherited it from her father. She was a good farmer, and she treated the people who worked for her very well. But she died. It was tractor accident."

Big Lou winced. "Poor woman."

"Yes," said Bob. "It was bad luck. She left the farm to her

nephew in Glasgow. He drank, and he owed a lot of money. So he sold it to a man who wanted to do the whole thing himself. He gave my father his notice, and, well, he became ill. My mother said it had nothing to do with losing his job, but it was a bit of a coincidence, if you ask me. There are people who can die of disappointment, Lou. I'm sure of it."

Big Lou agreed. "They used to call that dying of a broken heart. It's the same thing, don't you think?"

"Yes. And it was what did it for my father, I think. I was sixteen at the time, and it was really difficult for my mother. We lived in a tied cottage on the farm. And so we had to move out. That was hard, and we ended up living in a tiny, damp flat in Perth. My mother had to scrape about to get enough money just for food, let alone anything else, so I left school and got a job so that I could contribute something to the household. We were really poor. We had nothing, you know."

Big Lou waited for Bob to continue. "I'm sorry," she said. It was difficult to think of anything else one might say.

"There was no work where we were," said Bob. "I tried to get an apprenticeship in a panel-beating workshop, but the owner took on his nephew instead of me. I tried to get a plumbing apprenticeship. Nothing doing. So I went off to Glasgow. I was sixteen and still wet behind the ears. I had one suitcase and fourteen pounds that I had saved up. That was all. Fourteen pounds, Lou."

"What happened, Bob?" She experienced an uncomfortable sense of foreboding. Cities beckoned to the children of farmers. They always had. The promises they made were rarely kept. But Bob smiled.

"Don't worry, Lou. Sometimes the world surprises us, don't you think? Not all outcomes are bleak; not everybody is ready to take advantage of the weak; there are good people about, Lou – there really are."

"Yes," said Big Lou. Bob was right; but why, she wondered, was it even necessary to say what he had said? How had cynicism, suspicion, and distrust assumed such a role in our lives? What had happened, she wondered, to trust, goodness, and courtesy?

32

Harry and Josephine

"I arrived at Queen Street Station in Glasgow," said Fat Bob, "thinking that everything would be just fine."

Big Lou smiled. She remembered what it was like to be sixteen. You were still immortal then – just; your future was something that you would shape, and its possibilities stretched out before you.

"My mother had written to a cousin of hers," Bob continued. "She lived not far from the river, and my mother had asked her if I could stay with her for a few weeks while I found a job and some lodgings. She was called Cousin Josephine, I was told, and she was married to a man called Harry. Harry had a good job with a furniture company on Byers Road. They were good people, my mother said, and Harry might help me to find work. She was unwilling to ask him directly, but she was sure that he would do his best. He had been in the Navy, she said, and he was still in contact with a lot of his naval friends. He had influence.

"Their flat was above a laundrette. It was a nice enough place, I suppose. Some of those Glasgow tenements have ornamental tiles on their stair, and this was one of those. You know the sort, Lou? Those tiles with whirly designs?"

"*Art Nouveau*," said Big Lou.

"If you say so," said Bob, and grinned. "Anyway, I turned up there with my suitcase and my fourteen pounds and rang their bell. I had been excited and, as I said, quite confident when I arrived at the station, but now that was fading a bit. Now I was faced with explaining myself to people I had never met and on whom my future seemed to depend. Josephine was a relative, and might be expected to behave like one, but what about Harry? Why should Harry welcome a complete stranger into his house and be expected to help him to get a job? What could I do? I had no trade, no skills, and no real idea of what I wanted to do.

"Josephine answered the door. I'll always remember her expression when she saw me. You know how people say, *They looked at me as if I was something the cat brought in?* Do you know that expression, Lou?"

Lou nodded. "Aye, Bob. I know that one."

"Well, that's how she looked at me. I started to introduce myself, and she said, 'I ken exactly who you are. You're Betty's boy and your name's Bob. I ken all that. And you're to stay with us for a day or two, so you'd best come in.'"

"A day or two!" exclaimed Big Lou. "Oh, Bob, what an awful start."

"Yes, it was. I didn't say anything. I didn't correct her and say that my mother had told me that it would be a few weeks – I did not feel that I could say anything, really; I felt that anxious. But anyway, she took me to a room at the back of the flat and showed me my bed and the cupboard where I could store my clothes. Then she said that she and Harry would be having their tea in ten minutes and that I should come into the kitchen when I had unpacked my things and washed my hands.

"Harry was sitting at the kitchen table when I went in. He was reading the paper, and when I came in, he looked up and nodded. Then he went back to his paper. Josephine pointed to a chair opposite Harry's. 'We don't speak at meals,' she said. 'Some folk do, as you may know, but not in this house, you'll understand.'

"Harry looked at me sternly, as if to underline the warning. I said the first thing that came into my mind, which was 'My ma says hello.'

"Harry turned to his wife. 'So his ma says hello,' he said to Josephine. Then he addressed me. 'You tell her hello when you see her next, will you? You tell her that Harry and Josephine say hello.'

"I said that I would. I felt miserable. I had not asked to come to these people. This had all been arranged by my mother and had nothing to do with me. It would have been far better, I thought, if they had told my mother that it was inconvenient for me to come to stay with them. I could have found somewhere myself. I could have gone and asked somebody if they knew of a room to rent. That was the way that most people did things, I thought. Of course, I knew nothing of how things worked, but I thought I did. We all think that when we're sixteen, don't we?"

Big Lou frowned. "They were very unkind. Imagine treating a wee boy like that. Just imagine it. Shame on him, Bob – shame on him."

"Thank you, Lou. Anyway, there I was, and somehow I got through the meal without crying. Boys are told that they're not meant to cry. They still said that in those days, Lou. I think these days boys are allowed to cry, but it was different then. So I didn't cry, and I put up with it."

"Did Harry do anything for you?" asked Big Lou. "Did he find you a job?"

Bob laughed. "The subject came up the following day. He asked me what I wanted to do, and I said that I would do anything. This seemed to amuse him. He said that if you wanted to get anywhere in this life you had to know what you wanted to do. He said that if you didn't know what you wanted to do, then that meant that you would never be good at anything.

"I asked him whether I might get a job in the furniture trade. He was very discouraging. He said that you needed skills to get into the furniture trade. He said that it took years to make a good French polisher or upholsterer. He said that he didn't think that I would find anything there. Then he said, 'Have you thought of joining the Navy?' He said that he knew a chief petty officer who had something to do with recruiting and that he would have a word with him. I told him that I was not sure about the Navy, but he brushed my doubts aside. He said that a lot of people who signed up were unsure about it, but they quickly got used to naval life. It was a good career, he said, and they would teach you a trade if you were lucky. He said that he would speak to his friend and he was sure something could be fixed up. There would be a medical, of course, but he thought I looked strong and fit enough and that they would almost certainly take me. I should get a haircut before the interview, he said, and that he could take me to the barber the next day because he knew somebody who would cut hair half-price if you went before ten in the morning."

Big Lou was appalled. She did not like the sound of Harry. "Uncle Ebenezer," she muttered.

Bob looked puzzled.

"It's a familiar story," Big Lou explained. "Young man has introduction to a relative. The relative tries to get him to fall down the stairs. Stevenson's *Kidnapped*."

"Nobody tried to make me fall down the stairs," said Bob.

"Aye, but some stairs are metaphorical," said Big Lou. She dwelt on the word *metaphorical*, allowing its syllables room to breathe. Words need air.

Bob looked at her with growing fondness. He loved big words almost as much as he loved big women.

33

Sleeping Rough

Big Lou's coffee bar had been a second-hand bookstore before she bought it, and with the purchase she acquired the complete remaining stock of books. She had disposed of some of these, bestowing on charity shops multiple copies of Edward Heath's book on sailing, Delia Smith cooking tomes, stained by countless splashes and splodges, and any number of out-of-date guidebooks. Books of a more challenging nature were transferred to her flat in Canonmills, where she methodically made her way through piles of titles on philosophy, history, and theology, while making occasional sallies into nineteenth-century poetry, biography, and popular psychology. Her formal education had been limited, but now she made up for that with her voracious reading and her openness to new ideas. The autodidact always fears that the knowledge that he or she has taken such pains to acquire may prove to be pointless; Big Lou had no such concerns. She thought that the more you knew, the better, even if your mind came to be filled with irrelevant detail. Big Lou had no desire to impress anybody with the breadth of her learning: scholarship, of whatever nature, was a good in itself, she thought.

She had recently read rather a lot about life in the Royal Navy, having reached that region of her bookshelves where books on naval history were to be found. She had already read three of Patrick O'Brian's Jack Aubrey novels, and was saving up the remaining seventeen for a later date. These books were full of naval detail, and she soon learned the difference between *aloft* and *aloof* and between *astern* and *athwart*. She learned about what went on in the gunroom and the captain's cabin, about beating to quarters and bagpiping the mizzen, and about how press-gangs captured men of marine experience as well as those who had no desire to gain marine experience. She had assumed that sailors now were all volunteers, and was alarmed to hear that Bob might have been cajoled into a life at sea.

Bob sensed her concern. "Don't worry," he reassured her. "I wasn't going to let myself be forced into anything. I removed myself that night."

Big Lou was relieved. "You ran away?"

"Yes. I went along with Harry's suggestion, trying to appear enthusiastic in case he should lock me in until such time as he could get me to the recruiting office. I waited until they had both gone to bed before I repacked my suitcase and slipped out of the flat. I tripped in the corridor, dropping my suitcase with a loud thud, and I froze where I was, in the darkness, my heart beating wildly in my chest. I thought my heartbeat alone would be enough to wake them up, but no sound came from their room, and I was able to make my escape."

"Did you head for home?"

Bob said that he felt he could not do that. "It would have been a real humiliation to go straight home. Remember that I had gone off because I wanted to relieve my mother of a mouth to feed – if I returned, I would have achieved nothing, and we would have been back where we started. No boy setting off on his life's journey wants to come right back with his tail between his legs."

Big Lou said that she could understand that. But where did he go? He was alone in Glasgow, and he was only sixteen. Did he mean to sleep rough?

"That's exactly what I had in mind," said Bob. "I thought I might find a corner that might give me shelter somewhere. In a park, perhaps, or under a bridge. I thought that a big city like Glasgow was bound to have nooks and crannies where you could tuck yourself in. I knew that people lived on the streets – I had read about it in the papers – and I thought that I'd probably find a place to sleep if I poked about enough.

"I actually found somewhere quite quickly. I'd only been walking for half an hour or so –with no real idea of where I was going – when I found a yard behind a pub. It was the place where they stored the empty beer kegs and various other bits and pieces, but it had a small shed in a corner, and this was unlocked. It was dark, and it had a musty smell to it, but it was dry. Better than that, there were several old hessian sacks piled up in a corner, and that made a comfortable bed for me. I moved in there and then.

"When I woke up the next morning, I heard voices coming from the back of the pub. A man brought out a dustbin and a sack of rubbish. He stood in the middle of the yard and looked up at the sky, as if he was doing yoga. I held my breath. I thought that if he came into the shed I would simply push past him and run. It was not as if I was a thief, or anything like that – I was simply somebody who wanted to take advantage of an empty shed. I was not harming anybody.

"But there's the thing, Lou. A lot of the things that people want to do can't possibly cause any harm to other people, but they are still not allowed. Don't you think that's unfair? Don't you think we should let people do the things they want to do as long as they don't cause harm to any other folk? I believe that, Lou – I really do."

Big Lou thought for a moment. "John Stuart Mill," she said.

Bob looked at her. He was waiting for an explanation.

"Yes. What you said is exactly what a philosopher called John Stuart Mill said. I read a book on the subject."

"Oh yes? So, he agrees with me?"

"You could say that. It might be better, though, to say that you agree with him. He said it first, you see. And he says that the only justification for exercising power over another – in a civilised community – is to prevent harm to others."

"He's dead right, Lou. This John Stuart . . . What's the boy's name? He was dead right, I think."

Big Lou smiled. "John Stuart Mill. Well, there you are, Bob. Sometimes we do philosophy without knowing it, if you see what I mean."

Bob held up his hands. "I'm no philosopher, Lou. I'm an ordinary working man."

"Anybody can be a philosopher, Bob. You, me . . . anybody."

He made a self-deprecating gesture. "Not me, Lou. I haven't had the education."

She wanted to say to him: never, ever sell yourself short. You can think just as clearly as any of them. And what is philosophy but common sense? Hadn't there been a Scottish school of common-sense philosophy? Surely that would embrace people just like Bob? But there was so much we *could* tell people that we can't tell them. That is what she thought.

"What happened next?"

"I'll tell you, Lou," he said. "I'll tell you."

34

Bertie's Outing

Nicola was determined that Bertie's last day in Edinburgh before his three months in Aberdeen would be as enjoyable and memorable as she could make it. She had arranged for Ulysses to spend the day at a high-security nursery so that she could devote her full attention to Bertie, and to this end she had booked him into the Stockbridge Advanced Infancy Experience (High Security), a child-care centre for challenging under-threes. Two programmes were available – Normal Advanced and Gifted Advanced, with all but one or two of the children being booked into the latter. Nicola had no time for parental pushiness and had arranged for Ulysses to spend the day in the Normal Advanced programme. She had read the centre's syllabus with some amusement. "Our aim," it had stated, "is to provide a stimulating and supportive environment for your child. We are acutely aware that your future doctor or lawyer will need every encouragement to meet the exacting intellectual standards of their professional futures. Those futures start now."

Bertie had chosen a visit to Valvona & Crolla's delicatessen and restaurant. After that, he said, they might go on to the National Museum on Chambers Street.

"Two very good choices, Bertie," said Nicola.

"And I'd like Ranald Braveheart Macpherson to come with us," added Bertie. "He's my friend, you see."

Nicola smiled. "I know that, Bertie. I know that Ranald is very important to you." She paused. "And I imagine you'll miss him badly."

Bertie lowered his eyes, making Nicola immediately regret what she had said.

"Of course, three months will be over in a flash," she gushed. "And before you know it, you'll be back in Edinburgh. You and Ranald will be reunited again, and you'll have so much to tell him about all your adventures in Aberdeen."

Bertie was unconvinced. "Ranald may have another friend when I come back," he said. "He's bound to forget me."

"Oh, I don't think so," said Nicola breezily. She wanted to sound as cheerful as possible, although she knew that what he said might prove to be true. Children were notoriously fickle in their friendships; we all remembered the pain we experienced when the friends of childhood found others to divert them. For many of us, it was our first experience of disloyalty, and, like all first experiences, not easily forgotten.

Bertie did not share Nicola's optimism. In Olive's crowing, he had already had some warning of the shoals that lay ahead.

"When you go away to Aberdeen, Bertie," she had intoned, "you're going to lose all your friends. That's one-hundred-per-cent definite. You know that, don't you?"

Pansy had agreed. "Olive's right, Bertie. People who go to Aberdeen never hear from their friends again. That's a well-known fact. I read about it on Wikipedia."

Bertie doubted that. "But you can't read yet, Pansy," he pointed out mildly.

Olive papered over this crack in her lieutenant's credibility. "Mind you," she continued. "You don't have all that many friends anyway, do you Bertie? Perhaps you won't notice it so much."

Pansy nodded. "That's true," she said. "There's always Ranald, though."

"Hah!" exclaimed Olive. "Ranald Braveheart Macpherson. Him indeed. I can tell you that Ranald is already advertising online for new friends. I imagine he's probably already deleted you from his list of contacts. In fact, I'm sure he has."

"I feel sorry for you, Bertie," said Pansy. "It's no fun being deleted."

But now, doubts as to Ranald's loyalty put to one side, Bertie was on his way with his grandmother and his friend to Valvona & Crolla's delicatessen at the head of Leith Walk. As they made their way, Nicola tried to ensure that the conversation was as cheerful as possible, avoiding all reference to Aberdeen, journeys, cold, or the North Sea, gamely making upbeat comments about how time flew and how easy it was to communicate with friends in the electronic age.

"People used to use pigeons," she said, "to send messages to one another. Can you believe that, boys? Pigeons with messages tied around their legs."

Ranald and Bertie remained silent.

"Pigeons have an inbuilt sense of direction," Nicola continued. "They can always find their way home. It's quite miraculous."

"Not really," said Bertie, glumly.

"But it is, Bertie!" Nicola persisted. "You or I would never be able to find our way home if . . ." She stopped herself. This was not the direction in which she wanted the conversation to go.

"They use the stars," said Bertie flatly. "They may also use energy fields that we can't see, Granny."

Nicola raised an eyebrow. She was constantly finding herself astonished at the things that Bertie seemed to have picked up. He at least was well-informed; Ranald Braveheart Macpherson, by contrast, seemed to know rather less.

"Well, fancy that," she said.

"Birds know more than we think they do," Bertie went on. "They may have very small heads, but their brains are quite clever."

Ranald Braveheart Macpherson seemed surprised. "Do birds have brains?" he asked. "Just like us?"

"Yes," said Bertie. "Everything has a brain, Ranald."

"Even a worm?"

Bertie nodded. "They have tiny brains that have three hundred and two cells. We have billions."

Ranald whistled. "Even Larch?"

Larch was a boy at school not noted for his intellectual sophistication.

"Even Larch," said Bertie.

"And Olive?" Ranald asked, a certain yearning in his voice. He very much hoped that Olive and Pansy might be revealed to have fewer brain cells, but Bertie had to tell him that even the two girls, long their heartless persecutors, had the same number of brain cells as they did.

"That's a pity," said Ranald.

Nicola smiled indulgently. "There's no difference between boys and girls," she said.

Bertie looked at her. This was further evidence, he thought, of his grandmother's cognitive decline: everyone, possibly even Ulysses, knew that there was an important difference between boys and girls; one could hardly miss it, not that one should stare. How could anybody be unaware of that? He looked away. It was sad, really, that by the time he returned from Aberdeen it might be too late. She might have only a few weeks left, if she was saying things like that. That was another reason for him not to go – so that he might spend more time with his grandmother in her declining months.

His thoughts were interrupted by their arrival at Valvona & Crolla. The sight of the gastronomic mecca, home of all things warm, Italian, and tasty, helped him momentarily to forget Aberdeen and the three months of exile that lay ahead, a cloud no bigger than a man's hand, but imminent now, and almost upon him.

35

Bertie's Farewell to Ranald

Ranald Braveheart Macpherson had never stepped inside Valvona & Crolla before and was wide-eyed with wonder as they crossed the threshold of the famous Edinburgh delicatessen.

"Can you eat all of these things?" Ranald asked, his gaze moving from the shelves stacked with pastas, via the stacked wedges and circles of cheese and the bowls of bright peppers, to the hams and salamis hanging up behind the counter.

Bertie, who had regularly accompanied his mother on forays to the shop, was on familiar ground. "You can eat all of these things, Ranald. And they're very tasty – I can tell you."

Nicola pointed to the boxes of Panforte di Siena on a low shelf behind them. "That's Bertie's absolute favourite over there," she said. "Panforte di Siena. It's a sort of flat cake."

"Full of fruit, Ranald," said Bertie. "Orange peel and raisins and things like that. You'd like it, I think."

Ranald Braveheart Macpherson had started to salivate. A small trail of saliva ran down from his lower lip, dribbled over his chin, and fell in a tiny drop on the front of his shirt. Noticing this, Nicola extracted a handkerchief from her pocket and dabbed at Ranald's chin.

Bertie looked at his friend with sympathy. "I know how you feel, Ranald. I know that you don't get much nice food at home."

"Bertie!" exclaimed Nicola reproachfully. "I'm sure that's not true."

"But it is, Mrs Pollock," said Ranald. "My mother's not a very good cook. She drinks, you see. She drinks wine when she's meant to be cooking, and she gets the ingredients wrong. She doesn't mean to, but she does."

"That's rotten luck, Ranald," said Bertie. "Having a drunkard for a mother."

"I know," said Ranald. "We're both jolly unlucky, aren't we? My mummy's a drunkard, and yours is a well-known hate figure. We've both had bad luck, I think."

Nicola glanced around them. "Now, boys, you mustn't talk like that. Ranald, I'm sure that your mother only has the occasional glass of wine. There's nothing wrong with that."

"Oh, no," said Ranald. "She drinks far more than that, Mrs Pollock."

"And Ranald's father was had up in court," said Bertie. "Tell my granny about that, Ranald."

Before Nicola could stop him, Ranald started to explain about his father's prosecution, for a technical company law offence, and the resultant community payback order that had been imposed on him at Edinburgh Sheriff Court. "He has to do over one hundred hours of Scottish country dancing," Ranald said. "He hates it."

"He shouldn't have been a crook then, Ranald," said Bertie, helpfully.

"No," said Ranald. "You're right, Bertie."

Bertie remembered something else. "And now he's planning to overthrow the British Government, isn't he, Ranald?"

Ranald Braveheart Macpherson nodded. "My daddy wants Scotland to rise up," he explained to Nicola. "He thinks the rising might start in Morningside and then spread to Fairmilehead. He says there are lots of people in the area who are ready to rise up."

"Goodness me," said Nicola.

"He and some friends tried to raise a standard in

Morningside Road," Ranald continued. "But the traffic wardens came and moved them on."

Nicola supressed a smile. "I see," she said.

"He says the French will come to Scotland's aid," Ranald continued. "He says that they will definitely send ships."

"That's interesting," said Nicola. "I'm not sure if Scotland can count on the French. That was one of the problems that Bonnie Prince Charlie had, I think."

Ranald remained confident. "The English will run away when the French come," he said. "My dad says he has heard this from the man who cuts his hair. He knows all these things. I've heard him – he cuts my hair too. He's one of the people who will rise up, my dad says."

"Very interesting," said Nicola. "We shall have to watch this space, as they say. In the meantime, I think we should buy some olive oil and some Panforte di Siena. Then we can go through to the restaurant, and you boys can have some special Italian ice cream, and I shall have a cup of coffee."

Their purchases made, they made their way into the restaurant at the back of the delicatessen and sat down at one of the tables. A waitress appeared and took their order for ice cream (three flavours) and a *latte* for Nicola. Bertie placed the order in perfect Italian, much to the delight of the waitress, who pinched his cheek, kissed him on the top of his head, and patted his wrist in admiration. Then she kissed him again on the forehead, ruffled his hair, and exclaimed, *Accidenti, è carinissimo!*

Bertie blushed red with embarrassment as the waitress left him to make her way back to the kitchen.

"The Italians are a very demonstrative people," said Nicola. "They're tactile, Bertie – which means they like to touch things. The important thing is that they mean well."

After their visit to Valvona & Crolla, Nicola took them, as promised, to the Chambers Street Museum, where they spent an hour or so in the machinery department, marvelling at the vehicles and the antiquated rockets. They saw an instrument for the administration of chloroform and a Van der Graaf generator. They saw a model of the workings of a coal mine, with a tiny cage in which men, minute painted dolls, their faces darkened with coal dust, were poised to descend into the depths. Nicola gazed at this, while the boys moved on to another exhibit. She thought, *There were so many stunted lives.* She saw a picture of a Highland blackhouse, a windowless but and ben, outside which the members of a family were standing, and she thought of the Clearances and all the sorrow of life in Scotland. And then she thought: perhaps that is what one should think in a museum, and one should not be surprised to feel that way.

Then they caught a bus that took them to Morningside, where Ranald Braveheart Macpherson lived. On the doorstep of Ranald's house, Bertie said goodbye to his friend. Nicola, sensing the importance of the moment, stepped to the side, pretending to admire a fuchsia in the Macpherson garden, while Bertie spoke to Ranald.

"I hope that you come back, Bertie," said Ranald, grasping Bertie's hand in a handshake.

"I'm sure I shall, Ranald," said Bertie, not with any real conviction.

There was a silence. Then Bertie turned and began to walk down the path. He stopped. He looked back at Ranald Braveheart Macpherson, standing there on his doorstep with his spindly legs.

Bertie looked up at the sky. It was blue and empty. He raised a hand to wave, and Ranald Braveheart Macpherson, his friend, his only true friend, did the same. Nicola watched. She struggled with the tears that were just below the surface; a struggle that most of us have, when one comes to think of it, most of the time.

36

Retro's In

When Bruce heard the unexpected voice at the other end of
the speaking tube, he gazed in astonishment at Ed and Gregor,
who seemed to share his surprise. For a moment, Bruce
entertained the possibility, absurd thought though it was, that
he had fallen into a time warp. Time warps were a regular
hazard in television dramas, and Bruce, being a follower of
at least one of these, was able to believe in the possibility
of slipping back a few years, or centuries – at least for an
hour or so. He had read, too, of physicists who suggested
that such ideas were not entirely fanciful. According to them,
our present world could well exist just a hair's breadth away
from a completely different dimension from which we were
separated by wormholes and a few unintelligible mathematical
equations. Such theories were taken seriously, Bruce believed,
along with other ideas about space and time that most of us
found impossible even to envisage, let alone to understand.

Had he somehow slipped into that other dimension a
century or so ago, when in this very house a kitchen maid
on duty in the nether regions of the building might pick up
the speaking tube and reply to a request for a tray of tea for
the drawing room? Of course not, he thought, as he stared
at the tube in his hand and wondered whether he should say
something more – just in case he had imagined the whole
thing. But he could not have imagined it, he decided, because
Ed and Gregor had obviously heard it too, and the whole
point about auditory hallucinations was that you heard them
when nobody else did.

Then Ed laughed. "Give me the tube," he said.

Bruce handed him the instrument warily. "There's somebody there," he said. "I heard . . ."

"Of course there's somebody there," said Ed, giving him a condescending look. "You don't get voices coming out of nowhere."

And then, raising his voice, Ed bellowed down the tube, "Is that you, Katie?"

A compressed voice came back up the tube. "No need to shout, Ed. I can hear you perfectly well. Who was that?"

Ed was enjoying Bruce's surprise. "That was Bruce," he replied. "He's my surveyor friend. Remember?"

"Oh yes," came the reply.

"What are you doing in the kitchen?" asked Ed.

"Checking on something. I've just arrived."

"See you up here, then," said Ed, putting the speaking tube back in its place. Then, turning to Bruce, he said, "That's going to be a feature in the sale, you know. How often do you see that in a set of sale particulars? 'Speaking tube in good condition.' That's the business. People like things like that. Original features, see? Lots of places have had them ripped out."

Greg now expressed a view. "Retro," he said. "That's what people are yearning for. They want retro. E.g. speaking tubes." He paused. "Retro is now, Bruce. Right now."

"Greg's right," said Ed. "This city is full of retro people. It's a real magnet for them. Take the New Town, for instance. There are people down there – people like you, Bruce, no offence – who lead an entirely retro life. They live in Georgian flats. Their furniture is in period, or as close as they can get to period. They'd drive around in carriages if they had somewhere to keep the horses."

Greg liked that. "Yes. Spot on, Ed. And they pay for retro style. They don't want modern."

"Who wants modern?" asked Ed.

Bruce thought of his shower, with its power features. He thought of his Italian coffee machine – gleamingly modern. He thought of the robot vacuum cleaner he had recently bought and of how it sensed where the chair legs were and successfully worked its way around such obstacles. He felt slightly embarrassed by his taste for these modern conveniences. Had he missed the zeitgeist so completely?

But there were more pressing questions. "So, who's this Katie?" he asked.

"She's the person who works for the lawyers," said Ed. "She's the one who'll be showing people round this place. She has keys."

Greg took up the explanation. "They're the selling agents. They're acting for me as owner and developer. She's in their conveyancing department. She's my friend." He paused. "She's in on our . . . our plan."

"Greg was at school with her," Ed remarked. "Like I was at school with you, Bruce. Big pals."

Greg looked out of the window. "She used to be engaged to a guy called Laurence. It's over now. He was bad news. He was a lawyer. He used to criticise her all the time."

Ed confirmed this. "Yes, I heard him. He kept telling her that she was wearing the wrong things. He even laughed at the way she pronounced certain words. She came from somewhere in Fife, didn't she, Greg?"

"Yes. Kirkcaldy, I think. He came from Barnton. He had airs. He thought himself superior. I couldn't stand him. I wanted to punch him. You know the feeling, Bruce? There are some people you just want to punch in the gob."

Bruce nodded. "Like that guy at Morrison's. Remember him, Ed? The one who clyped on Danny Fairgrieve when he put purple dye in the swimming pool?"

"Yes," said Ed. "Him. He shouldn't have clyped. They

almost suspended Danny. It was that close."

"The dye did nobody any harm," said Bruce.

"It made that girl purple, though," Ed admitted.

"She deserved it. Catriona Hodge. You know she married a guy who owned a garage in Perth? He had had really bad skin, and you could still tell, you see. I think she felt sorry for him."

"You forget about teenage skin issues," Greg mused. "I never suffered from them. I was lucky. But there was this boy in my class who had those issues, and he was so embarrassed, poor guy. He avoided eye contact for years. Then you know what? He got some pills that fixed his skin, and he went on to do engineering in Glasgow."

"What sort of engineering?" asked Ed.

"Mechanical. He was a serious petrol-head, and he ended up getting the job he always wanted. He's a design engineer for one of those Formula One teams down near Oxford. No, seriously, that's what he does. They're always fiddling with those cars. They have whole teams of engineers. It's big money."

"It's a stupid pastime," said Ed. "Those cars go round at two hundred miles an hour. You can't see who's where. Then it's all over."

"And not one of those drivers," said Greg, "is in touch with his feminine side."

Bruce looked at him, but Greg just laughed. "You don't want to take yourself too seriously, Bruce," he said, and added, "Ever heard of irony?"

37

Bruce Snubbed

Bruce turned round to see Katie coming into the room. He saw a young woman in her mid-twenties, perhaps, with auburn hair swept back under an Alice band. She was tall – slightly taller than Ed, although Bruce still had a few inches on her. She was wearing a white linen blouse and black jeans. Her appearance and bearing suggested calm and confidence.

Bruce fingered the cuffs of his jacket. It was a mannerism that affected him when he felt anxious. Why should he feel that way now? He was not sure. This young woman was attractive enough, but he was often surrounded by attractive young women – that was his regular lot. I can't help all that, he sometimes said to himself; bees go to pollen, don't they? Some things just *are*. So, why do I feel ill at ease meeting this Katie?

Ed introduced Bruce. "You two have spoken on the tube," he said, and laughed.

Katie glanced at Bruce, and then quickly transferred her gaze to Gregor.

Excuse me, thought Bruce. *No point barking up the wrong tree.*

"Hi, Greg," she said.

"Hi, sweetie," replied Greg.

Hi, sweetie! thought Bruce. How *cheesy!*

"How's things?" Katie continued, still addressing Gregor.

"*Comme ci, comme ça*," Gregor replied. "Actually, not too bad – all things considered. I went to the dentist yesterday."

"Oh, poor you," said Katie. "I hope it wasn't sore."

Oh really! thought Bruce.

"I'm a bit of a wimp. I go for the injection the moment I sit down in the dentist's chair."

"I don't mind a bit of pain," interjected Bruce. "It doesn't last long."

Katie threw him a quick, dismissive glance and then turned back to Gregor. "There's no shame in asking for a local anaesthetic," she said. "And besides, injections are like quiche, you know."

Bruce smarted. He had detected a note of contempt in her voice, and he was not at all sure what she meant in comparing injections to quiche. What a ridiculous thing to say. Was she trying to be clever? Who did she think she was? She was *nobody*. He had never seen her in any of the places in town that counted. Never.

Ed moved about impatiently. "We need to get down to business," he said. "What's the situation, Katie?"

Katie had been carrying a small attaché case. Now she opened this and extracted a piece of paper. "I've done twelve viewings over the last two days," she said. "There's really strong interest in this flat."

"Good," said Ed. "That's exactly what we expected – and wanted."

"You only need one offer," Bruce pointed out. "When I was in practice, that's what I said to sellers: 'You only need one offer.' Land that offer and the place is sold."

Katie looked at him almost pityingly. "I don't agree," she said. "In fact, I can't think of anybody who would agree with that these days. You need competition to get the price up."

Bruce seethed. He did not like being corrected by this rather superior young woman – he was a surveyor, after all, and she was . . . what was she? A paralegal at best.

"Excuse me," he said. "I've bought and sold rather a lot of properties in the past. And I can tell you: you only need one good offer."

"One *good* offer," said Katie. "But what if it's not that good? Oh yes, you only need one buyer if you are to get rid of a property, but it may not be the result you want. Sellers want a good price – and a single offer doesn't always have the right sum attached." She looked at him in a challenging way. "See? That's how it works."

Bruce struggled to control himself. "I know all that," he said, from between pursed lips. "I wasn't born yesterday." What was wrong with this woman? Why had she taken against him in this way? It was probably resentment, he decided: people resented what they did not have. She wanted him to notice her, and evidently he had not done so markedly enough. Her behaviour, then, was a cry for attention – that was it. It was as simple as that. Well, that was easily enough remedied.

He smiled at her. "You know a lot," he said. "And those jeans . . ." He rolled his eyes.

She stared at him briefly, and then looked pointedly away, addressing Ed now. "We've had seven notes of interest, Ed. Seven is pretty good, bearing in mind it's only been on the market for three days."

This information pleased Gregor. "Supply and demand," he said. "There aren't enough double-uppers available. And some of them are going on the private market. They're not even advertised."

"You're quite right," said Katie, glancing at Bruce as she spoke, as if to suggest that at least somebody knew what he was talking about.

Bruce seethed – again.

Ed did not appear to notice the undercurrents. "So," he said briskly, "seven notes of interest. Good. Who are they?"

Katie passed Ed a piece of paper. "Here we are," she said. "I've shown all of these people around. One of them came to see it twice."

"Keen," said Ed.

"It was two people together, actually. Two women."

Ed waited. "Buying together?"

"I think so," Katie said. "They were going on about what they'd do to the place. There was a lot of discussion." She paused. "Those people will be serious bidders. You can always tell."

"Good," said Ed. "So, this is what we'll do. Let's set a closing date for offers. Next Friday at twelve. Agreed?"

Gregor nodded. "It's the usual time."

"The offers will come in to your firm," Ed continued. "By email, right? PDFs?"

Katie nodded. "I get them. I usually pass them on to my boss. He always has lunch on a Friday at Mortonhall Golf Club. He doesn't get back until three. That's when he looks at them."

"That gives us three hours," said Ed. "Just before twelve you identify the highest bid. You pass on the info to Bruce here, who puts in a bid that's twenty grand higher. Then you go back to the original highest offer and tell them they're going to have up things or they'll be the under-bidder."

"We can probably drive the thing up by fifty grand," said Gregor.

Ed agreed. "At least." He turned to Bruce. "Katie's boss has no reason to suspect anything. He comes back from lunch and sees an increased offer from one of the bidders, but won't know that it's come in after twelve or that it's higher because they heard what you had offered. So, if anybody suspects anything, it all looks dead gen. And nobody can pin anything on Katie."

"Nor on you and Gregor?" said Bruce.

"Exactly. The trail stops dead and nobody would be able to prove anything."

"Convenient," said Bruce, adding, "For you."

"Well, yes," said Ed. "But you get a cut, Bruce. We all benefit." He paused. "It's good to co-operate, remember. It's called enlightened self-interest."

Gregor smiled. "We are *very* enlightened," he said archly, winking at Katie, who responded with a coquettish giggle, cutting Bruce dead where he stood in his tracks.

38

In the Elephant House

Bruce was not in a good mood as he made his way back to his flat on foot. He drew a couple of admiring glances while crossing the Meadows, one from an earnest-looking young woman on a bicycle, who swerved, but made a quick recovery, and another, more wistful perhaps, from a matron walking a rheumatic Schnauzer. Bruce ignored these shy tributes – there was nothing unusual in them, but he was not in the mood to enjoy the attention. On George IV Bridge, as he walked past the Elephant House, the café where he occasionally met a friend who lived nearby, he noticed his reflection in the window and stopped, through ancient habit, for a brief moment of self-admiration. What he saw reassured him and put Katie's rebuff in its proper place: the problem was hers, not his. Her antipathy, he decided, spoke not to any defect on his part, but to . . . well, it could only have been frustration on hers.

Poor girl: she was to be understood and forgiven rather than disliked, and that was what he would do. He would forgive her, which made him the moral victor in that brief and rather distasteful encounter – and the psychological victor, too: Bruce had always found that forgiving somebody who slighted him resulted in the most delicious feeling of superiority. Poor girl, he thought; how sad.

On impulse, he decided to go into the café for a cup of coffee and a piece of cake. His light breakfast, of a boiled egg and smoked salmon, had left him hungry, and although it was too early for lunch, Bruce felt that a mid-morning snack was justified. He rather liked the Elephant House, which was a bustling place popular with students and literary tourists. Occasionally there would be queues, but he saw that there was none now, and within a few minutes, with a steaming cup of coffee in one hand and a plate in the other, he made his way to a table near one of the large, rear windows.

There was a newspaper on a nearby table, and Bruce paged through this while he waited for his coffee to cool. He began to read a report on a potential volcanic eruption in Iceland, and was barely half-way through this when he became aware that somebody was approaching his table.

"So this is another of your haunts," said a familiar voice.

He looked up. It was Sister Maria-Fiore dei Fiori di Montagna, whom Bruce knew from an occasional meeting in Big Lou's coffee bar or in the natural food store in Broughton Street. He had seen the nun shopping for lentils and dried beans there on more than one occasion, and they had exchanged snippets of conversation.

Bruce set aside the newspaper. "Sometimes," he said. "I haven't been here for ages, though."

"The places we go to infrequently are more frequently in our minds than those to which we go more regularly," said Sister Maria-Fiore. "The tracks of the heart are not always well-trodden."

The nun sat down. Bruce felt a momentary irritation that she did not ask his permission: one did not sit down at another's table in a café without at least some enquiry as to whether one's presence might be welcomed. He almost said, *Please sit down,* in a pointed tone, but stopped himself. It was ill-mannered to be rude to nuns.

"I have been in the library," said Sister Maria-Fiore dei Fiori di Montagna. "I needed to do some reading for a trustees' meeting tomorrow at the National Gallery."

In the course of her meteoric rise in the higher reaches of

Edinburgh society, the nun had been appointed to the Board of Trustees of the National Gallery, where she had quickly made her mark as a conscientious board member, always ready to deliver an aphorism that might clarify the debate. She also had proved to be a useful mediator, somehow managing to bridge the gap between differing opinions in such a way that neither side felt either humiliated or triumphant. "A decision that we both think is our own idea is always best," she observed. "Two snails do not argue about whose shell is the more attractive." The relevance of this latter observation may not be immediately apparent, but it brought nods of agreement from all sides of what had been, until then, a divided table.

Recently there had been intense discussion by the board of a plan to lower the paintings on the gallery's walls in order to make them more readily accessible to people from cities where the average height was on the low side. Sister Maria-Fiore dei Fiori di Montagna found the discussion fascinating. Rarely had she witnessed, outside Italy, a discussion as heated as the one that followed a committee recommendation that the paintings be lowered by four inches. Not only had a raw nerve been touched by this proposal – an entire nervous system had gone into spasm.

The plan had been condemned as tactless at best, and outrageous at worst. "You know who will think it's aimed at them?" said one opponent. "They'll think this a typical bit of Edinburgh arrogance. This is the most offensive plan anyone could imagine."

That view met with some support, but a few voices were raised against it. "Nobody said anything about the Weeg . . . I mean, the Glaswegians," said one member. "This is emphatically not aimed at them."

This brought silence, followed by a few embarrassed groans. "You can't say that sort of thing," said a voice from the end of the table.

"Even if it's true?" asked the maker of the original comment.

"But it isn't true."

"Why can't one take account of the evidence of one's own eyes? Why is that unacceptable?"

There was sigh. "Because it doesn't help to draw attention to stature issues. It shows a lack of respect. And anyway, where's the hard evidence?"

"There's plenty of evidence. Urban Scotland has big problems. Life expectancy figures tell the story. Poor diet, smoking, damp housing, chronic unemployment, drug abuse: these are all pieces of the whole tragic picture."

"And whose fault is all that? Who deindustrialised Glasgow, may I ask? Answer me that."

And so the debate continued until Sister Maria-Fiore dei Fiori di Montagna caught the chairman's eye. "May I suggest a compromise?" she said. "If there are indeed dear brothers and sisters who might find themselves craning their necks to see the paintings, then why don't we have a supply of elevator shoes at the entrance that people can put on for the purpose of their visit? The shoes can then be returned at the end of the visit."

There was complete silence in the room. Sister Maria-Fiore smiled benignly as she looked around the table at her fellow trustees. Then she said, "The idea occurred to me when I thought of Poussin's painting of blind Orion searching for the rising sun with Cedalion, the servant, perched on his shoulders, showing him the way."

There was a further silence.

"Dear Poussin," she mused.

39

The Omnipresence of Hierarchy

Now, sharing a table with Bruce in the Elephant House, with the light falling in shafts, butter-yellow and thick, through the windows, Sister Maria-Fiore dei Fiori di Montagna took a sip of her coffee and exhaled with pleasure.

"When I drink a good cup of coffee," she said, "I am always reminded of dear Sister Angela of Charity. She was one of the cooking nuns in our order back home in Tuscany. We used to call her Sister Angela of the Medium Roast, because that was the sort of coffee she preferred to make. She made such a delicious *latte*. I can still both smell and taste it when I close my eyes."

In spite of himself, Bruce was being drawn into Sister Maria-Fiore's conversation. "Cooking nuns? Is that all they did?"

"And other domestic chores," said Sister Maria-Fiore. "The order was a bit old-fashioned, you might say. We had the nuns whose main job it was to deal with our dear, deluded patients – the ones who had been affected by Stendhal syndrome. And then we had the nuns who did the cooking. They were mostly – indeed entirely, as I recollect – women from very ordinary backgrounds: the daughters of small farmers, for example – what we call the *contadini* – or from working-class parts of Milan and Turin: the daughters of men who laboured in factories of one sort or another. All postulants were divided into two groups on their third day with the order. All were invited to have lunch with the Mother Superior, who set them a simple test by laying each place at the table with five or six knives and forks and then asking what it was about Dante that most appealed to them. Those who failed the test – who had no idea how to deal with the cutlery, or who were not too sure who Dante was – would be allocated to the cooking stream, as we called it. Dear limited ones – even if they managed that first hurdle, there would be other tests down the line that could separate the wheat from the chaff, so to speak. And by and large, the system worked. People found their niche."

Bruce raised an eyebrow. "Rather hierarchical, surely?"

Sister Maria-Fiore dei Fiori di Montagna replied calmly. "Hierarchies are everywhere, Bruce. They are to be found in the natural world as much as the human world. Be under no illusion about that."

"But still, I would have thought . . ."

She cut him short. "Even amongst angels there are hierarchies – very complicated ones, too. There is no Presbyterianism in the ranks of angels, I can assure you!"

"Well, I imagine . . ."

He did not finish.

"We are so fortunate to have had Pseudo-Dionysius," said Sister Maria-Fiore dei Fiori di Montagna. "I can't imagine where we would have been without him."

"No," said Bruce.

"It's a great pity that his *De Coelesti Hierarchia* is not more readily available," she went on. "It really is most helpful when it comes to sorting out the exact order of precedence. I have a little *aide-memoire*, of course, which sets out the various angelic ranks, but there are plenty of people who don't have that."

Bruce decided to let this all flow over him. Every conversation that he had in the past with this extraordinary woman had been largely one-sided – it was too late to change that now. "You're most fortunate," he said.

"Yes. There are Seraphim, Cherubim and Thrones at the apex. Seraphim, you may recall, have six wings. That's how I remember them."

"Rather like those more expensive drones?" Bruce ventured.

Sister Maria-Fiore nodded. "You could say that, yes. Cherubim, by contrast, have two sets of wings. Not two wings – that's a common mistake – two *sets* of wings."

Bruce nodded.

"And the Thrones. They represent humility and submission, while Dominions, another order of angels, have a sort of administrative role. At least, that's the way I look at it. They are the civil servants, so to speak. Just like people who work for the Scottish Government down at Victoria Quay, although the Scottish Government doesn't use quite the same terminology, I believe."

"I believe not," said Bruce, patiently.

"Indeed. Sometimes, I expect it overlaps. So Principalities, for instance, who are lower down in the pecking order perform, I suspect, some of the tasks that Dominions undertake. They are more accessible to us, though – they understand our language, so to speak." She paused. "And then we have the ordinary angels – the foot soldiers of the heavenly choirs. These are the ones who watch over the likes of you and me, Bruce – who offer their assistance in difficult times."

She took another sip of coffee. "Enough of angels, Bruce. I must let you into a little secret."

Bruce was encouraging. "I can't resist a secret, Sister Maria-Fiore."

"I'm sure you can't. Who can? Our secrets are the truths we dare not reveal; and the secrets we dare not reveal are the truth."

Bruce was still thinking about this when Sister Maria-Fiore dei Fiori di Montagna leant forward and whispered, "Antonia and I have found a delightful flat in the Grange. We have decided to buy it."

Bruce caught his breath.

"And we have so many plans for it," the nun continued.

"I've already ordered some curtain material and shall make the curtains myself. I learned stitching from Sister Perdita. We used to call her Sister Perdita of the Threads – such a suitable name, that she loved, actually. We never chose a hurtful name for any of the sisters, you know – we always spoke with charity."

Bruce was silent. It was a terrible, unanticipated coincidence. He hardly dared ask her where the flat was, as he dreaded the answer she would give him, but he steeled himself and asked the question. He was proved right.

I am about to defraud a nun, he said to himself.

"I don't know whether you have experienced this yourself," Sister Maria-Fiore continued, "but there is a particular sense of contentment in finding just the right place for oneself. It's a sort of homecoming, I think. You have been on a long journey, and then you find yourself in the place that you know is just right for you. You have come home. You know it. You feel that there simply cannot be another place for you – that this is it."

He heard, with a sinking heart, how this double-upper flat in the Grange was, for Sister Maria-Fiore, that place – that haven in an unsettled and sometimes trying world.

"Are you certain?" was all that he could think of saying.

And she replied. "I am completely certain, Bruce."

He hesitated, but then said, "Of course, you realise in our system that you might not get the property. There may be others who will put in higher bids."

"Impossible," said Sister Maria-Fiore. "We have funds at our disposal. There are my modest assets and Antonia's slightly larger resources. We are in a very good position to buy this house which, *Deo volente*, we are assured of getting."

She added, "If you want a house, Bruce, then you can be sure that the house wants you."

And with that she finished her coffee, wiped her lips, and smiled a smile of serene confidence.

40

Poppadoms and Theology

As the onion bhajis were consumed and the pile of poppadoms steadily lowered, Fat Bob continued the story of his arrival in Glasgow. He had been a youth of sixteen, he told Big Lou, with no more than a few pounds in his pocket and an introduction to an unhelpful cousin, and now he found himself sleeping rough in the courtyard of Wee Jimmy's pub. He was already homesick and fearful of discovery, but felt unable to return to the home he had only so recently left.

"Oh, Bob," said Big Lou. "I can just imagine how you felt. When I went up to Aberdeen as a young lass at least I had somewhere to go to. You had nowhere. And you had nothing – or next to nothing."

"That's right, Lou. But when you're that age, you don't necessarily realise how little you have. It doesn't seem to matter so much."

Big Lou said that she thought that by and large that was true. "And yet, where was your next meal coming from?"

"I wasn't so much worried about that," said Bob. "What I wanted was a job. I thought that if I got work, everything else would sort itself out. So I decided that I would simply go down the street and knock on every likely-looking door. I thought that sooner or later I would find somebody who could do with some help."

"And did you have any luck?"

Bob laughed. "A lot. The first door I knocked on was a builder's merchant's. He was a big fellow, and he looked at me and laughed. "Does your mammy know you're oot?" he

said. He was very pleased with himself for that remark. But
then he said that, as it happened, he needed somebody to shift
piles of timber. He would pay me in cash, he promised, at the
end of each day for the first week, and that if I worked hard,
he would take me on properly.

"Then he asked me where I lived. I said that I had been
staying with a cousin, which was true, I suppose, but that
I was hoping to find somewhere else. He looked at me as if
he didn't quite believe me, and then asked me whether the
police were looking for me. I think that my indignant reaction
to that convinced him that I wasn't on the run, and so he
didn't wait for me to deny it. He explained that he had to be
careful. A few months previously he had taken on a boy who
had stabbed somebody and the police had given him a lot of
trouble over that. Glasgow had gang issues at the time – it still
does – and people were jumpy."

Big Lou saw Bob look longingly at the last of the poppadoms. "You have it," she said. "I've had enough."

He reached for the poppadom and broke it in two. "Let's
share," he said.

Big Lou was pleased: sharing the last poppadom was a
good sign. She had known plenty of men who would have
eaten it all themselves.

"It was hard work," Bob went on. "I was given thick work
gloves – I can still smell them – and shown the timber that
had to be moved. Then I was left to get on with it, which I
did. At twelve o'clock I was told I could take an hour off if I
wanted to go and buy myself something to eat. The boss gave
me money for this and to buy a pie for himself. He said that I
would have to pay for my own lunch the following day, but by
then I would have my first day's wage in my pocket.

"He was as good as his word about paying me. I got the
cash in my hand and was told that he was pleased with the
work I had done. He said that the following day he would fix

me up with a set of overalls as he didn't think my clothes were quite suitable for the job I was doing.

"I went out into the street. I had no idea of where I was going to find a bed for the night, so returned to the shed I had left that morning. It had started to rain, and I was getting wet. At least that would give me a roof – of sorts – over my head.

"There was nobody around in the yard. I slipped in and let myself into the shed and lay down on the sacking. The work had tired me, and although I felt hungry, I decided to rest before I went out in search of fish and chips for my supper. Oddly enough, I felt quite happy. I had done a day's work; I had money in my pocket; and I had somewhere to go that night. Obviously, I would have to find somewhere better to stay, but for the time being, I thought the shed would do fine.

"I slept rather longer than I had planned. When I woke up, it was almost ten o'clock, and I thought that I would have to rush if I were to find a chippie open. I need not have worried – there were plenty of places still serving, and enough people coming out of pubs to keep them open for a good while yet. I ordered fish and chips and a pie for good measure. I stood outside and ate the meal, watching what was going on about me. Somewhere down at the end of the street there was a brawl – an angry shout and the sound of glass being smashed. Then the police arrived, the blue light of their car illuminating figures in the road. A woman was shouting at the police. It had never occurred to me that you might shout at the police; that never happened where I had been brought up. But this was Glasgow, with rules of its own, and I thought that I would have to learn a whole new way of behaving if I was to fit in here.

"I went back to the yard behind the pub. Nobody was about, and I was able to slip back into my shed. I took off my boots and prepared for bed. In those days, Lou, I said my prayers every night – my mother had always insisted on that.

She was a Catholic and said that if you died in the night, the state of your soul might depend on having said your prayers before you went to sleep. I don't believe any of that now, Lou, but I did then."

"You were sixteen," said Big Lou.

"Yes. And I believed what they told us about Hell. It was a place of eternal torment, they said, and any of us could end up there if we weren't careful."

Big Lou sighed. "The Devil's just a tattie-bogle. And there's no such place as Hell, Bob."

Bob hesitated. "No, I don't think there is. But why did they tell us all that?"

"It was a useful threat, Bob. Fear works. It secured compliance."

"What a wicked thing to do," said Fat Bob.

"Aye," said Big Lou. "But the Catholic Church has changed, Bob. It's not the same. It's now more about love and charity, which is what it should have been all along." She paused. "You can't condemn the present for the wrongs of the past."

Fat Bob listened. He wanted more love and charity in this world. He wanted that.

"Mind you, it's high time they allowed women priests," said Big Lou.

"You're right there, Lou," agreed Fat Bob, adding, "Shall we order more poppadoms?"

She looked at him fondly: here was a new man who was nonetheless strong, and who liked poppadoms. It had been a long search.

41

Given Lodging

Big Lou would have been happy to discuss theology at greater length with Fat Bob had it not been for her eagerness to find out what happened next. This was *Oliver Twist,* she thought – the universal story of the young man cast adrift in the city. Predators circled, ready to dazzle and then devour the innocent in all their guilelessness. Being press-ganged into the Navy might not be as unattractive a fate as it seemed, when conscription into a street gang was a possible alternative.

"Tell me one thing, Bob," she said. "Does this have a happy ending?"

Bob looked puzzled. "My story? A happy ending? I'm not quite there yet, Lou, not quite at the end . . ."

She smiled. "Oh, I know you're not, Bob. But this particular chapter of your life – this bit in Glasgow: does it end well? You see, I can't bear an unhappy story. I just can't."

Bob reassured her. "There's no unhappy ending, Lou, so you can stop worrying. You see, I don't like unhappy endings either."

"People tell me it's burying your head in the sand," Big Lou continued. "They say that life is hard – cruel even. They say that the only story worth telling is one of how things go wrong."

Fat Bob snorted. "That's just not true, Lou."

"Of course it isn't. There are plenty of good stories. There are plenty of people who go through life without . . . well, without anger. Who are kind to other folk. Who don't rant and rage."

Fat Bob nodded his vigorous agreement. "You're right. Because if there weren't, then would any of us carry on? I don't think so, Lou. There'd be no point."

He spoke with such feeling that Big Lou felt there was nothing she could add. And she knew then, as if she had not known before, that this was the man whom she had always hoped would exist. The others – the Elvis impersonator, who had shown his true colours at that desperate Elvis convention at the Crieff Hydro, the slightly seedy chef, the Jacobite plasterer – were all a distraction. This man was the person for whom she had been destined all along. She had read somewhere that all of us, no matter what our personal predilections might be – and creative Eros bestowed so many options – all of us cherished the hope that there would be one whom we could love with all our heart because he or she was just *right*; that we knew what we were looking for, even if we sometimes seemed to pursue the very opposite, and consequently, and with utter predictability, were unhappy, unbelieving of the optimistic lies we told ourselves.

As she looked at Fat Bob, thinking just this, he looked at her and thought much the same thing. He closed his eyes. She was real, because she was still there when he opened them; she, who could have been sent by some divine agency charged with the consolation of those from whom the world, thus far, had withheld much consolation.

"I'll tell you what happened, Lou," Bob continued. "I got back to my shed and lay there in the dark, wondering what I would do the following day about some clean clothes. I could get away with what I was wearing for one more day, perhaps, but I had left the rest of my things in the house I had run away from, and I was not going to go back there.

"We take a lot for granted, don't we – those of us who have somewhere to live; who have a washing machine to launder some clothes; and somewhere to wash ourselves and clean our teeth? If you live on the street, you don't have any of that, and you have to work out every day how you're going to do any of those very ordinary things."

Big Lou nodded. "I can imagine it, Bob."

"I got to sleep eventually and slept through until I heard a delivery lorry grinding its gears in the road outside. I opened the door of my shed and looked out – and saw a girl staring at me. She was about my age, and she was standing there, holding a lead with a small black dog at the end of it. I did not know what to do. I wondered whether I should run away – it would have been easy enough to push past her and disappear down the road, but something stopped me from doing that. I think it was the fact that she was looking at me with concern.

"The first thing she did was to ask me my name. I told her, and then she said, 'Why are you in my Uncle Billy's shed?' I said that it was because I had nowhere else to sleep. She took a moment or two to take this in, and then she asked where I had come from. I answered that question, telling her that I had come to Glasgow to find a job and to send money back to my mother and family. Then she said, 'You can't live in a shed, you know. You can come back and stay at our place. It's just round the corner.'

"I said, 'But what will your parents say? They won't want me.'

"She did not seem to be worried about that. 'They won't know,' she said. 'You can have my big brother's room. They never go in there. It's full of his stuff – you can hardly get in.'"

Big Lou's mouth was wide open with astonishment. "You went?" she asked.

"Yes, and I moved in. She meant it. She let me in at nights and brought me food. She brought me some clothes from a charity shop."

"And they never found you?"

"Not for a whole week," said Bob. "Then her mother came in and found me asleep on her big brother's bed. I woke up to find her father standing over me. He was called Jock."

"And then?"

"He listened to my story and then went off to discuss the situation with his wife. Then he came back and said that it was an awful pity that people like me had to sleep rough and that there should be a law against it. He said I could stay."

"And did you?"

Fat Bob nodded. "For four years," he said. "They were so kind to me. They treated me as a member of the family. They also gave me a job in their bakery. And that was where I discovered my strength. They had large sacks of flour, you see, and these needed to be shifted from time to time. Usually, it took four people to do this – one at each corner of the sack – but I could do it by myself. Jim said that he had never seen anything like it, and it was his idea that I should compete in the Largs Highland Games. They took me down there in the bakery van, and I won all the events I entered. That was the beginning."

He had been talking for some time. Now he stopped.

"You were so lucky to have found those people," she said. "It could have worked out very differently. For so many young people, it probably does."

"There are plenty of folk like that in the world," said Bob. "We don't hear enough about them because we're so busy looking at all the wretched things that happen."

"Yes," said Big Lou. "The good things that happen – the acts of kindness, the concern for others . . ."

"Are forgotten about," said Bob. "I wish it were otherwise."

"So do I," said Big Lou. "But it isn't, is it?"

42

Bruce Reflects, and Conducts

For Bruce it was an entirely unfamiliar feeling: shame. As he made his way out of the Elephant House on George IV Bridge, past a group of giggling Japanese teenagers, leaving Sister Maria-Fiore dei Fiori di Montagna at the table that they had, until a few moments ago, shared – the table at which she had revealed to him her dreams of a double-upper flat in the Grange – Bruce barely had time to glance appreciatively at his profile in the reflective front window of the café. Had he allowed himself to dwell on that image, he might have experienced that shock that greets us all when we engage fully and frankly with our face in the mirror, and are confronted, if we are prepared to open our eyes, by our faults laid bare for all to see.

But he did not, such was his eagerness to get away from this place, the site of his perfidy. *I sat there*, he thought, *and listened to the voice of my intended victim.* And then he added to this dire soliloquy, *And I said nothing.*

He walked on. It was early afternoon, and the Old Town was bathed in the charitable light of summer. Obscure corners, moody when in mist, sinister in night-time darkness, were now friendly under the warm benison of the sun. If there were secrets and sorrows in these winding streets, these sharp descents and mysterious closes, then these seemed a long way off. Bright flags fluttered briskly; from a side street somewhere drifted the accusing notes of a pipe tune – Edinburgh *en fête*, welcoming the world's visitors, inviting them to the party.

Bruce was in no mood for any of that. As he walked down the Mound, a Glasgow-bound train, emerging from its tunnel, gave a blast of its two-tone whistle, a familiar enough sound in the Princes Street Gardens, but to Bruce, in his mood of regret and self-recrimination, a note of sharp reproach, like the trumpet that summons the guilty to judgement. He thought now of how easy it had been to fall in with Ed's plan. How quickly had he agreed to be part of it, without any weighing of pros and cons. Why had he done it? Was it because he was concerned that Ed would think him too cowardly to join in? Was it because he always wanted to be one of the boys, whatever the boys were getting up to? When was he happiest? The question came to him out of the blue, and he answered it without hesitation. Bruce liked the fellow feeling of the rugby team. And more than that, he was happiest when in the communal bath at the rugby club, after a game, in the warm soapy water with the rest of the team. The thought almost stopped him in his tracks. It could not be true; it simply could not be true. And yet he had thought it.

He put it out of his mind. He had to. There were times when one thought the opposite of what one really felt. That was very common, and this was an example of exactly that. It was true that he had acted impetuously by agreeing to Ed's plan, but there was no point in engaging in self-analysis to work out why he had done that. And it was not too late to pull out. He would phone Ed and tell him that he wanted no further part of the scheme. He would be careful not to be too judgemental – he would not criticise Ed for what he was planning to do – he would simply stand back from it himself. But then he would have to decide what to do about Sister Maria-Fiore dei Fiori di Montagna and Antonia Collie. Should he warn them? If he did, he might end up exposing Ed and Gregor, who might then be prosecuted for fraud. He would have to give evidence and denounce them in court. Did he really want that? *Anderson the clype*: the playground insult, no more than a threat at this stage, made him shiver.

He crossed Princes Street and began to walk up Hanover Street. His mobile phone rang, and he took it out of his pocket to glance at the caller's number. He recognised it as Ed's, and for a few moments he hesitated. It would have been easy enough to answer and to inform Ed of his decision. "I'm out," was all he would need to say. And then Ed would . . . Well, he was unsure what Ed would do, but there were not many options open to him. This was not like leaving the Freemasons. No callers would drop in to remind one of solemn oaths. All he had to do was to say to Ed that he was no longer involved.

For a moment he allowed himself to fantasise. Ed might say that he knew too much. That's what criminals said when members of their gangs threatened to leave. And if they even thought that, then they might – even if reluctantly – order that he be . . . what was the term they used? That he be *terminated*? That was ridiculous. This was not a gangster operation; this was a perfectly ordinary middle-class fiddle – an attempt to drive up the price of a house. There were probably plenty of countries in the world where that sort of thing was perfectly permissible. It was just bad luck that Scotland was so holier-than-thou, thought Bruce.

The thought cheered him, and with his improving mood, he began to abandon the resolve to withdraw from the scheme. He should get a grip of himself, he decided. He should stop these unhelpful, self-recriminatory thoughts; he should stop being such a *wimp*. It was bad luck that Sister Maria-Fiore was involved, but it was probably mostly Antonia Collie's money, and that woman was clearly more than comfortably-off. She could easily afford an extra fifty thousand or so for the privilege of securing that double-upper in the Grange. In a year or two it would be worth what she paid, anyway, if house prices continued to climb as they were currently doing.

He reached the top of Dundas Street. Now the Queen Street Gardens were on either side of him as he made his way down the hill. He looked up at the sky, which had suddenly become dark and threatening. A great cloud had moved in briskly from the south-west and was towering above, an ominous anvil of cumulonimbus. Bruce gazed up at the swirling cloud mass, and was marvelling at its size when the bolt of lightning descended with a gigantic crack. It struck him with a crash, flash, and shower of sparks, making of him a brief and glorious firework. Then it flung him into the air, twenty feet or more above the pavement and the road, giving him a last vision of grey sky and trees and, tilting wildly, the distant shores of Fife.

43

Against All Medical Odds

Annette McFarlane was a nurse. She was twenty-seven and had recently become engaged to Rab Cameron, a civil engineer from Falkirk. Annette was from Oban, where she had been a keen member of a kayak club. She had met Rab at a kayak rally on Skye, and they were engaged within three months. Annette's mother ran a small garden centre, and got on particularly well with Rab's mother, whose hobby happened to be the cultivation of roses. Annette had studied nursing at Queen Margaret University, Edinburgh and had been given her first job at the Royal Infirmary. That had been in the Accident and Emergency Department, to which she had returned after a brief spell in Paediatrics, which she left after being bitten by several of her young patients.

"I like the drama of A&E," she remarked to Rab. "You get all of life there, you know. And then some."

Rab was not sure whether he wanted to see all of life. "But you must see some pretty horrible things," he said. "People with knives sticking out of their backs and so on."

Annette laughed. "That's actually quite rare. You do see knife wounds from time to time, but it's usually people cutting themselves with the bread knife, or something like that. Those very expensive German bread knives – you know, the ones that actually cut the bread – they're the worst. We had a guy in the other night who was making himself some toast and he took the bread knife and . . ."

Rab stopped her. He was squeamish. "Okay, I get the drift."

"I was just going to tell you about his thumb," Annette continued. "You see the knife went . . ."

"I don't want to hear about it," said Rab. But he added, "He was all right, was he?"

"Yes," said Annette. "Although there was a bit of a panic when we weren't sure where we'd put the thumb. They wanted to sew it back on, you see, and this nurse I was working with – she's called Julie – she had it. I swear I gave it to her, but she said I didn't. She should have owned up – she really should. Anyway, we found it on the floor and I gave it a bit of a wash. Have you ever washed somebody else's thumb under the tap? It's really odd, you know . . ."

"All right," said Rab. "He was fixed up. Good."

"And there was this boy who swallowed a light bulb," Annette continued. "No, I'm serious. He swallowed a light bulb. One of those screw-in ones. He was about sixteen, which is a bit late to be swallowing things. Over at the Sick Kids Casualty they get small kids who have swallowed all sorts of things – but he was brought in to us. He had an X-ray, and there it was – an actual light bulb."

"What did they do?"

"I don't know," said Annette. "I went off duty shortly afterwards."

But now Annette was on duty and was standing outside one of the examination rooms when Bruce was wheeled in on a trolley by the paramedics who had retrieved him from Dundas Street.

"He's had a shock," one said.

"A big shock, I think," said the other.

Annette looked at Bruce, who was staring back at her, his eyes wide and unfocused. She noticed his hair, which was standing straight up, bristling like the coat of a cat that has had a bad fright. She smelled something unusual – was it cloves?

She reached out to take his pulse. "Hello," she said. "What's happened to you?"

Bruce struggled to say something.

"I think his tongue's swollen," said one of the paramedics. And then he addressed Bruce. "Don't bother to speak, Jim. You can tell us later."

He drew Annette aside. "Lightning," he said. "This chap's been struck by lightning. Down in Dundas Street. He was in the middle of the street – in the middle – and there was a muckle great burnt patch about five or six metres away. That's where he was standing when the lightning hit him. There were two witnesses."

"They swore it was lightning," whispered his colleague. "They said there was a great bang and sparks – the lot. This poor guy was thrown up in the air like a doll."

Annette looked down at Bruce. "Where does it hurt?" she asked. It was not perhaps the most intelligent thing to say to somebody who has been struck by lightning, but she found that it was usually a good way of getting a history.

Now Bruce managed to speak. "My ribs," he said. "I landed on my front. I've hurt my ribs."

A junior doctor arrived. "What have we here?" she asked.

"A lightning strike," said Annette.

The doctor looked at her. "You serious?"

The paramedics repeated their report. The doctor listened, frowned, and then began an examination of Bruce.

"You're very lucky," she said. "You appear to be largely unscathed. I think you may have broken some ribs, but not much else."

Bruce groaned. "It's sore when I breathe."

"That's cracked ribs for you," said the doctor.

A consultant was called. Lightning strikes were unusual, and word quickly got round the hospital. Notes were taken, and a medical photographer was summoned. Bruce attempted to tidy his hair before the photographer got to work, in spite of being assured that it did not matter. What interested the consultant, and in due course the photographer, were the thin lines, like exposed veins, that ran down Bruce's side. That, the consultant said, was where the current had passed down into the ground. They were surface burns, but so slight as to be inconsequential. "Lightning is a very peculiar thing," said the consultant. "I attended a case in India where a mother who was holding her baby was struck. She was badly burned, but the baby was completely unharmed."

Bruce listened to this. This was no accident, in his view. It was a judgement – a punishment. These people would not understand that, but he did.

Once the consultant and the photographer had left, Bruce said to Annette, "I'm really sorry."

She looked at him. "You've been no trouble. And it wasn't your fault."

"No, I'm sorry about what I did. I'm sorry about what I did to make this happen."

She looked bemused. "Lightning is . . . just lightning. It's nothing to do with what you did."

But then she thought: *I wonder what he did.* So she said, "I'm sure it wasn't all that bad." And added, after a brief pause, "What was it, anyway?"

44

'You are troubled in your soul'

Bruce was kept in overnight in the Royal Infirmary. An X-ray had confirmed the diagnosis of cracked ribs, and an ECG had established normal heart function, apart from a slight and, as it happened, temporary irregularity. This was what justified his remaining in hospital, even for a brief period. Further observation, though, revealed nothing untoward, and by ten o'clock the following morning Bruce was informed that he could return home, but was to take things easy for the next few days. "And avoid lightning," added the doctor, somewhat unnecessarily.

The incident had been picked up by the press. *The Scotsman* had reported it under the headline *Man Struck in Capital Strike*, while *The Sun* wrote 'Bolt Batters Bruce'. Always interested in near-escapes of any sort, there were several journalists and photographers waiting to greet Bruce on his return to his flat in Abercromby Place. He replied courteously to their questions, and posed without demur for the photographs in which he was pictured looking up at the sky, as if awaiting further intervention from that quarter. His hair still seemed to be holding an electrical charge and was sticking up from his scalp in an irrepressible fashion, and this was of some interest to the photographers, who took close-up pictures of the phenomenon.

One of those to read the news reports of Bruce's misfortune was Sister Maria-Fiore dei Fiori di Montagna. She saw the item in Antonia Collie's copy of *The Scotsman* and immediately drew her friend's attention to it.

"Toni, there's the most remarkable thing here," she said. "You know that young man who lives in Abercromby Place – the one with the hair . . ."

"And the curious hair gel? Brian, or Bruce or . . ."

"Bruce Anderson. Yes."

Antonia nodded. "I call him Apollo."

Sister Maria-Fiore said that she thought this very appropriate. Then she continued, "He was struck by lightning yesterday. In Dundas Street, of all places."

"Oh, my goodness," said Antonia. "One doesn't expect people one actually knows to be struck by lightning."

"No, one does not. Fortunately, to no ill effect, according to the paper."

"He must have been well grounded," remarked Antonia, and then added, "Not that I mean to make light of it. I would wish lightning on nobody."

"Wish lightning on another," said Sister Maria-Fiore, "and you wish it upon yourself."

As Antonia thought about this, Sister Maria-Fiore continued, "I must have been speaking to him no more than a few minutes before it happened. For in the midst of life, we are in death; of whom may we speak for succour?"

"Indeed," said Antonia.

Sister Maria-Fiore put down the newspaper. "I shall go and see him," she said. "I shall take him some honey, I think. It has curative properties for those who are in a state of shock. We always gave it to our Stendhal syndrome people when they came to recover with us."

"I'm sure he would appreciate it," said Antonia.

It was not only honey that Sister Maria-Fiore took to Bruce's flat, but also a salami, a bunch of grapes, and a copy of a small booklet entitled *The Pensées of Sister Alphonsine of Tours*. Bruce welcomed her warmly and was clearly touched by the gifts.

"I love honey," he said. "I always have. And salami too. You're very kind, Sister Maria-Fiore dei Fiori di . . ." His voice trailed off.

"Dei Fiori di Montagna," Sister Maria-Fiore prompted. "But I have always been content to be simply Sister Maria-Fiore. A name is only as good as the heart of the one who bears it."

"Of course," said Bruce. He gestured towards Sister Alphonsine's book. "There will be many fine thoughts in this book, I imagine."

"That is indeed true," said Sister Maria-Fiore. "Dear Sister Alphonsine spent years in Indochina. She was much loved there and makes frequent reference in the book to her many friends in that part of the world. She died in Algeria about ten years ago. She wrote a book called *My Dear Pieds-Noir*, which did not meet with the success it deserved. But you will find a great deal of value in these *Pensées*."

Bruce invited Sister Maria-Fiore to sit down on the sofa next to him. "I have had a terrible experience," he said. "It happened a few minutes after you and I had our conversation in the Elephant House."

"I know," said Sister Maria-Fiore. "I read about it in the papers. What a ghastly accident."

Bruce hesitated. "Except, it was not an accident."

"But it was lightning, wasn't it?"

Bruce stared out of the window, seemingly deep in thought. "Not all accidents are accidents," he said. "Some are sent. They are sent because of something that we have done."

"Surely not," protested Sister Maria-Fiore. "God does not intervene so directly in our affairs. He sets the stage. He gives us our freedom, and then it is up to us."

Bruce shook his head. "I used to think like that," he said. "I used to reject anything that seemed vaguely superstitious. Not now." He looked at Sister Maria-Fiore, who knew immediately that he was troubled.

"That lightning strike was a judgement," said Bruce. "I was part of a plan to drive up the price of that double-upper you and Antonia are interested in. I feel so ashamed, but I was part of that."

"*Were* interested in," Sister Maria-Fiore corrected, in a matter-of-fact way. "Now no longer."

Bruce frowned. "You've decided against it?"

"It decided against us," said Sister Maria-Fiore. "The building was declared unsafe yesterday. We heard from the solicitors."

Bruce wanted to say something, but found that he could not speak.

"Yes," continued Sister Maria-Fiore. "It's an awful shame, but apparently a load-bearing wall collapsed. Nobody was hurt, but there was substantial damage."

"Oh heavens," whispered Bruce, struggling to take this in.

"Yes. But we must remember this: God destroys a building here, and builds another there. In this way the equilibrium of the world is maintained."

Bruce rose to his feet. "A great burden of guilt has been lifted from my shoulders," he said.

"Then give thanks for that," said Sister Maria-Fiore.

"May I ask you one thing?" said Bruce. "Will you forgive me if I confess that I lied to you? Not a direct lie – more a withholding of the truth."

"Of course I shall," said Sister Maria-Fiore. "Forgiveness is the greatest of the virtues – greater even than love. Forgiveness enables us to get on with the future unembittered."

There was more. "If something is true," the nun continued, "then it does not matter how you express it – its truth will shine out, even in the darkest of darkness."

"You put it so well," said Bruce. He paused. It was not easy for him to utter the words he was about to say. "I feel so ashamed of myself."

She looked at him. "You are troubled in your soul, Bruce. I can tell, you know." She looked at him with compassion. "And those who are most troubled in their soul are often those who deny they have a soul. Did you know that, Bruce?"

He lowered his gaze. She was right. He had been so proud; he had never spoken like this to another. He felt himself beginning to cry. Him! Bruce Anderson! Crying! Was that the effect of lightning? Was that what it did?

She reached out to embrace him. Her arms were so thin, as are the arms of pity, wherever, whenever.

45

The Road to Aberdeen

The day after Bertie's visit to Valvona & Crolla with Ranald Braveheart Macpherson, Nicola drove him up to Aberdeen. She had not been looking forward to the trip. Not only would she be saying goodbye to her grandson for a full three months, but she would have to hand Bertie over to Irene, and maintain a cheerful disposition during what was bound to be a trying meeting with her ex-daughter-in-law. Nicola was prepared to be tactful – for Bertie's sake – but she had always found that more than fifteen minutes in Irene's company strained comity to near breaking point. Irene would lecture her or condescend to her, or, more likely, do both. For her part, Nicola would bite her tongue, purse her lips, and resort to whatever other muscular and facial contortions that might help her get through the encounter, and then, in the car journey home, would think about what she should have said to the various comments that would be bound to come her way. That was always the case, she thought: the perfect riposte, the *mot juste*, inevitably occurred well after the event, and one could not really write to somebody and tell them what you would have said had you thought about it in time.

As they drove across the bridge spanning the Firth of Forth, Bertie gazed out of the car window at the water far below, a rippling field of greyish-blue. Two working boats, a tug and a pilot vessel, ploughed the surface of the sea, a white line of wake behind them; a little further out, attached to an oil terminal, a long tanker poked out into the waterway. In the distance, pale shadows against the sky, were the islands of the Forth, half-veiled in a mist rising from the sea. The ragged coast of Scotland stretched out to the north, an indistinct, disappearing line that would eventually become Aberdeenshire. Bertie shivered.

"How long before we're there?" he asked.

"About three hours," said Nicola.

Bertie considered this. "Could you not drive a little slower?" His tone was pleading.

Nicola glanced at the speedometer. She was travelling at forty miles an hour – slowly, by most standards – but would speed up to sixty once she was off the bridge.

"I don't think I'm going too fast, Bertie. Are you feeling nervous?"

"Couldn't we break the journey somewhere?" Bertie continued. "We could spend the night in Montrose or somewhere, and then go on tomorrow – or the day after that."

Nicola made light of this. "But we don't need to break such a short drive, Bertie. We don't need to do that."

"I'm sure Mummy wouldn't mind if we didn't arrive for a few days. That would give her more time to get things ready."

Nicola tried to change the subject. "Oh, look, Bertie. Look down there. That's Rosyth, if I'm not mistaken. That's where the Royal Navy fixes ships."

The distraction succeeded. "There's a boy at school called Robbie. His dad is a sailor, and he works there," said Bertie. "Or he thinks his dad works there."

Nicola frowned. "How can he not be sure? Hasn't he asked him?"

"Oh, he knows that he goes there to work. It's just that he's not sure that it's his dad."

Nicola waited, but Bertie offered no further explanation. "Has this person – the man who works in the dockyard – said that he might not be his dad?" she asked.

"No," said Bertie. "It's just that Robbie says that when

the man who says he's his dad goes off to sea, a friend of his mummy comes to stay. Robbie says that he thinks this friend might be his dad."

The car swerved, but Nicola quickly regained control. She tried not to smile. What Bertie said was perfectly feasible, as she had heard that there was a lot of swapping of partners and spouses in Rosyth. One sailor might move out, but another was always available to move in.

"Does Robbie like this . . . this other dad?" she asked.

"Yes," said Bertie. "He has red hair – just like Robbie."

"And the other dad?"

"He has black hair, Robbie says."

"I see." And then, "And do you get on well with Robbie?"

Bertie thought about this. "Mostly," he said. "He has a tattoo."

Again the car swerved.

"Are you sure about that, Bertie? It's against the law to give children a tattoo, you know."

"His mum's friend gave it to him," said Bertie. "He did it himself with a pin. It's a small anchor."

"Not a good idea," said Nicola.

"Robbie likes it."

"Be that as it may," Nicola insisted. "That's not the point."

She decided to change the subject again. "We shall be going fairly close to Falkland Palace, Bertie," she said. "We can't stop this time, but maybe someday I'll take you there. After you come back to Edinburgh."

Bertie was silent. He would not be back for three whole months – an eternity at his age.

"Falkland Palace," Nicola continued, "was where James V heard of the birth of Mary, Queen of Scots. He was on his deathbed, and they brought him news of Mary's birth. He was hoping for a son, but he got Mary instead, and the whole unhappy story began."

Bertie looked thoughtful. "Why are so many stories unhappy, Granny?" he asked.

"There's no simple answer to that, Bertie," Nicola replied. "Perhaps it's because of all the things that are wrong with us. Not you and me, of course, but people in general – what we call humanity." She paused. "People are unkind to one another. They are thoughtless in their dealings with others. They want what other people have, and they try to take it from them."

"Ranald Braveheart Macpherson says that the English have always tried to take Scotland from us," said Bertie.

Nicola thought about this. "There's some truth in that," she said. "The English have many virtues, Bertie, but they may be said to have shown a slight tendency to take things from other people."

"Like the Benin bronzes?" said Bertie.

Nicola was unprepared for this. And yet it was typical of Bertie – his eclectic reading meant that he picked up all sorts of snippets of information. "Yes, Bertie, you could say that."

"I think you should give back the things you've stolen," said Bertie. "It's only fair."

Yes, thought Nicola: it was only fair. And yet when you had stolen so much . . .

She decided on another change of subject, and the conversation moved on to all the news that Bertie would have to give his mother once he was safely settled in Aberdeen. "There's so much for you to tell her," said Irene. "What Ulysses has been getting up to, for instance."

Bertie agreed. "She'll be pleased to hear that he's so much better now that she's gone," he said. "He's not sick as often. And he doesn't scrunch up his face so much and yell."

"Possibly," said Nicola.

"And I could tell him about some of Daddy's new friends. That nice lady who wrote poetry. I could tell Mummy about her."

"Best not to burden her with too much news," Nicola counselled.

"I could tell her about how you threw away most of her things," Bertie went on.

"I did not throw them away," Nicola pointed out sharply. "I rearranged them. That's all."

"I saw some of the things you rearranged in an Oxfam shop in Stockbridge," Bertie said.

"Let's listen to Radio Scotland," said Nicola, leaning forward to switch on the car radio. And then, "Oh listen, Bertie. Jimmy Shand and his Band! *The Braes o' Auchtermuchty!* How about that, Bertie?"

46

My Ordeal, by Bertie

Irene had initially lived in a flat when she arrived in Aberdeen but had since moved to a small terraced house in Granite Drive, Ferryhill. The house itself was solidly built – of granite – and so constructed as to withstand the gales and storm-force winds that regularly assailed it from the North Sea. Irene had converted one of the house's two bedrooms into a study, where she was writing her thesis on Melanie Klein, and so Bertie was to be accommodated in the scullery, in which she had installed a folding bed and a small chest for his clothes.

"This," she said to Nicola, "is where Bertie will be staying." And to Bertie, she said, "Your new bedroom, Bertie. Isn't it snug?"

Nicola's eyes narrowed – involuntarily. She struggled to control herself. It was so important, she felt, that Bertie be spared overt arguments within the family.

"How very sweet," she said. She lingered on the word sweet, knowing that Irene would pick up her disapproval.

"Isn't it just?" said Irene. "Such a change from Scotland Street."

Nicola was not sure what this implied. She pursed her lips. "It's a pity the window is so small," she said quietly.

Irene turned round. "I don't think one wants large windows in a bedroom," she snapped. "Such windows leak heat, Nicola – as I'm sure you know. The emphasis now is on insulation."

"Of course," said Nicola. "Mind you, I don't see an obvious heat source here. No radiator – as far as I can make out. Therefore no heat to leak, surely?"

The gauntlet had been thrown, and Irene was not slow to pick it up. "It's bad for children to be in overheated rooms," she said. "They are far healthier in a more invigorating environment. There's no substitute for fresh air, Nicola – as I'm sure you know."

Nicola addressed Bertie. "Remember to wear a vest," she said. "At all times."

Irene glowered at her. "You'll be wanting to get back down the road to Edinburgh," she said. "I won't delay you by offering you tea . . . or anything."

Nicola drew in her breath. "I assumed that," she said icily. "I took the precaution of packing some sandwiches. And I have a flask of tea. I can stop on the way back." She paused. "But do tell me, Irene, how is your PhD going?"

"Extremely well," said Irene. "But let me not detain you."

"Oh, don't worry about that. I'm so glad that you're happy here in Aberdeen. No need to rush back to Edinburgh."

Irene looked down at the floor. "I really must get on," she said. "And Bertie needs to settle in."

Bertie had remained silent throughout this encounter. Now he heaved his small suitcase onto the bed and opened it.

"My goodness," said Irene. "All those woollens, Bertie! You should have let your grandmother pack for you."

"I did indeed pack," said Nicola. "Bertie was concerned about being cold. I sought to reassure him."

Irene bit her lip. "Quite unnecessary," she muttered. "However, let's not waste time on these small things. Bertie, shall we see your grandmother to her car? She'll want to get home before it gets dark. A dark road is not easy if you have aging eyesight."

Nicola froze. This was too much. But then she looked down and saw Bertie, standing in dejection, and thought: it's hard enough for him as it is; a showdown would simply make it worse. So she limited herself to saying, "Your mother is so considerate, Bertie – always to be thinking of others. I wish I could be as selfless as she is. Very few are, I fear."

Irene threw her a suspicious look, but said nothing, and the three of them made their way out to Nicola's car.

"Goodbye, darling Bertie," said Nicola, bending down to embrace her grandson. And whispering to him she said, "I know you'll be strong. Just remember that three months is not very long and we'll be waiting for you in Edinburgh. Tell yourself that every morning when you get up, and it'll help you through the day."

"What's that?" asked Irene, struggling to hear what was being said.

"Nothing," said Nicola, and Bertie, taking his cue from his grandmother, his co-conspirator, also said, "Nothing".

That night, after he had been put to bed, Bertie switched his bedside light back on and opened a small notebook he had hidden in his suitcase. On the cover of this notebook he had written, in large letters, MY ORDEAL by BERTIE POLLOCK. This was to be his diary, his secret record of his durance in Aberdeen. If he had to be here, then he might as well use his time to keep a record of his experiences. He had read somewhere that there was a large market for what were called *misery memoirs* and he thought, therefore, that there might be many potential readers of an intimate diary kept over three months. He would hide the notebook under his mattress, as people did when they wrote their diaries in prisoner-of-war camps. He might even begin to dig an escape tunnel, as some of those brave men did in those days.

He opened the notebook and began to write on the first page. "Chapter One," he wrote. "I was transported from Edinburgh by road . . ." He liked the sound of that. Being *transported* seemed just right for a story of this sort. "My driver took me over the new bridge over the Forth and then headed straight for Aberdeen, where my Mummy was awaiting me." He liked the sound of all that. He did not mention that his driver was his grandmother, as that rather spoiled the tone, and although readers would want a certain amount of detail, they did not need to know everything.

He wrote a few more sentences. There was a description of his room, which he said was cold and dark. "I know that my Mummy wants me to be happy. I think she likes me. She also likes Dr Fairbairn, who phoned her today while I was eating my dinner. I knew it was him because he has a way of clearing his throat while he is speaking (Ulysses does the same thing – it's very strange). Dr Fairbairn is mad, although he tries to hide it. One of these days they will get him and take him off to Carstairs, but in the meantime he is living up in Aberdeen quite openly.

"My Mummy says that Dr Fairbairn is keen to see me to discuss some more of my dreams. I do not want to see him, but I know that I shall have to. I shall make up some dreams for him so that he is kept busy writing them down in his notebook. If he is kept busy like that, he is less dangerous.

"I have to go to school tomorrow. I am not looking forward to that. There is a school called Robert Gordon's, and I am going to be going there for three whole months. I will put a chalk mark on my wall for each day, and I shall strike out each group of five, which will be a full school week. But now I shall stop writing this because it is time to go to bed and my fingers are already so cold that I can't hold the pencil properly. And this is summer here. End of Chapter One: (signed) Bertie Pollock (7)."

47

Edinburgh Past; Glasgow Future

While Bertie was committing to paper in Aberdeen the first pages of *My Ordeal*, in Edinburgh Angus Lordie was making his way up Dundas Street in the direction of the National Gallery of Scotland. Angus was that evening due to attend a lecture there entitled *New Directions in Scottish Conceptual Art: Glasgow Leads the Way.* The lecturer was unknown to Angus, but had been described in the advance publicity for the event as "one of the most exciting artists to come out of Scotland in recent years" and "hotly tipped for a future Turner Prize". Both of these recommendations had sounded warning signals to Angus, as had the title of the lecture itself. To describe somebody as an artist who had "come out of Scotland" was, he felt, vaguely ridiculous. How did one come out of Scotland? The expression seemed to conjure up a picture of a large map of Scotland with a hidden trapdoor through which, Houdini-like, an artist emerged. And if one came out of Scotland, where would one be going? As for being a front-runner for the Turner Prize – that was even more damning, in Angus's view. He was convinced that it was impossible for anybody with any interest in painting in any form, or any feeling for the role of art as an expression of the beautiful, to get anywhere near the Turner Prize – even onto its longlist. Those were his views. He knew that not everyone shared them, and that there were others who thought the opposite, but he told himself that there always would be people who were utterly wrong – whatever one was talking about.

By the time he reached Hanover Street and was beginning the descent to Princes Street and the Mound, Angus had worked himself up into a mood of despair. How could it be that the artistic establishment – or a substantial part of it – should be so incapable of seeing pretentious posturing for what it was? How could it enthuse so over people whose sole talent seemed to lie in the arranging of found objects, the switching on and off of lights, or the making of unintelligible, self-obsessed videos of themselves or their domestic surroundings? He had recently seen one such video – highly praised by the critics – which was entitled *My Chair*, and which consisted of a twenty-minute film of a kitchen chair, shot from different angles. In the final scene the chair disappears and the room in which it stood is solemnly filmed for a further five minutes, during which the artist performs a small dance. "Utterly memorable," said one of the newspapers. "Immensely promising," said another.

The audience was composed of familiar gallery supporters and a small cohort of intense and slightly disapproving-looking people occupying the front seats. These Angus immediately identified as the lecturer's friends: they had that special conceptual-art look about them – a look he had long since learned to spot at any formal artistic function. It was born, he suspected, of discomfort at being in the presence of others who might not understand – or, at least, understand in the way in which they understood. As such, it was not a sentiment that was out of place at any occasion where a mystery of any nature was being celebrated. These people, Angus thought, are convinced of their vision, but know that they are vulnerable in the way in which the Emperor with No Clothes knew he was vulnerable: at any point a small boy, with the innocence of youth, might point out that the emperor was naked. Huddled together in the front rows, they cast occasional glances towards the audience filing in behind them. Seeing nobody of any consequence, they turned to talk to one another in hushed, expectant tones.

The lecture began. "I am not a painter," said the lecturer. "Nor would I wish to describe myself as an artist. I am one who has a practice, and that practice is art. Why is it art? To quote a well-known practitioner, it is art because I say it is art. Art is not something that needs the endorsement of an establishment, of an academy. An academy is nothing but a self-appointed bureaucracy that purports to endorse one particular view of the world and in doing so to delegitimise the work of those who do not meet with its approval. That may have worked in the past, but no longer. Now we are free of the constraints of the officialdom that stifled and distorted the creative impulses of people in the past. Now we are free to be ourselves – to look at the world through eyes that are beholden to nobody, through eyes that can truly see. And to show you – the public – what we see, we do not need to put paint on a canvas. That has been done, and done again. There are no new landscapes to depict; there are no new jugs and flowers to portray. All these things have been done. They are stale. They are the fixations of the stale mind located in a stale world-view. We no longer need paintings. We need experiences. We need ideas that spring not from the material, but from the inner experiential universe. That is why the focus of Scottish art is now firmly on Glasgow. Glasgow is alive. Edinburgh is dead."

Angus looked about him. The front rows were nodding; behind them, though, there were several stony faces. A well-dressed woman turned to her neighbour and whispered something; the neighbour smiled. Angus stared at the lecturer, who had appeared in his short sleeves, with no jacket. There were damp patches under his arms. He was sweating. He was free, of course, but he was still sweating, Angus noted.

Then Angus saw that Sister Maria-Fiore dei Fiori di Montagna was there, seated towards the back, and next to her was Antonia Collie, looking a bit bored. He realised that he should not have been surprised to see Sister Maria-Fiore – the nun was everywhere, and of course she was now on the gallery's board of trustees. He made no attempt to catch her eye, but she spotted him shortly after he had noticed her, and she waved in a friendly way. That was not something that happened all that often at an Edinburgh lecture: people did not wave to one another. Perhaps that happened in Glasgow, of course: he might ask the lecturer at the reception afterwards. Or he could present it to him as confirmation of the point he had made about the vitality of intellectual and artistic life in Glasgow.

Angus waved back. He was fed up with accusations that Edinburgh was stuffy. It may have been a bit like that in the past, but things were different now. Edinburgh had taken off its metaphorical tie, and what the lecturer had said was just an old canard. It was he who was stale. He was stale through and through – with a stale practice. "You have a stale practice, you know," Angus might say to him.

Why were these people so dismissive of painting? Angus asked himself that question as the lecture drew to its conclusion. Was it because they could not paint? Was that the real reason underneath the pretentious banality of conceptual art? Everyone, Angus thought, who cannot do something, experiences at least some resentment of those who can do it. Human nature.

Angus felt that he needed a drink. There was a reception, although he realised that the word *reception* was a bit old-fashioned. It suggested ownership of the space and the event to be held in that space. *Gathering* was perhaps more acceptable. Or what about *rammy*?

48

Sister Maria-Fiore Confides

Clutching a glass of National Gallery of Scotland white wine, Angus surveyed the crowd gathered outside the lecture theatre. The lecturer was surrounded by acolytes congratulating him on the content of his talk. He accepted their plaudits with a grave nod of the head, shaking hands with one or two, blowing a kiss to more favoured others. Angus turned away. Perhaps he's right, he thought. Perhaps I am exactly what he was talking about – I'm a *stale man*. My time has passed. Nobody wants to hear from me because I paint the sort of things that have been done to death. I am a portrait painter, and who is going to get excited about anything a portrait painter does – particularly a portrait painter who happens to be a *man*? Ramsey and Raeburn were all very well in their time, but now people want a whole new approach, and that approach does not include portraits, particularly portraits of other *men*.

He was thinking these somewhat destabilising thoughts when he became aware that Sister Maria-Fiore dei Fiori di Montagna was at his side, accompanied by Antonia Collie. Angus greeted them warmly. He did not want to talk to anybody new, he had decided, and the familiar presence of these two was just what he needed. Both had glasses of wine considerably larger than his – reserved for trustees and their guests, Angus decided.

"You've heard about our friend, Bruce?" asked Sister Maria-Fiore.

"Struck by lightning," said Antonia. "In our very midst. In his prime, so to speak."

Angus said that he had read about the incident. "A narrow escape," he said.

"Of course, in one sense he's fortunate," observed Antonia. "They say, do they not, that lightning never strikes twice in the same place. That means that statistically Bruce can discount any possibility that he will ever again be struck. It's rather like having measles – you are unlikely to get it again."

"But the chance of being struck by lightning is infinitesimally small," said Angus. "About the same as you or I being the victims of a shark attack."

Sister Maria-Fiore thought about this. "Of course that depends on where you live," she said. "If you live in a landlocked country – let's say Switzerland – then surely the chances of being attacked by a shark are non-existent. Whereas you or I, being residents of an island, at least face some such odds, small though they may be."

Antonia took a sip of her wine. "I think this is Italian," she said. "Goodness knows where from." She paused. "Perhaps you might be able to identify it, Floral One."

It was the first time Angus had heard Sister Maria-Fiore addressed by this soubriquet. It was, he thought, rather touching.

Sister Maria-Fiore sniffed at her wine before tasting it. "Veneto," she said, after a moment or two of thought. "I have an uncle who produces wine exactly like this. Not on a big scale, of course – no more than four hundred bottles a year. But his wine is much appreciated. We bought some for the convent a few years ago. The sisters enjoyed it greatly. It was a change from the red wine that we produce ourselves."

Angus looked at her with fascination. She really was a most *refreshing* nun. And her social ambitions, although plain for all to see, were harmless enough. Sometimes those with social aspirations simply wanted to be loved – that was all there was to it.

Angus sought their views on the lecture.

Antonia shrugged. "I was thinking of other things," she said. "There's a limit to what one can take in."

Sister Maria-Fiore smiled. "Dear Antonia has so much on her mind," she said. "What with her book on the lives of the Scottish saints and one thing and another. As you know, Angus, we were thinking of moving over to the Grange, but that will no longer happen."

"The house fell down," said Antonia, in a melancholy tone.

"Not altogether," Sister Maria-Fiore corrected her. "It was declared structurally unsound after somebody interfered with a supporting wall. One should never do that. Supporting walls are called supporting because of the support they give. And without support, they are unsupported."

"No," said Antonia. "That is not quite correct, dear Floral One. Supporting walls are not themselves supported – they *give* support. It is the overall structure that is not supported."

"You are quite right, Toni," said Sister Maria-Fiore. "I sometimes speak in general terms and lose sight of the particular."

Angus now asked Sister Maria-Fiore what she thought of the lecture.

"He has a point," said the nun. "Art can become stale. We all know that. When I contemplate the endless Holy Families painted by Neapolitan Baroque artists, for instance, I am overwhelmed with a sense of déjà vu." She paused. "St Joseph usually looks so uninspiring in those paintings. He looks rather like the chairman of a branch of Rotary International."

Angus was inclined to agree. There could be a sameness to certain stock images. But then so many of our cultural images were afflicted by that sameness: there was a limit to the human imagination, after all, and we revisited and revisited certain popular themes. What was the current word for those? Tropes? Memes?

Sister Maria-Fiore had more to say. "But at the end of the lecture, I found myself thinking: who is the stale one here? And do you know what? The answer that came to me was: *they are.* Yes, the conceptual artists who are so busy attacking conventional painters for being stale have themselves become stale. They are the ones who are saying the same thing over and over again. Whereas anybody now who paints in a conventional style is the radical, the outsider."

Antonia was nodding her agreement. "Maria-Fiore is absolutely right, you know," she said.

Angus smiled. "Am I then in the avant-garde?"

"Of course you are," said Sister Maria-Fiore. "Anybody who has painterly skills is the progressive now, ploughing a lonely furrow. You are definitely in that category, Angus."

He was pleased. It was rather like being rehabilitated after a long exile.

Sister Maria-Fiore looked about her. She had the look of a conspirator, and now she leaned forward and whispered to Angus. "Antonia knows about this, so she can hear. But I wouldn't want some of those people to hear just yet." She glanced over at the lecturer and his knot of supporters. "I learned only a few days ago that I have been chosen to be on a rather significant committee."

Angus waited. It seemed to him that there was barely a committee left in Scotland on which Sister Maria-Fiore had not been invited to serve. "Tell me all about it," he pressed. "I'm the soul of discretion."

"I have been appointed to the panel of judges of the Turner Prize," said Sister Maria-Fiore. "The Board of the National Gallery of Scotland was invited to nominate a member, and I proposed myself. It was at the end of a trustees' meeting, and people were keen to get away. Nobody objected, and I was on."

Angus struggled to regain his composure. "You?" he stuttered. "A Turner Prize judge?"

"Yes," said Sister-Maria Fiore. "And I can tell you this, Angus, the prize will not be going to people like tonight's lecturer who belittle the tastes of ordinary people. These people are incorrigible elitists. They are the epitome of intellectual arrogance. No, I'm going to do everything within my power to make sure it can go to somebody who can actually paint. Perhaps even to a landscape artist. Who knows?" She paused. "And I shall use such skills as I have to ensure that I am elected to chair the panel."

Angus clapped his hands together, forgetting he was holding a glass of wine. The wine went everywhere, but it was worth it.

"This is very welcome news," he enthused. "And I suspect you might just be able to pull it off."

Antonia Collie beamed. "Of course she will. She's a Daniella come to judgement."

Sister Maria-Fiore dei Fiori di Montagna lowered her head demurely. "I merely do my duty – to art and to beauty," she said. "That's all."

49

A Martini Is Planned

While Angus was receiving the extraordinary news of the appointment of Sister Maria-Fiore dei Fiori di Montagna to the Turner Prize panel of judges, Domenica Macdonald was back at their flat in Scotland Street mixing a martini for her student neighbour, Torquil. They had met on the stair earlier that day, and she had invited him to come in for a drink that evening. He had readily accepted.

"I wouldn't want to distract you from your studies," she said. 'But I thought that . . ."

He cut her short. "I never do any work after six," he said. "And neither do any of my flatmates. In fact, some of them never do any work *before* six either."

"I'm sure you exaggerate," said Domenica, smiling.

"Of course I do," replied Torquil. "But some of them are . . . well, I think they don't over-exert themselves. Take Rose, for instance. She gets up really late, you know, even when she has a lecture at ten. She says, 'I can learn the stuff out of a book. I don't need to be told.' And so she doesn't go into the university until well after eleven. She's writing a novel by the way – or claims to be doing that. She's fairly secretive about it, but if you press her, she'll tell you a bit about it. It's science fiction, I suppose – about a woman who finds that her new car has a time-travel feature. She thinks it's the air-conditioning switch, but it isn't. It's a time-travel device that will take you back to minutes before some important historical event is about to occur. She gets transported back – in the car – to Dallas on a November day in 1963. That was the date that President

Kennedy was assassinated. This woman finds herself parked outside the Texas Book Depository, and she sees a man going inside carrying an object that looks as it might be a rifle."

Domenica smiled indulgently. "How far has she got?"

"Page three," Torquil replied, and laughed. "Anyway, what time shall I come up?"

"Six-thirty," said Domenica. "Angus will be at a gallery lecture and usually doesn't come back from those until eight, or so. He and I shall be having a late dinner, which means there's plenty of time for a cocktail. Do you like a martini?"

Torquil nodded. "Do I like a martini? I certainly do. I had a mystical experience once after drinking a martini. I've never forgotten it."

"You can tell me about it later. Gin or vodka?"

"Oh, gin," said Torquil.

"I have a bottle of McQueen Gin," said Domenica. "They make it up near Callander. I don't suppose you remember *Dr Finlay's Casebook*. That was set in Callander. With Janet and the miserable Dr Snoddie, and Dr Cameron being every bit what a country doctor is supposed to be. It was an old Scotland that, well, seems to be slipping away."

Torquil was listening. He said, "I think I know what you mean."

She looked at him. "Do you?"

"Yes."

She returned to the subject of martinis. "With an olive perhaps?"

"Good idea."

The plan was laid, and at various points in the day Domenica thought with pleasurable anticipation of what lay ahead. Every so often, she reflected, one met somebody to whom one felt one had just so much to say. It was a curious phenomenon, and occurred quite unexpectedly. People talked about being on the same wavelength, and perhaps that was all it was – being attuned to the interests and concerns of another. She and Angus talked, of course, but much of their conversation was what she would describe as comfortable, covering well-worn tracks, involving references that both understood perfectly, involving no surprises. They were fortunate in that: some couples, she knew, lapsed after a time into near-silence, as if they had said to one another anything they possibly could say. When all the words were used up in a marriage, what was left?

Domenica remembered a previous discovery of a conversational soulmate. It had occurred before her first marriage, when she had been involved in a research project with a young anthropologist from Cambridge, a man a year or two older than she was, but seemingly so much more worldly and sophisticated. He had been a junior fellow of one of the colleges and had a set of rooms overlooking a quad. He had the ease and self-confidence of the expensively educated and the privileged, but none of the negative qualities that sometimes went with that background. He was modest and unassuming, and it was only by accident that she discovered that his family lived in an Elizabethan manor with a dovecot and tennis court. He referred to the tennis court as a *lawn tennis* court because he played real tennis, a different game altogether with its strange score calls and its half-roofed court. She remembered now how she had looked forward to the time they spent together and the ease with which their conversation ranged over every conceivable subject.

That was different, of course. She had been single then, and she could afford to immerse herself in the company of a brilliant and entertaining young man. They were near co-evals; she and Torquil were not, and this friendship, if that is what it was, had predetermined boundaries. It would be unwise to become too close to this young man because . . . She asked herself why, and she came up with the answer immediately. It was because they inhabited different worlds, and she understood that; he might not. She had to remember the inescapable realities of age: he was twenty – she was not.

And there was scope for misunderstandings. How would she feel if Angus started meeting a much younger woman for coffee, or – and here she brought herself up sharply – martinis? Platonic friendships existed between men and women, but even the most trusting of spouses or partners might feel a twinge of jealousy in such circumstances.

She thought about cancelling the invitation. She could find some credible excuse that would not involve any embarrassment for her nor offence to Torquil. She could truthfully claim a deadline or, less honestly, a forgotten prior engagement. And then she would simply not reissue the invitation and could avoid any situation in which a substitute invitation might be expected or extended. But although she considered these possibilities, she did nothing to bring them about, with the result that when six-thirty arrived she found herself looking anxiously at her watch, her breathing shallow, an odd feeling in the pit of her stomach, like somersaulting butterflies – if such a thing does not strain to breaking point the tendons of analogy.

50

Post Martinis Omnia Animalia . . .

"You said that you once had a mystical experience after drinking a martini. You did say that, didn't you?"

Domenica was addressing Torquil as she handed him the martini she had just mixed for him. He took it, smiled appreciatively, and replied, "Yes, I did." And then, after a moment's hesitation, he continued, "I'm not sure if I should tell you, though. We don't like to hear about the dreams of others, do we? Perhaps the same goes for mystical experiences."

Domenica disagreed. "No, mystical experiences are different. We're not interested in others' dreams because we know that dreams are unreal. That's why we forget them so quickly. Have you noticed that?"

He had. "It's odd, isn't it? You wake up remembering a dream and then, in two seconds flat, it's gone."

"That," said Domenica, "is because the brain knows that it can't clutter itself up with useless phantasmagoria."

Torquil, taking a sip of his martini, looked at her over the rim of his glass. "What a great word."

"Phantasmagoria? Yes, it is, isn't it? It was invented by a French playwright to describe magic lantern shows of disturbing images – ghosts and what we would call bogles. People liked to frighten themselves with them."

Torquil rolled his tongue around the word. "Phantasmagoria . . ."

"Whereas," Domenica went on, "a mystical experience is something that really happens, even if it is elusive. So we're interested in that. And most of us have had one, even if we wouldn't necessarily describe it as such." She paused. "All of which means you can speak about it, you know. My eyes won't glaze over."

Torquil took another sip of his martini. "All right. It was in New York."

"Ah. Place is important for such things. It's easier to imagine having such an experience in exotic locations. Trebizond. Dar-es-Salaam. Does New York belong in such company?"

Torquil thought it did. "I know that if you live in New York – work there – then it's probably just the place you live or work. But if you don't, then it hits you when you first see it. You can't be indifferent to it. There it is. Those buildings. The scale of it. The feel. The sounds. The sirens. The yellow cabs. The steam coming out of the subway vents. The smell of hot dogs on street corners."

Domenica dipped the tip of her tongue into her martini. The alcohol was sharp. A madeleine cake dipped in tea. A bar in London. A man in a fur-lined coat, his hair still wet from the rain outside. A red London bus going past the window. She shook her head. "You were in New York. Go on."

"It was at the end of my first year at university," Torquil said. "Two years ago. As a birthday present my parents offered me an air ticket to New York. They said they would pay for my cousin Chris to come too, although we would have to live in a cheap backpackers' hostel – not that anywhere in New York is cheap.

"I accepted the offer like a shot, and Chris and I went off for two weeks. My parents had friends there, and they were in touch to ask us to drinks at their apartment on the Upper East Side. We went to the address expecting to find just a . . . well, an ordinary apartment. It wasn't. It was massive; on the very top of a building, and with a garden terrace of its own. They had invited other people too – members of their crowd – and these people were milling around making us look seriously shabby, as you can imagine.

"They had a piano on the terrace, played by a small man in a double-breasted blazer and a bow tie. He had an oddly shaped head – rather like a bullet – and a pair of tiny round glasses. He was playing show tunes, singing some of the lines in a thin, reedy voice that sounded as if it was coming out of an ancient radio. Chris said, 'That guy is the real McCoy, you know.' I agreed. He was. I think he may have overheard us because he turned and said to us in his thin, rather whiny Midwest voice, 'Thank you, boys. Take care now.' Then he carried on playing.

"Chris went off to talk to a girl in a green dress. I walked over to the parapet around the terrace. It was topped by an ornate bronze rail, with Art Deco features – the style you see on the Chrysler Building. I looked over the edge, down twenty-six storeys to the street below, which was Madison Avenue. It was early evening, about seven o'clock, and the slanting sun was on the tops of the skyscrapers, making them warm and gold. The sky was empty, and I remember thinking it was so pale a blue as to be almost white.

"I turned round. I had just finished the martini I had been given when I arrived. I saw that Chris was on his second, but one was more than enough for me, as it had been generous. I looked at the people there, at these New Yorkers, and I suddenly felt a rush of affection for them. It was very strange – a feeling of love, in the *agape* sense – a feeling of being *with them* in a curious way. It was a feeling of tenderness; I suppose you might call it that.

"And everything, it seemed to me, was just right. The people, the terrace garden, cars crawling along the road down below, New York in all its extravagant, unapologetic glory, was all *just right* – benevolent and well-meaning and utterly human – not the indifferent, money-making machine it is sometimes portrayed as being, but a place of human tenderness. These were kind, generous people who had just given me, a perfect stranger, a life-changing martini; and now the pianist had started to play *As Time Goes By* from *Casablanca*, and was singing the words, almost under his breath, as if unconcerned whether any of the guests might hear him. *A kiss is just a kiss,* he sang; *the fundamental things of life . . .*

"He looked up. Chris had come back to join me. 'The fundamental things of life. Remember that, boys,' the pianist said, from the corner of his mouth."

Torquil stopped. He put down his glass and rose to his feet. Then he took Domenica's hand in his. She caught her breath. Then she said, "Perhaps not." And he looked away. He seemed neither hurt nor surprised.

They started to discuss something quite different – an essay that Torquil was writing on how cruelty is portrayed in the final scenes of Homer's *Odyssey*.

"Odysseus was very unforgiving," said Torquil. "I ended up not liking him at all."

"Neither did I," said Domenica. "A very unsympathetic type."

At seven-thirty he left. Angus came back half an hour later.

"I had Torquil up for a few minutes," said Domenica. "We chatted for a short while." Then she added: "We held hands. Very, very briefly. It was his doing, not mine."

Angus seemed uninterested. "You'll never guess what I heard from Sister Maria-Fiore dei Fiori di Montagna," he said.

51

Room Issues

Torquil went downstairs. He had declined a second martini, not because the atmosphere had soured after his ill-advised taking of Domenica's hand – it had not – but because he found that the boundary between the feeling of exhilaration following the consumption of one martini and the collapse into maudlin incoherence following two was a fine one, and easily crossed unawares. Domenica had similarly shown restraint, and they had ended up having a cup of tea before Torquil looked at his watch and remembered that Rose and Dave had agreed to make dinner for the entire flat that night. They would be expecting him to be there.

"He's back," Dave called out from the kitchen when he heard the door open and close. "Torquil has returned from his intimate little tête-à-tête with his friend upstairs. Let's hear all about it, Torquil, you dark horse, you."

Rose appeared from her bedroom – the one she shared with Alistair. "What do you two talk about?" she asked. "Or do you just, you know, commune with one another?"

Torquil ignored the taunt. "We talk about all sorts of things. She's an anthropologist, you know. She's worked in some amazing places. Papua New Guinea. The Malacca Straits."

"And you know all about that sort of stuff?" asked Rose.

"No. But we talked about other things."

Rose took Torquil aside. "Torquil, can we talk?" she said, her voice lowered.

Torquil nodded. "Of course."

"In there." She nodded in the direction of the room she had just left. Torquil followed her back into the room, closing the door behind him. Rose gestured for him to sit down.

"I don't want to talk about this in front of the others," she said. "But I feel I can talk freely to you."

"Of course you can."

"And you can talk freely to me," Rose continued. "You know that, don't you?"

He nodded. "We always have. You remember when we discussed your relationship with your sister. And I told you about how I felt when Sally chucked me. That wasn't my fault, you'll remember."

Rose frowned. "You have to move on, Torquil. You can't live in the past. Sally is history as far as you're concerned. And Phoebe said that your star signs were completely incompatible."

"That's nonsense," he snapped back. "You don't believe any of that rubbish, do you? She picks up all those ideas from Findhorn. You know how weird they are up there. The problem with Sally was that she was looking for somebody exactly like her father. I worked that out eventually. She wanted somebody who was just like him. I wasn't."

Rose looked doubtful. "I'm not so sure of that."

"Well, I am. I met her father. I think that he liked me. He said he did. He said to me, 'I quite like you.' Those were his exact words."

"You have to forget Sally. You have to move on."

"I have moved on," protested Torquil. "I used to be . . . be *there*." He pointed to one side of the room. "Now I'm here. I've moved on."

"Then stop talking about her."

"I wasn't. You brought her up."

Rose sighed. "This is not about Sally. It's not about you. It's about me and Alistair. Or mostly about Alistair."

Torquil waited.

"I don't dislike Alistair," Rose began. "I wouldn't want you to think that."

"I never thought you did."

"It's just that I don't see why I have to share a room with him."

He gave her a reproachful stare. "You chose to share with him."

"I know I did. But that was at the beginning – when we first moved in. Remember? And it was you, I think, who said that we weren't going to allocate rooms on a gendered basis."

"I did. Yes, that was me. But it was also you. You were in favour of it, remember. You and Phoebe both said that was fine by you."

"I know. But that was because we were so keen to show that we had risen above all that stuff – all that single-sex nonsense."

"Well? Nobody said they were unhappy with it, did they?"

Rose laughed. "You're talking about the boys. Of course, they're not going to object. Ask a guy if he wants to share with a female, and he'll say 'Sure'. Ask a girl the same thing, and you won't get the same answer."

"But you both said you wanted to," Torquil pointed out.

"That's because we didn't want to appear uncool," she said. "Then we discovered it wasn't such a good idea."

Torquil hesitated before saying, "Is Alistair making things difficult for you?"

She shook her head. "No, he's not like that."

"Then?"

"I think he's thinking things," said Rose.

"What things?"

"Things. I'm not sure exactly what – but you can tell he's thinking. He looks at me sometimes, and I realise that he's . . . he's thinking."

Torquil resisted the temptation to laugh. "Do you think he fancies you?"

Rose shook her head. "No. Well, maybe. Who knows?"

"So what do you want me to do?" asked Torquil.

"Why don't you let Alistair share with you? You're both guys, and your room is bigger than the other two bedrooms put together."

"And you?" asked Torquil. "Who will you share with? With Phoebe?"

Rose shook her head. "No, with Dave. Phoebe can have a room to herself. She's too weird to share with anybody really."

"Let me get this straight," said Torquil. "Alistair moves in with me. You move in with Dave. Phoebe has a room to herself. Is that what you want?"

"More or less. In fact, yes, that's what I want."

"But I don't want to share with Alistair. Why can't he share with Dave and you and Phoebe share? Two guys sharing and two girls sharing. What's wrong with that?"

Rose gave Torquil a sullen look. "Why can't I share with Dave?"

Torquil thought for a few moments. Then he said, "You fancy Dave, don't you?"

Rose looked away. "Maybe. In the past. Not now."

"You've moved on?"

"Yes."

"And do you think he wants to share with you? Have you spoken to him about it?"

"Not in so many words. I thought if you said that you were doing a reorganisation, he'd accept it."

Torquil asked what Rose thought Phoebe would want – if she were to be asked.

"You don't ask Phoebe for an opinion," came the reply. "She can't handle these things."

"And Dave? Did you ask Dave what he wanted?"

Rose shrugged. "Dave doesn't mind either way."

"Do you think Alistair's into guys?"

"Maybe."

"Maybe he'd like to share with Dave. Have you thought of that?"

Rose's tone was dismissive. "I don't do hypotheticals," she said.

"Why don't you share with me?" asked Torquil, adding, "Hypothetically."

"Because you aren't Dave," Rose replied. "Sorry, Torquil. No offence, but you just aren't."

52

Elspeth Reflects

Elspeth had enjoyed having Angus and Domenica to dinner. She liked both of them, but in particular she found Domenica's company stimulating. At the same time, she found the evening of friendly conversation curiously unsettling. As she and Matthew said goodbye to their guests, waving them down the drive towards the narrow passage through the encroaching rhododendrons, she felt a nudge of regret. Only twelve miles or so separated them from Scotland Street, Drummond Place and the world in which Angus and Domenica lived, but it seemed to Elspeth to be rather more than that. Angus and Domenica led an urban existence – one in which the facilities of Edinburgh were there at hand, only a short walk away. They could go out of the front door of 44 Scotland Street and expect to meet, within a block or two, people with whom they could pass the time of day. They could drop into Big Lou's coffee bar whenever they wanted, and the odds were there would be somebody whom they knew. Or if there wasn't, there would be Big Lou herself, whose reassuring presence, it seemed to Elspeth, was so much a part of Edinburgh life – like the One o'Clock Gun or the Floral Clock. Big Lou always had time to chat, even as she made her bacon rolls and coffee, and of course Matthew was now part-owner of her business, which meant they could, if they wished, go round to the other side of the counter and lend a hand.

It seemed to Elspeth that Domenica had a far more interesting life than she did. She knew that this was not a line of thought one should pursue: all of us know of others whose lives seem more colourful, more fulfilling than our own. Other people, it often seems, have more friends than we do. Other people have more going on in their lives; have more interesting things happen to them; have more disposable income, more attractive clothes, fewer problems with their weight, their cholesterol levels, or their hair. Other people, Elspeth thought, don't have triplets, or live in a place where for large parts of the day there is simply nobody around with whom to have a chat. If she felt lonely, as she often did with Matthew off at work in the gallery, then to whom could she talk? James, the au pair, might be around, but his working time was now shared between them and Big Lou's coffee bar, and anyway James was young and there was a limit to the company he could provide. He was planning something, Elspeth felt, but she had no idea what it was.

"Are you happy with these arrangements?" she had asked him.

"What arrangements?"

"The deal we agreed. You work here so many days a week and then so many at Big Lou's."

He assured her he was. "This suits me fine. It really does. I love helping out in the coffee bar – I really do. You meet all sorts of people. And I like Big Lou. She makes me laugh. We have a great time."

She was pleased with that, because they liked having him about the place. He was by far the most successful au pair they had had: he was good with the boys, who adored him; he was a talented cook; he was good with his hands, and had recently fixed not only a washing machine but also a leaking water tank, a malfunctioning computer, a fence, and a window that had been broken by a ball kicked by one of the boys. James was in every respect perfect, and if Elspeth was discontented with her lot, it had nothing to do with him. She had heard stories from other young mothers of nightmare au pairs, including one who had been dealing in stolen goods from the house, another who drank, and a third who spent several hours a day, every day, washing her hair. Elspeth knew that she was lucky to have James, but what she needed were friends, and that, it seemed, was more difficult, living in the country.

There was the Duke of Johannesburg, of course, who was James's uncle, and who lived just a few miles away. He was always happy for her to call in for a cup of tea, and he sometimes called in to see her on his way back from West Linton, where he played bridge two afternoons a week. Recently, though, he had had trouble with transport, and these calls had become less frequent. His Gaelic-speaking driver had gone back to Stornoway and had taken the Duke's old Land Rover with him, promising to return it, but failing to do so. That left the Duke only with the car that he had bought from a man at Haymarket Station, and that had proved to be temperamental. It was a strange-looking car: it was difficult to tell at first glance which was the front and which was the back, and it was only when one opened the door and saw the position of the steering wheel that one could work out which way it was meant to go. A further problem was the fact that nobody had as yet identified what make it was. The garage man to whom the Duke went, a mechanic whom he had used for years, had expressed the view that it was Belgian, but he was not certain about that. When spare parts had been needed, they had found that Alfa Romeo parts appeared to fit, but then so did some made by Ford. This had left the *garagiste* scratching his head.

"The important thing is that the car goes," he said. "That's the bottom line, Duke – believe me. If your car goes, you're happy. If it doesn't, you're unhappy."

"True," said the Duke.

That afternoon, on the day after the dinner with Angus and Domenica, Elspeth was thinking about her situation when she heard the crunch of tyres on gravel and looked out to see the Duke of Johannesburg's unusual car drawing up outside. It was exactly what she wanted. She felt in the mood for a chat. James had taken the boys to play in the woods, and she had been sitting there, looking at the hills. The arrival of the Duke was very well timed.

She went outside to greet him.

"Car's playing up again," he said. "I had to drive half the way from Carlops in reverse. Then it got unstuck and went forward again."

Elspeth expressed sympathy. But then she said, "There comes a time when you have to get rid of a car." She paused. "Have you thought of going electric?"

"It would be an awful bother changing the batteries," he said.

Elspeth smiled. "Let's have tea on the terrace. Have you been playing bridge?"

"Dreadful hands," said the Duke. "I had the wrong cards. But you have to make do with the cards you get."

Yes, thought Elspeth. You do.

53

We're All of Us Lost

"It's an odd thing, corrosion," remarked the Duke. "I'm fairly convinced that the problem with my car is that some of the leads have corroded."

Elspeth poured his coffee as they sat out on the terrace, taking advantage of the warm mid-afternoon sun. An area of high pressure had settled over Scotland, and the sky was devoid of cloud. Elspeth had put on a battered sunhat, and the Duke had taken an ancient Tam o' Shanter out of his pocket, brushed it down, and then planted it firmly on his head.

"This tam belonged to my father," he said. "He was with Fitzroy Maclean in the desert during the War. And in the Balkans."

The Duke looked at Elspeth. "Do you know who Fitzroy Maclean was?"

Elspeth looked embarrassed. "It sounds as if I should."

The Duke shook his head. "No, I wouldn't say that. I wouldn't expect your generation to know about him. He was one of our finest men, though. He had an adventurous life – the sort of life nobody leads today. He sat through Stalin's show trials; he fought in the Western Desert and with Tito in Yugoslavia; he was in Parliament for a long time. He wrote travel books and spoke numerous languages and ran a hotel in the Highlands . . . My father knew him well. I went to his funeral. It was the last funeral Scotland will ever have for a hero, a clan funeral that everybody attended, with a piper playing a lament, and crofters and fishermen rubbing shoulders with smart Edinburgh people, and everybody aware that the country had lost a great man . . ."

He stopped. "I shouldn't be talking about the past. It's only too easy, but I don't want to wallow in nostalgia."

"You started off talking about corrosion," said Elspeth.

The Duke took a sip of his coffee. "Yes, corrosion. Living here, a few miles from the sea," he continued, "we don't see as much corrosion as they do down on the coast. I have a friend over on Mull who is right on the shore. He gets wind coming in from the Atlantic, and it's laden with salt. You don't see it, of course, but the salt is there. And do you know what? He went to open his front door one day, and the door fell off. Right off. It landed on the ground with a great bang. The hinges had corroded."

"No!"

"They were meant to be brass. He always went for brass, because it's not meant to react to salt. It's the same with stainless steel. But the problem is that they sell stuff that claims to be stainless, but isn't."

The Duke took another sip of his coffee. "Talking of doors, do you know I'm having some alterations done to the house? I've been putting it off for some time, but I've decided to bite the bullet. You may recall that when you and Matthew came to dinner at my place, we ate in a rather poky little dining room at the back of the house. Remember?"

"I rather liked it."

"Oh, it's all right. It's just that I find it a bit small. If you have more than four people for dinner, as I sometimes do, it gets a bit crowded. So I decided to incorporate a large pantry with the dining room. Together the two will make a good-sized room."

"That seems reasonable enough. Who's your architect?"

"Actually, I'm not employing an architect. No need to, in my view. If you get a builder who knows what's what, then they can do the drawings in-house. A competent draughtsman can do much of what an architect does."

"Perhaps that's what *we* need. Matthew has been talking about building a conservatory. On that side of the house, over there. It's south-facing."

"And has lovely views too," said the Duke. "The Lammermuir Hills."

"I can imagine sitting out there a lot," said Elspeth. "We have this terrace, of course, but it can get a bit chilly – even in summer – if there's much wind about. Anything from the north or north-east can be a bit chilly." She paused. "Have you got a good builder, Duke?"

"The best. He lives in Penicuik. People speak highly of him around here. An Orangeman, I believe. He's had a look at the house, and it was he, in fact, who suggested that we simply remove the wall between the existing dining room and the pantry. He says we don't need planning permission. I assume he's right. Anyway, he says he can do it as early as next week. He said the messy bit will last only two days – then it can all be finished off pretty quickly. I must say . . ."

The Duke suddenly stopped talking. He looked at Elspeth quizzically, as if unsure about something. "Elspeth," he said, "may I ask you a very personal question?"

She nodded. "I don't mind."

"Are you unhappy?"

She had not expected this, and for a few moments she was unsure what to say. Then she answered, "For the most part, no. But sometimes . . ."

"It's just that you seem unhappy to me. I'm not sure why I think that – perhaps it's something in your eyes. The eyes give us away, you know."

She looked away, unsettled.

"I don't mean to embarrass you," said the Duke. Then, "Is it your marriage?"

She shook her head. "No, it's not Matthew. He's a good husband to me. And I love him dearly."

"Good, so it's being out here, with the boys. Trapped? Am I right?"

She sighed. "Perhaps."

"And not having any sense of purpose? Or is that putting it too strongly?"

"Maybe. I mean, no, you're not putting it too strongly."

The Duke sat back in his chair and looked up at the sky. "We're all of us pretty lost, I think. We have no purpose to our lives because we don't believe in anything. And because we don't believe in anything, there are no challenges for us. It's all flat and featureless. Empty."

"Isn't that a bit extreme? Some people still have a cause."

"Yes, they do. And in Scotland, what is that cause for many of our compatriots? A new Scottish state – because the existing state is not one that some people find easy to believe in any longer. We want to have a sense of something we can create ourselves. A chimera, perhaps, but *our* chimera. We want to have a mission in our lives, and the national cause provides one. I can see that."

"And where do you stand?" asked Elspeth.

The Duke hesitated. "I can see both sides, quite frankly. And surely one shouldn't deny that there are always two sides to such issues." He paused again, before adding, enigmatically, "Head or heart?"

Elspeth waited. And then the Duke continued, "There are patriots on both sides, we might remind ourselves. Perfectly reasonable people have quite differing ideas of the good. And remember that people may take up a position enthusiastically because it is something that they are invited to believe in. And when you haven't believed in anything for some time, that's an attractive invitation. Therein lies the appeal of identity politics throughout the world."

"Heal Scotland, and I heal myself?"

The Duke turned to look at Elspeth again. "These are big

questions, and the real issue is what can be done to make *you* feel better?"

"Talking to you seems to help," said Elspeth. She barely thought about the words before she uttered them, but, once she had spoken, she immediately realised that what she said was true.

54

At Doddie's Hoose

It was on the third day of his sojourn in Aberdeen that Bertie reached the view that his only hope was to escape – by whatever means possible – and make his way back to Edinburgh. He had by then started at his new school, Robert Gordon's, where he had been handed over to a small group of boys in the class who had been instructed by the teacher to ensure that "this poor boy from Edinburgh" be made welcome. "So you're the new loon," the leader of these boys, Doddie, had said. "Is it yersel', then?" Bertie had been uncertain how to respond to what was clearly intended to be a friendly greeting, but had replied, "Aye, it's mysel'." This appeared to satisfy Doddie, who looked him over while muttering, "So, a new loon . . ." Bertie had not known what this meant. Loon? What was a loon? Was it an insult, or was it something else – perhaps even a compliment? But if it was a compliment, why was he described as *peer?* Bertie's grasp of Scots was sufficient for him to know that *peer* meant *poor*, but if it was Scots that these boys were speaking, it was certainly a very strange version.

His subsequent conversation with his new friends was equally unenlightening.

"Fit are ye cried?" asked Doddie at this first encounter.

Bertie stared at the other boy. "I'm not crying," he said.

Doddie frowned. "Naebody said you're greeting. Fit are ye cried?"

"He's cried Bertie," said Jake.

"Aye," agreed Jeems. "Bertie Pollock. He's cried Bertie Pollock."

"Aye, ye're nae far wrang there," joined in Jeems. "Bertie

Pollock fae Edinburgh."

Doddie now had a further question, "Fa div ye bide?" he asked politely.

Bertie looked up at the sky. He had no idea what Doddie meant and hoped that inspiration might come from above. But it did not. All he saw was a cold, empty sky. And he wondered, for a moment, how far they were from the North Pole. Fifty miles, perhaps.

Getting no response to his question, Doddie went on to say, "Foo ye deeing?"

Bertie smiled. In desperation he said, "Aye." This appeared to satisfy Doddie, who himself then said, "Aye" – a sentiment echoed by Jake, Jeems and Andra, each of whom in turn said, "Aye."

Having broken the ice in this way, the four Aberdonian boys then told Bertie a bit about themselves. Doddie explained that he lived at Mannofield, but that he spent every weekend at his grandfather's farm near Cults. Or that was what Bertie thought he said, although he was by no means sure. Jake came from Milltimber and had two brothers, he said, Hamish and Willie. Jeems told Bertie that he was not sure where he came from – or again that is what Bertie thought he said. "He kens fine," said Doddie. "Aa folk ken where they bide."

This exchange was followed by a suggestion – from Doddie – that they play *steelers*. Not having any steelers himself, Bertie was given a couple of round metal marbles by each of the boys on the understanding that he could pay them back once he had won a few more himself. The game was ready to start, but before that happened, Doddie solemnly pronounced a formula that was taken up by the others, as a Greek chorus might pronounce on a character's fate:

Eetle, ottle, black bottle,
Eetle, ottle oot;
Tak a roosty roosty nail

And pit it straight oot,
Shining on the mantelpiece
Like a silver threepenny piece,
Eetle, ottle, black bottle,
Eetle, ottle oot!

In the silence that followed, Bertie asked what this meant.

Doddie shrugged. "That means you start, Bertie, and I dinnae ken fit it means. We've aye done it."

Back in the classroom, it was time for instruction in Charles Murray's *The Whistle*. The class appeared to know several verses of this poem, and recited it with vigour while Bertie, embarrassed at not knowing what was going on, made an attempt to mouth the words. He felt ashamed. He felt isolated and ignorant. And the following day, when Doddie kindly invited him to come home to tea at his house – the invitation having been approved by Irene, who had engaged in conversation with Doddie's mother at the school gate – Bertie's sense of alienation simply grew.

Doddie was welcoming, and showed Bertie his collection of birds' feathers, his electric train set, and the rugby ball signed by Stuart Hogg and Gregor Townsend that his father had bought at a charity auction. Then he escorted Bertie into the garden, where Bertie helped him take the tea bags off the line.

"Why do you hang tea bags on the washing line?" Bertie asked, as they released the small shrivelled squares from their pegs before putting them into a jar.

Doddie seemed surprised by the question. Was this not something that everyone did? Perhaps Edinburgh, he reflected, was different. "To dry them," he replied.

He was now speaking English to Bertie, and there was no difficulty in their understanding one another.

Bertie was puzzled. "But you've already used them," he

pointed out. "Why dry them out?"

"To use them again, of course," said Doddie. "You dry them, see, and then you can use them again. We use our tea bags three times. Jeems say that at his house they get six cups of tea out of each bag. That's a lot, I think."

Bertie had heard that there was a certain degree of parsimony in Aberdeen, but he had not expected this. Nor had he expected what happened next, which was for Doddie to show him how to repair a hot-water bottle after it perished.

"You can fix them with a bicycle puncture repair kit," Doddie explained. "We keep our hot water bottles for thirty years, you know. This one here, Bertie, belonged to my grandfather. My Dad still wears his slippers. Patched up a bit, of course, but still all right."

Tea consisted of a bowl of oatmeal porridge and half a rowie, a buttery roll on which a very small amount of jam had been spread.

"My granny makes that jam," Doddie explained. "She collects the berries from the hedges. The only thing she has to pay for is the sugar."

Bertie was collected by Irene at six o'clock.

"You'll have had your tea?" Irene asked.

Bertie nodded.

Irene drove them home. "I'm so pleased you're enjoying yourself here, Bertissimo," she said.

Bertie said nothing. Before he had left Doddie's house he had had an urgent conversation with his new friend. Doddie, it transpired, knew how to use his father's solar-powered computer and had agreed to Bertie's request that he send an email to Ranald Braveheart Macpherson, who not only knew the combination number for his father's safe, but knew, too, all his computer passwords. Ranald's reading was not all that good, but he could get that girl next door to read it to him. And Ranald had, of course, told Bertie that if he needed help, he was only to send a message. With this in mind, Bertie had written out a message for Doddie to send.

"Please help me, Ranald," it read. "Please help me to get home. Very unhappy here. Your friend, Bertie."

55

Ranald Leaves a Note

When Ranald Braveheart Macpherson received Bertie's
email, as dictated to Doddie and as read out to him by his
neighbour and amanuensis, Shirley, he lost no time in packing
his school satchel with a change of clothing, a compass, and
a water bottle. Then, making sure that his parents were fully
engrossed in their favourite soap opera, he crept into his
father's study and began expertly to twirl the dial of the safe's
combination lock. With a satisfactory series of clicks, the
mechanism slipped into place and the door of the safe swung
open. Inside, Ranald saw the neatly stacked piles of euros that
he knew his father kept for some unexplained eventuality,
along with several expensive-looking men's watches, and a
pouch of Krugerrands. Behind the euros were smaller piles
of five- and ten-pound Bank of Scotland notes, and it was to
these that Ranald now helped himself, tucking them into the
zip-up compartment of his satchel. Then he went out briefly
– to speak to the girl next door – before returning to his own
house for final preparations.

Being as quiet as he could, Ranald let himself out of the
door, and darted down the garden path. Within a few minutes
he boarded a bus that would take him down to Princes Street
and to Waverley Station. Once there, he used some of the
purloined Bank of Scotland notes to purchase a one-way
ticket to Aberdeen.

"How old are you, son?" asked the official in the ticket booth.

Ranald hesitated. "Eighteen," he said, eventually, making
his voice as deep as he could.

The official burst out laughing. "Do you want to pay an adult fare?" he asked. "Is that what you want, son?"

Flustered, Ranald shook his head, and was given a half-fare ticket.

"You're not running away, by any chance?" asked the official. "And what's your name, by the way?"

Ranald cleared his throat. "Ranald Braveheart Macpherson," he replied. "And I'm going to Aberdeen on a humanitarian mission."

The official laughed again. "Oh, goodness! Humanitarian. That's a big word, Ranald Braveheart Macpherson! I must remember that."

Ranald made his way to the platform from which the Aberdeen train was scheduled to leave. Once on the train, he made himself as unobtrusive as possible, sheltering behind a newspaper left in the carriage by a previous traveller. Ranald could not yet read, and was concerned that he might have the newspaper upside down, but a glance at a photograph on the front page reassured him. It was the First Minister, and she was opening something, or closing it – Ranald could not be quite sure. As the journey began, he gazed out of the window, thinking of what he would do when he arrived in Aberdeen. He had an address for Bertie, and he had a street map of the city that showed quite clearly where Irene's house was. He would go there, he thought, and help Bertie to escape through a window. Then they would return to the railway station and start the journey back to Edinburgh. With any luck they would have a head start on any pursuers – especially Bertie's mother, for whom Ranald had a healthy respect. He would not like to be caught by Mrs Pollock, Ranald thought, because he had heard it said that mad people sometimes had the strength of ten ordinary people, and there was very little doubt in Ranald's mind that Bertie's mother, even if not entirely mad, was at least half-mad, and was therefore very probably as strong as five normal women.

Ranald had given some thought to what his parents might think and do when they realised he was not there. He was a conscientious boy, and had asked Shirley, the girl who lived next door and who was famous for her neat handwriting, to pen a note for him. This note, written in what Shirley described as "my exemplary joined-up writing" had cost thirty pence. "And no credit terms are available, Ranald Braveheart Macpherson!" Shirley warned. Ranald had given her one of the five-pound notes from his father's safe and told her that she could keep the change.

Shirley had outdone herself. "To whom it may concern," the note began. "This is to inform you that Ranald Braveheart Macpherson has been called away. He will be back tomorrow. During the period of his absence, he will not have access to email or to a telephone, but will attend to your issue immediately on his return to Edinburgh."

"What do you think of that?" Shirley asked proudly.

"It's very good, Shirley," Ranald said. But then he asked, "Are you sure it says what you say it says?"

Shirley looked at him disdainfully. "Of course it does," she snapped. "Why would I tell fibs in one of my notes? I've got more sense than that, Ranald Braveheart Macpherson. I want to get customers coming back. If you fib, then they don't." She paused, and finished, "Your call is important to me."

Ranald had left the note on the dining-room table where it would be sure to be seen by his parents. He did not want them to worry, and he thought that they would probably be reassured by the tone of the message. This was not a simple *back soon* note – this looked, and sounded, official.

Slowly the train wound its way through Fife. Kirkcaldy came and went, and then there was the Tay Railway Bridge, curving across the river, with Dundee nestling on the other side. Then the towns of the east coast, with their hinterland rolling out behind them; farms and villages amongst which lives were led according to nature's designs: spring, and planting, summer and growth, the harvest of autumn.

Ranald felt increasingly anxious. What if he could not find Bertie? What if he arrived too late and Bertie's mother had sent him off to boarding school, or apprenticed him to a cruel ship's captain and he was, even now, being forced to climb the rigging on some Jamaica-bound ship? Ranald had been read a story very much like that not all that long ago, and he could just imagine poor Bertie in the position of the boy in that tale. Bertie's mother was a desperate character – everybody knew that – and she was quite capable of packing him off to sea.

Ranald shivered. He was beginning to feel homesick. Scotland was much bigger than he had imagined it to be. And what was that smell? Fish. They were approaching Aberdeen now, and it occurred to Ranald that Bertie might even have been put to work on a fishing boat. That was very tough work – and dangerous too. And you came home and you smelled of fish for days, Ranald had heard. It wouldn't matter to him, of course, because Bertie was his friend, and if your friend smells of fish you should try not to let it affect your friendship. Everybody, thought Ranald Braveheart Macpherson, knows that.

56

Thank You for Having Me

Bertie heard the pebble hit his window. He looked up sharply. A second pebble clattered against the glass, and he caught his breath. His heart raced as he approached the window and stared out into the darkness.

An urgent voice came from below. "Bertie!"

He peered into the darkness. "Ranald? Is that you?"

Now Bertie saw his friend's face emerging from the shadows. He should never have doubted that Ranald would come. Of course he would come. Ranald had never let him down, even in small things, and now, in this, his moment of greatest need, he was here. Bertie opened his window and reached down to help Ranald clamber up to the sill. Then with a wriggle and a twist, Ranald was in the room, dusting himself off, beaming with pleasure at his achievement.

Bertie stuttered his thanks. His heart was almost too full for him to say very much, but he left Ranald in no doubt as to the intensity of his relief.

"We can go back tomorrow morning," Ranald said. "I've got money for our tickets, and I've also got a compass and a torch."

"You think of everything, Ranald," said Bertie appreciatively.

Ranald accepted the compliment with a nod of his head. "We can set off tomorrow," he said. "It's easier to travel by daylight."

Bertie agreed. He remembered what he had read in *Scouting for Boys*, a clandestine copy of which he had secreted under

his bed in Edinburgh. Baden-Powell had said something
about how easy it was to get lost during the night, especially
when there was no moon or the moon was obscured by
clouds. He knew what he was talking about, thought Bertie,
as he must have been lost many times in Matabeleland. And
Matabeleland and Aberdeenshire were probably more similar
than many people realised.

"You're right," said Ranald. "You could end up going in
the completely wrong direction if you can't see where you're
going."

"You can sleep at the other end of my bed," Bertie said.
"There's plenty of room." He paused. His mother usually
came in to say goodnight, and Ranald would have to hide
until that visit was over. He could go under the bed, Bertie
decided. Then, when Irene had switched off the light, he could
be made more comfortable.

As it happened, Ranald had just enough time to hide under
the bed before Irene appeared and told Bertie it was time to turn
off his light. The following day was a Saturday, and although
there would be no school, Irene said that she was planning
an hour of Italian *conversazione* after breakfast, and Bertie
would need to be alert for that. "We have so much to catch up
on, Bertie, *troppo*, in fact." Afterwards, she announced, they
would go out to have morning coffee with Dr Fairbairn.

"You remember Dr Fairbairn, don't you, Bertie? You loved
going to talk to him in his consulting rooms."

Bertie remained tight-lipped. Not wanting to prolong his
mother's presence in the room, he merely made a sound of
general assent.

"Dr Fairbairn is so looking forward to seeing you again,
Bertie," Irene said, and then added, "Sweet dreams," innocent
of the irony in such a wish, given Dr Fairbairn's known and
unhealthy interest in the dreams of others.

Irene hesitated in the doorway. Bertie hoped that Ranald

would not suddenly sneeze or have a coughing fit, or do anything else that might give away his presence. He thought that he could hear Ranald breathing, and if he could, then presumably Irene could as well. To mask the sound, Bertie decided to hum a tune as loudly as he could.

"Do stop that noise, Bertie," Irene said. "Humming is such a mindless exercise."

"But I feel so happy," Bertie said. "It makes me want to hum."

"There are other ways of expressing a positive state of mind," said Irene.

Bertie thought he heard a noise from under the bed. He froze, thinking it inevitable that Irene would hear, but she did not, and now the door was closed and he and Ranald were left alone.

Waking early the next morning, Bertie and Ranald were out of the house by seven. Irene had taken to sleeping in since she moved to Aberdeen, and would not be getting out of bed for another hour. When she arose, she would find the note left for her by Bertie. "Dearest Mummy, I have had to return to Edinburgh," he wrote. "I am so sorry. Please say hello to Dr Fairbairn for me. Tell him I have been having lots of interesting dreams and I shall write some of them down for him so that he can think about them. Tell him not to worry. Thank you so much for having me. Love, Bertie."

It did not take long to get to the railway station, where Ranald used more of his father's Bank of Scotland notes to purchase two tickets to Edinburgh. Then, after buying themselves a bacon roll and a bar of chocolate, they sat down on a platform bench and waited for the Edinburgh train to draw up for boarding.

In retrospect, neither boy could work out how they made the mistake. Ranald, at least, had the excuse of not being able to read; Bertie had no such excuse, but he still failed to see that the train manifestly proclaimed itself as being bound for Inverurie and not for Edinburgh. And so it was that when, after its short journey north, the train drew to halt at Inverurie Station, both Ranald and Bertie were surprised to find themselves somewhere that did not look at all like Edinburgh Waverley.

"I think we've come the wrong way," said Bertie. "This sign says *Inverurie*. See? That's what it says, Ranald. Inverurie is north of Aberdeen – I've always known that."

Ranald tried to put on a brave face. "Oh well," he said. "It's better than still being in Aberdeen."

Bertie had to agree. "We can go and look at the timetable," he said. "We probably won't have long to wait to get a train to Edinburgh."

Ranald looked miserable. "I want to go home, Bertie," he sniffed.

Bertie put his arm round his friend's shoulders. "You mustn't get upset, Ranald," he said. "We'll get home eventually."

Ranald tried to control himself. But soon his shoulders started to heave as the full extent of their plight sunk in. They were far from home, and presumably by now they would have been reported as missing. Their photographs would be on the television news, and the police would be looking for them, perhaps even using dogs to track them down. As he thought this – and shuddered – Ranald imagined he could hear the baying of a bloodhound, although it was not that at all, but the sound of a flock of geese passing overhead, squawking to one another as they dipped and wheeled across the northern sky.

57

Bless You

From behind the counter of her coffee bar, Big Lou watched Fat Bob in discussion with Angus and Matthew at Matthew's favourite table on the other side of the room. The three of them had taken to sharing morning coffee together and would spend an hour or so chatting before Matthew would look at his watch and remember that he had a business to run. Angus would do the same, and remind himself that not only did he have a canvas awaiting him on an easel, but he had his dog, Cyril, to exercise. Cyril, of course, was in no hurry, and was as happy to be in one place as in any other, and to remain there indefinitely. He was on dog time, which is quite different from human time, being punctuated only by meals, periods of wakefulness or sleep, and by the occasional salience that comes with the pursuit of a cat or squirrel. Apart from that, an hour is much the same thing to a dog as a day, a week, or a month – and of course there is no terminus. No dog knows that he or she must die: what we have now is what we will have forever, in the mind of a dog, just as it is in the mind of a small child.

Big Lou knew that the three of them were planning something, but she was not sure exactly what that might be. It pleased her, though, to see Angus and Matthew getting on so well with Fat Bob. They came from such different worlds, with Angus being a portrait painter, Matthew being the director of an art gallery, and Fat Bob being a professional, or semi-professional strongman – he also had a job in a stone merchant's yard, where he cut and polished marble for kitchen surfaces. Scotland's democratic traditions, though, meant that people talked to one another as equals whatever the difference in their level of education or their station in life, and that was just how it should be, thought Big Lou. It did not matter in the least what bed you were born in: what counted was what you were inside. People in England, she suspected, sometimes just did not grasp that, and that was a pity: their society was more stratified than Scotland's; they needed to read Robert Burns' *A Man's a Man for a' That*, she felt, because that said all that had to be said on that subject. If you understood what Burns was saying in that poem, then you understood how Scotland felt – at heart.

That morning her curiosity got the better of her. "You boys," she called out, "you're sitting there like a pickle of conspirators. What are you talking about?"

Angus looked at Fat Bob, expecting him to answer.

"Just a wee set of Highland Games," Bob replied.

"In Drummond Place Garden," added Angus.

Big Lou came over to hear more. They were planning, she was told, to have an afternoon of Highland Games the following Saturday. "It will be in aid of charity," Fat Bob said. "We'll charge a pound to get in . . ."

"And two pounds to get out," said Angus. "That was my idea."

"And I've approached the George Watson's Pipe Band," chipped in Matthew. "They've agreed to come and play."

Fat Bob ran through the events they had agreed to include. There would be a tug-of-war, he said: lawyers against accountants, and Catholics against Protestants.

Big Lou raised an eyebrow. "What a good idea," said Big Lou. "Who thought of that last one?"

"I did, actually," said Angus. "These things are community-building."

Fat Bob nodded. "And then tossing the caber and throwing

the hammer, of course. And a few track events for the weans. A sack race, maybe."

"Good," said Big Lou. "It should be a very good afternoon."

Big Lou got up to attend to a customer, leaving Bob, Angus and Matthew to their planning. She looked over her shoulder at Fat Bob; she was so proud of him. Her previous men had been loners, for the most part – rather moody types who would never have sat down with people like Matthew and Angus and hatched a plot to hold Highland Games. She had known Bob for a few weeks now, and there had not been a single day, nor indeed a single moment, when she had entertained so much as scintilla of doubt about him. He was a man of complete honesty – that was just so obvious – and he was kind and attentive too. The previous evening, he had insisted on cooking for her and had persuaded Finlay to help him prepare the meal. She had heard the two of them chuckling in the kitchen, and she had seen the look of pride on Finlay's face when he and Bob had served the meal.

And then, before Finlay went off to bed, she had seen Fat Bob down on the floor fiddling with the points on Finlay's train set, while the young boy adjusted the tiny benches and trollies on the miniature platform.

"That should do it," said Bob. "There, that's working now."

And she heard Finlay say, "Thanks, Fat Bob. I like it when you come round to our place."

"Aye, and I like it too," said Bob. "And thanks for making me so welcome, Finlay."

Big Lou took a deep breath. She wanted to cry. The sight of a man being gentle and kind towards a child is something that moves women profoundly – it just does. And she knew that she would never find anybody like Fat Bob again, and that if he were to ask her to marry him she would give a positive reply, immediately, there and then, without waiting to consider the matter. She would say, *Yes*, and then, just in case he had not heard, she would say, *Yes*, again.

Which is exactly what happened two hours later when, with Finlay off to bed and the two of them sitting together on the sofa, Fat Bob turned to Big Lou and said, "Lou, I have an important question to ask you."

And she had said, rather quickly, "Yes," as if in answer to a question that he had not, in fact, asked. She corrected herself, saying, "Yes?"

He said, "Will you marry me, Big Lou? I'm not much to look at. I haven't got a lot in this world – not when you come to think of it. But I have a good job, and we'll get by on what I earn, and I'll try to make you happy – I promise you that, Lou, I promise to God."

She gave him her answer, and he took her hand, and pressed it against his chest, where he believed his heart to be. And it was a broad heart, and a strong one too, and she felt it beat, which was such a strange thing, and so wonderful – the heart-beat of another.

She looked at him, and he at her. Their happiness required nothing else; it was complete.

"Bless you, Bob," Big Lou whispered.

She meant it. Whatever power there was to confer a benediction, she now invoked, in the sure and certain belief that it was the right thing to do.

58

A Thursday Meeting

Every Thursday the Professor of Philosophical Psychiatry at the University of Edinburgh – the holder of a personal chair conferred after the publication of his groundbreaking *The Brain, Identity and the Continuity of the Self* – held a lunchtime seminar meeting with a small group of like-minded colleagues. Also invited to these meetings were several of the more academically inclined medical students, particularly those who were showing an interest in pursuing psychiatry as a speciality. These meetings took place in the Professor's room at the Royal Edinburgh Hospital, where sandwiches would be provided, along with tea, coffee, and sparkling water. People were encouraged to bring occasional items to add variety – a few sticks of celery, for example, or cheese, or, as on this occasion, some fruit. The Professor's garden had recently yielded a crop of plums, and these were now being offered round in a small basket.

"Very delicious," said one of the students. "I love apricots."

"Thank you," said the Professor. Youth should be corrected gently. "Plums," he whispered. "We've had a large crop this year. It all depends on the weather."

"Everything depends on the weather," said one of the research fellows.

"Indeed," said the Professor. "You might well say that."

There was a short silence. The Professor began. "I may as well begin," he said.

One of the students licked his fingers after finishing a plum. Another looked surreptitiously at her phone. She was expecting a text message from her boyfriend. She suspected that he had stopped loving her. The Senior Lecturer in Abnormal Psychology dabbed at her lips with a handkerchief. She wanted another plum, but was not sure whether she should ask for one. She decided not to.

The Professor reached for his notes. "I thought that we might look today at the most extraordinary case," he said. "I have only just seen the patient and shall be seeing him again, but I thought some preliminary observations might be of interest."

They looked at him expectantly.

"The patient is a young man in his late twenties," said the Professor. "I shall call him Bruce. He was referred to me by a colleague in the Royal Infirmary who asked him if he wouldn't mind a psychiatric examination after he had presented with a non-psychiatric complaint." He paused. "He had been struck by lightning."

The Senior Lecturer in Abnormal Psychology let out an involuntary laugh. "I'd certainly complain if I were to be struck by lightning."

One of the medical students smiled. "Shocking," he said.

The Professor looked at him with slight disapproval. "Let us not make light of our patient's misfortunes," he said.

The student looked apologetic, and blushed. He had merely followed on the remark made by the Senior Lecturer in Abnormal Psychology. She had made the original joke, but he was getting the blame. That was hierarchies for you, wasn't it? It was.

"Bruce was quite prepared to see me," the Professor continued. "Physically, he had escaped largely untouched. A small area of very superficial burns – and a rib fracture or two where he had landed on the road. He was, apparently, thrown some distance into the air by the impact of the lightning."

"Astonishing," said the Psychiatric Registrar. "You'd think

that . . . how many volts are there in a bolt of lightning? More than 230, I imagine."

"As it happens," said the Professor, "I looked that up before I saw him. The figure is surprising. It's millions of volts, apparently. Millions. And yet I read that ninety per cent of those who are struck survive. Yes, I was surprised by that, given that we're talking about that many volts, but you're unlucky if you succumb."

"Unlucky if you're hit in the first place, surely," said the Psychiatric Registrar. "What are the odds of being hit? It must be pretty unlikely. Anybody here been struck by lightning? See? Nobody."

"Actually," said the Professor, "I looked at that too. There are wild variations in the estimate of the odds. I saw one in three hundred thousand being mentioned. But the *British Medical Journal* assured me that it's more like one in ten million. The Office of National Statistics, however, says that it's roughly one in a million each year. That means about sixty people are struck by lightning in the UK annually."

There was a short silence as this information was digested. It was not a comfortable thought. It could happen. It was not all that unlikely.

"But the point," the Professor continued, "is that this young man was, in fact, struck by lightning in Dundas Street."

One of the medical students thought, *I'm not going there. Not me.*

"He was walking down the street when it happened, and he was taken by ambulance to the Royal. As I said, there was little physical damage. But then, when I saw him, I realised that there was a far more interesting dimension to the case. Put simply, the lightning strike had led to what may amount to a significant personality change."

The Senior Lecturer in Abnormal Psychology frowned. She did not like it when people bandied the term *personality* around indiscriminately, and she had particular views on any reference to *personality change*. What exactly did that mean?

The Professor caught her eye. "All right, Alice," he said. "I'm aware of your views on this, but put it this way: there was a significant, not to say complete, change not only in *affect* but in *attitude*. Will you accept that?"

"So far as it goes, yes. But . . ."

The Professor raised a hand. "Bear with me. A notable feature of this case is that the patient appeared to have a significant degree of insight into his own behaviour. There was considerable self-awareness. He went to some pains to tell me of his defects. He used terms like *narcissism* and *selfishness* and painted a rather uncomfortable picture of what he had been like prior to this experience."

The Senior Lecture in Abnormal Psychology looked unimpressed. "Not all that uncommon, of course," she said. "People often refer to what they see as a past self in disparaging terms. It happens when they have a conversion experience, for instance. Talk to a born-again Christian about what they were like beforehand, and you may get a striking degree of self-abasement. Or to a reformed drinker. This doesn't mean that there has been any fundamental change in deep-seated traits. What it may mean is that there has been a conscious reappraisal, and a strategic decision to suppress certain urges, certain behaviours, if you like. That's not the same as so-called personality change. The underlying impulses may still be there."

The Professor looked out of the window. He felt slightly irritated. This was *his* seminar. She had been eating *his* plums. And if you couldn't talk about personality change in a case like this, then what could you say about it? Nothing, really.

He looked away from the window. "I take your point about caution," he said. "But let's put that to one side for the moment and look at what happened here. This is not about theoretical positioning on taxonomy or aetiology, or anything like that." He glanced disapprovingly at the Senior Lecturer in Abnormal Psychology. "This is about the experience of a real young man to whom something very unusual has happened. Let's look at that for a moment or two."

59

Pluscarden Abbey

"This young man," said the Professor, "was something of a Lothario – before he was struck by lightning, that is."

"In Dundas Street," muttered the Psychiatric Registrar. "*Il Lothario della via Dundas* . . . Donizetti, perhaps."

The Professor gave him a sideways look. The Registrar had a tendency to find an operatic analogy in everything, and he found it trying. *Obsessive behaviour*, he thought. *Reductio ad opera* . . . If that was the correct accusative . . . "Yes," he said. "In Dundas Street. He told me that he had a stream of girlfriends. He said they were queuing up."

One of the medical students, a thin young man still wearing cycle clips, closed his eyes. *Queuing up* . . . For a moment he saw himself looking out from the window of his flat in Gladstone Terrace, observing the line of attractive young women that started at the door of his stair and wound all the way down to the edge of the Meadows. Bliss. And he would be preparing to interview them before choosing one, with one or two in reserve, should his choice prove not to be quite up to his exacting standards. Oh bliss, bliss. And his MB, ChB done and dusted and with no further exams until some easy membership exam at some time in the vague future, and a good job lined up somewhere . . .

The Professor's voice brought him down to earth. "There is a range of possible explanations. One is the effect of trauma. PTSD springs to mind. That obviously has behavioural ramifications as well as implications for mood. Being struck by lightning is clearly traumatic . . ."

"I would have thought so," agreed the Psychiatric Registrar. "Electricity, you see . . . You know, by the way, that there was an opera called *The Electrification of the Soviet Union*. Nigel Osborne wrote it. The libretto was by Craig Raine – he of 'The Onion, Memory' – such a memorable poem . . ."

"Yes, yes," said the Professor. "But even if trauma in that conventional sense has a role in the aetiology, there is another possibility – that the exposure to a large jolt of electricity has had a physical effect on the brain."

"Interesting," said the Psychiatric Registrar. "In the same way as . . ."

The Professor, fearing an operatic reference, cut him short. "In the same way as electro-convulsive therapy. Yes. In that way."

They looked at one another.

"Of course, people argue about exactly how ECT works," said the Professor, in an explanation intended for the students. *They know so little*, he thought. "All we know is that in some cases it *does* work."

"Changes in regional cerebral blood flow and in glucose utilisation," said the Psychiatric Registrar. "My money's on that."

"Possibly," said the Professor. "But not everyone would agree."

"Not everyone agrees that night follows day," observed the Registrar.

"But they do," said one of the medical students. "Of course they do."

"I'm speaking metaphorically," snapped the Registrar.

"Just about all speech is metaphorical," said the Professor. "Look at a passage of prose and you'll see that the structure is almost all metaphor. Metaphor is deep in the bones of language."

"I don't think we need explore metaphor at these lunches," the Registrar sniffed. "The issue is behavioural change following electrical stimulation of the brain."

"Being struck by lightning is certainly stimulation," observed the Professor. "And I wonder whether this is just a further instance of the sort of result claimed by proponents of cranial electrotherapy stimulation. There are claims for the benefits of that for anxiety and depression. If that works on mood, then . . ."

The Senior Lecturer in Abnormal Psychology remembered something. "What was the name of that unfortunate man? The railway worker?"

The Professor looked impatient. This discussion was getting nowhere: metaphors, railway workers.

But the Senior Lecturer in Abnormal Psychology had recalled the name. "Gage," she said. "Phineas Gage."

One of the medical students brightened. "Oh, I read all about that," he said. "This is the guy who got a great big metal spike blown through his head. Right through. An explosive charge went off and blew it out of its hole all the way through his brain. And he survived."

"Yes," said the Senior Lecturer in Abnormal Psychology. "It was a well-documented case. The fact that he survived was astonishing, but what secured him a place in medical history was the personality changes that resulted. This drew attention to the physical basis of personality, that people at that point of the nineteenth century were only beginning to wrestle with. Apparently, Gage had been a reasonable, affable man before the accident and thereafter became what was described as a vulgar and aggressive."

"Not surprising," said the Psychiatric Registrar. "Consider what even a slight lesion may do to behaviour and personality." An idea had occurred to him. "The Phineas Gage case would make a good subject for an opera, don't you think? *The Case of Phineas Gage*. Quite a title, that. Almost as arresting as *Nixon in China*."

A medical student raised a hand. "Are psychopaths

psychopathic because of a brain abnormality?"

"Yes," said the Professor.

"No," said the Senior Lecturer in Abnormal Psychology. "We don't know that. But there does appear to be a genetic link."

"It can be inherited?" the student asked.

The Senior Lecturer in Abnormal Psychology smiled. "It would appear that a disposition to psychopathy may be passed on. We're not certain how the genes in question function – although there are theories."

"So you can't blame them for what they do?"

The Professor winced. "That's *very* complicated."

"I don't think so," said the Senior Lecturer in Abnormal Psychology. "Surely it's simple: the psychopath doesn't *choose* to be a psychopath. I thought that choice lay at the heart of any notion of blame, or fault, or whatever you want to call it. That's been so since the time of Aristotle, I believe."

"Then you exculpate roughly one third of the prison population," said the Professor. "That's the proportion of people in prison who are thought possibly to have psychopathic personality disorder. Am I right?"

The question was addressed to the Senior Lecturer in Abnormal Psychology, but before she could answer – and she would have agreed – the Psychiatric Registrar asked, "What did you find when you spoke to this patient?"

The Professor was pleased to be back on the topic in hand. "He was most impressive," he said. "There was good social presentation. He struck me as being modest and considerate. He was neither too self-effacing nor too assertive. He spoke cogently."

"And yet he was – according to his own account of himself – rather different before the incident?"

"Yes. As I said earlier, he was very pleased with himself. He was aware that women found him attractive, and he made maximum use of that."

"And you think that this self-assessment was true?"

The Professor nodded. "I had no reason to doubt it. It sounded credible. And in my experience, if somebody mentions his faults, they exist. It's different with virtues. Those may be entirely aspirational."

The Senior Lecturer in Abnormal Psychology looked up at the ceiling. "I think the real test will be what he's like in, say, three months. It will be interesting to see."

"By then," said the Professor, "he will be up at Pluscarden Abbey, I imagine. You know the place? It's up near Elgin. Benedictines."

They looked at him.

"Yes," he went on, enjoying the drama of his announcement. "He's going up there as a lay brother in the first instance – pending his acceptance as a novice. He's been put up to it by some Italian nun he became friendly with. Extraordinary – but there we are."

The Senior Lecturer in Abnormal Psychology raised an eyebrow. "Hysterical over-reaction," she muttered.

"Possibly," said the Professor. "But I'm not sure that we should completely discount that old-fashioned phenomenon – a change of heart."

The Senior Lecturer in Abnormal Psychology shook head. "Leopards don't change their spots," she said.

The Professor's tone was withering. "Forgive me for saying this, but is that what twenty years of studying the intricacies of the human mind have led you to conclude?"

The Senior Lecturer in Abnormal Psychology nodded. "More or less," she said.

60

Ca' the Yowes

Ranald Braveheart Macpherson was reported missing less than thirty minutes after he walked out of Albert Terrace, bound for Waverley Station. It was not until the next day, though, that a general alert went out to the police and public throughout Scotland to be on the lookout for him. And by that time, of course, Bertie's absence was similarly made public. It required little thought thereafter to conclude that the two boys had absconded together, and the bulletins were adjusted accordingly. *Look out for this boy* became *Look out for these boys*, with a photograph below of the two friends standing together, smiling into the camera – a moment of happiness caught by Nicola when she photographed them playing *Jacobites and Hanoverians* in Drummond Place Garden.

For the adults it was a time of chilling desolation and relentless anxiety. Stuart was beside himself and had to be calmed by Nicola, who did her best to reassure him that the two boys would undoubtedly turn up before the day was out. "Boys tend to do this sort of thing," she said. "They get an idea in their heads and act on it without thinking. They'll be fine."

Stuart's state of mind was scarcely improved by a series of recriminatory phone calls from Irene. Bertie must have run away because Stuart had encouraged him to get back to Edinburgh; the blame, by this logic, was entirely his, and how did he feel about it? "If you feel that you should reproach yourself," she continued, "then you are absolutely right. You should. This is your doing, Stuart."

Stuart had struggled to control himself. He wanted to point out that Bertie had run away from Aberdeen because he did not want to be there. He could have said that this was Irene's fault, for insisting that Bertie should spend time with her, but he did not. There was no point in rubbing salt into any wounds, and part of him felt a real sympathy for Irene. So he ended up saying, "Take a deep breath, Irene. Bertie will be all right. This is a childish escapade that will soon blow over."

When it became apparent that this was all a joint enterprise between the two boys, Ranald Braveheart Macpherson's father, thinking that Ranald and Bertie might be wandering around Aberdeen, decided to drive there immediately and to start scouring the streets for any sign of the boys. It was better than sitting at home and fretting, he decided.

Of course, the searches that were conducted in Edinburgh and Aberdeen, including a thorough search of Drummond Place Garden, Queen Street Gardens, and the Scotland Street tunnel, were destined to reveal nothing, as Bertie and Ranald by this time were in Inverurie, north of Aberdeen, examining the timetable of train departures displayed on the main platform of the railway station.

"We're going to have to wait for hours," said Bertie despondently. "Hardly any of these trains go to Edinburgh, Ranald."

Ranald looked anxiously at his friend. "Couldn't we hitch-hike," Bertie?" he asked. "I saw people do that in a film once. They stood at the side of the road and held out their thumbs. A car stopped and took them."

"We could try," said Bertie.

"But then in the film the people who stopped were bank robbers," Ranald continued. "They were being chased by the police."

"Maybe not then," said Bertie.

It was while this conversation was taking place that Bertie

noticed a boy walking towards them on the platform. He was a few years older than they were, Bertie thought, but his expression was friendly, and he seemed keen to speak to them.

"You seen my Dad?" the boy asked.

Bertie shook his head.

"He was going to pick me up here," the boy said. "We're taking some yowes down to Lanark – although we're going to my auntie's place in Balerno first."

"I haven't seen him," said Bertie. Then he thought: *Balerno*. Balerno was just outside Edinburgh – on the edge of the city. He looked at the boy.

"Can we come with you?" he asked.

The boy frowned. "In the back of the lorry? You wouldn't mind travelling with the yowes in the back?"

"No," said Bertie. "We wouldn't mind, would we Ranald?"

Ranald looked doubtful, but eventually nodded.

"Because my Dad might not say yes if I ask him whether you can sit in the cab with us."

"Of course," said Bertie. "But don't worry, we'll sneak in. He won't see us."

"In that case, you can come," said the boy. "And that's him coming. See that lorry over there? That's him."

Smuggled into the back of the lorry, they set off. Buffeted by the sheep, Bertie and Ranald eventually found a place to sit, and spent the next few hours in the rough warmth and odour of a herd of Scottish Blackface ewes. By the time the lorry drew up in Balerno, in the driveway of a well-set bungalow in a quiet street, Bertie and Ranald had had more than enough of their ovine travelling companions and were happy to start the walk back along the Water of Leith pathway. Signs erected for hikers obligingly showed them the way, and within a couple of hours, having said goodbye to one another under the towering arches of the Slateford aqueduct, they were standing before their respective front doors, worried about being scolded for absenting themselves, but relieved at having found their way home so easily.

Nicola opened the door to Bertie and fell upon him with shouts of inarticulate delight. Stuart appeared and picked him up bodily, hugging him so tight that Bertie struggled for breath. Similar scenes took place at Ranald Braveheart Macpherson's house, although Ranald's father was still in Aberdeen and was obliged to enthuse by telephone.

Nicola put Bertie straight into the bath and washed away the smell of sheep. "It could have been worse," she said. "It could have been pigs." Then, when he was thoroughly washed, and clad now in fresh clothing, she heard his account of his escape.

"I wasn't happy in Aberdeen," Bertie said. "Please don't make me go back."

"Of course we won't," Nicola promised.

It fell to Stuart to inform Irene of Bertie's safe return. "And I'm afraid he won't be coming back up," he said.

There was an ominous silence at the other end of the line. Then Irene's voice, severe and threatening, broke the silence. "We shall see about that," she said.

Nicola grabbed the phone from Stuart. "You listen to me, Irene Pollock," she said. "Bertie has voted with his feet. Do you understand that? With his feet. And let me make this one hundred per cent clear, in case you haven't taken it in: Bertie stays here. Full stop. End of story. Here, Scotland Street."

Bertie listened. He did not like conflict. He knew that his mother wanted the best for him. He knew that his grandmother wanted the same thing. And his father too. They all wanted the best for him. And that made him feel a whole lot better. He imagined how hard it would be to go through life without anybody at all wanting the best for you.

Bertie was composed of love – pure love. He wanted nobody to be unhappy. He wanted them to enjoy their lives.

He wanted that so much – more than he could express, in fact.

He went to Nicola's side. "Please tell Mummy something," he whispered.

Nicola looked down at him.

"Tell Mummy that I love her – I really do. But could I please love her from Edinburgh, rather than from Aberdeen?"

Nicola caught her breath. Into the receiver she said, "Did you hear that, Irene?"

There was silence on the line down from Aberdeen. No humming. No cackle. Just silence. Irene had heard what Bertie said.

"Tell him if that's what he wants," she said, "then that's all right by me. Because I *do* love him, you know."

Nicola struggled with herself. Plato's white horse would take her chariot one way, and his dark horse another. The struggle was resolved, for now she said to Irene, "I know that, Irene. I know that you love him a great deal."

Later, Nicola tried to work out how Irene could have managed such a volte-face. There are roads to Damascus, she told herself. People travel on them.

61

How the Cyclops Felt

The return of Bertie and Ranald Braveheart Macpherson took place on a Saturday. On that Sunday, Big Lou and Bob walked to South Queensferry and back, through Dalmeny, taking Finlay with them. Finlay was a keen walker and when unobserved would practise his leaps and pirouettes, sometimes using the bough of a tree as a barre or a fallen trunk as a platform from which to cast himself briefly into space. When he did this in Bob's view, he received enthusiastic applause – a compliment that would be returned when Bob, walking through the woods at Dalmeny, stopped to pick up the occasional felled pine and tossed it casually through the air – a caber arc across the sky.

Big Lou had left James in charge of the coffee bar. He had shown himself to be completely capable of running it single-handedly, and this had liberated her from the constant responsibility of ensuring a steady supply of cups of coffee, cheese scones, and bacon rolls. Like any owner of a small business, she had found the demands of work oppressive. Now she could take time off to spend in the company of Bob and Finlay, and she was luxuriating in the sheer pleasure of being with the two people who had come to mean everything to her.

Their plans for the Drummond Place Highland Games were now at an advanced stage. Permission had been obtained from the Gardens Committee, and several notices advertising the event had been prominently displayed in the area. Local businesses had donated prizes, and catering requirements were being met by Nicola's firm in Glasgow, Inclusive Pies, that had agreed to send over a large supply of Scotch pies at a very favourable price. James had been involved too: he had baked several trays of shortbread and obtained three kegs of ale to be served in biodegradable paper cups. Everything was ready and lined up, including the equipment needed for the events themselves – the caber, the hammers, the tug-of-war ropes, the sacks for the sack races, and bales of hay to prevent people from hurting themselves in the various contests planned as the afternoon's entertainment. Bob had even secured the services of a Scottish dancing team that would perform various dances on a raised platform, clad in short tartan skirts, tartan knickers, and white blouses with frills. A small pipe band, known for its enthusiasm rather than its skill, had agreed to play as the Games began, during the interval between events, and at the conclusion of proceedings. The prizes were to be awarded by Domenica's friend, Mary Davidson. Everything was in place.

As they walked through Dalmeny Estate, the Firth of Forth stretching out in front of them, Big Lou asked Bob whether he was proposing to enter any of the competitions himself. He thought about this for a while before he said, "I'm not sure, Lou. What do you think?"

"Some folk might think it unfair," Big Lou said. "It would be like giving yourself a prize, don't you think?"

"I wouldn't necessarily win," said Bob. "Some of my friends have agreed to take part. They're pretty good."

"Even so," said Lou. "Family hold back. You know that saying?"

Bob did. "You're right, Lou. As always."

She basked in his praise. Few people had ever said anything like that to Big Lou – indeed, throughout her life she had received very little praise from any quarter. She had worked hard on the farm as a child, and had received scant thanks or acknowledgement of her efforts. That was not because she had been unappreciated – it was simply because she came from part of the world where people did not think it necessary to say too much. You said what needed to be said and left it that. You did not waste words. And here was this man – this kind, considerate man, saying that she was right. Bless you, Bob, she said under her breath; bless you Bob, and thank you.

Over the days that followed, Angus helped Bob to install the platform, pitch the small marquee that had been hired, and generally prepare the grassy expanse in the middle of the Garden, where the main events were to take place. This was an open area, rather like a glade, which allowed adequate room for the tossing of the caber and the throwing of the hammer. The tracks events could take place on the perimeter of this space.

Observing the preparations from her window, Domenica reflected on the tribal nature of the forthcoming gathering. The prism through which anthropology viewed the world – the prism of *otherness*, had of course been abandoned, and not before time; now it was not the differences between societies so much as the similarities that engaged the attention of members of her profession. There was no difference, she thought, between these Highland Games and the trials of strength she had observed in the remote New Guinean village in which had spent six months in her early post-doctoral years. Human society, she felt, was much the same, whatever its external trappings. At heart we were all concerned with the same essentials: food, shelter, security, and status. All the rest was little more than the superficial complication of these eternal fundamentals. And complication, she told herself, was nothing of which to be proud. Complication was not the same as culture.

But what function, she wondered, did these trials of strength, these crude competitions to see who could throw things furthest, jump higher than others, or most effortlessly transfer heavy weights from one place to another? What was the point? Was it a form of mating selection: sorting out whose genes were the most likely to produce the fittest children, the offspring most likely to survive? Was it that simple, that socio-biologically focused?

And as for the strong men themselves – what went on in their heads? How did they see themselves? Were they concerned with strength because that was all they had?

It was not always a simple matter of being strong. She thought, rather inconsequentially, of Polyphemos, the one-eyed giant and son of Poseidon, who had trapped Odysseus and his crew in his cave. She thought of his rage and his throwing of boulders into the sea, and of his unhappiness. She thought of how he had been outwitted, because that was what such a person must fear above all – being outwitted by nimbler, more adroit opponents, who would laugh at you in your strength, would mock your ungainliness, and eventually, with impunity, evade your angry lashing out.

She felt sorry for Polyphemos. Odysseus and his men were interlopers, who stood for colonialism and intrusion. Polyphemos represented their horror of the *other*, the *indigène*, made to appear brutish when the brutishness, in reality, came from their own side – from those who would make the Cyclops creatures feel bad about themselves, feel inadequate, feel unentitled. Of course, such creatures would throw rocks into the sea in their rage. Who wouldn't?

62

Let the Games Begin

"Of course you're nervous," Big Lou said to Fat Bob on the morning of the Games. "These are the first Games you've ever organised yourself." She paused. "And dinnae worry, Bob – this is going to be a big success."

"Mega," said Finlay.

"Aye, mega," Big Lou agreed.

"I hope so, Lou," said Bob. "Last night I was lying there thinking, *What if nobody comes? What then?*"

Big Lou made light of his fears. "But of course folk are going to come. Lots have already said so: Angus, Domenica, Elspeth, Matthew; their wee boys. Matthew says he's had them all fitted with kilts for the occasion. They're all coming. Bruce. Antonia and that nun of hers. Those students who live in the flat below Angus and Domenica. You ken them, Bob? The tall one told me he was coming and that he'd bring some friends from the university who were good runners, he said. And James Holloway. He's coming. He said he was going to try throwing the hammer. He said he was already practising, but I had to tell him it wasn't an ordinary household hammer – the sort you get in toolboxes. He seemed a bit disappointed, but he's still going to try."

Bob looked a bit more cheerful. "That's reassuring, Lou. Having a big crowd makes a difference. Atmosphere, you know."

"You cannae have too much atmosphere," said Big Lou.

"There's atmosphere in the sky," joined in Finlay, who had been listening to the exchange.

"Aye, you're right there, wee fellow," said Fat Bob. "We'd be gey trochled if we didnae have atmosphere."

These predictions of a good turnout might have been optimistic, but, as eleven o'clock approached – the hour at which the Games were due to be inaugurated – a sizeable throng of people had assembled at the west gate of Drummond Place Garden.

"You see, Bob," Big Lou said, as the pipe band wheezed into action and the first members of the public were admitted. "It's already a big success."

Fat Bob was still slightly on edge, but it did not show, and within a few minutes of the opening of the gates he was beaming with pleasure, giving instructions to his helpers and greeting some of the professional strongmen whom he had lured into participating. The prize money – such as it was – would normally not have attracted any of these competitors, but favours had been called in. The fact that he was the organiser also helped: Fat Bob was popular on the Highland Games circuit, and most of the professionals present would have willingly supported him in any venture he undertook.

The pipe band paraded, the notes of *I See Mull* drifting up to the windows of the surrounding buildings. Dogs barked, children squealed with delight, the crackling sound of an ancient public address system announced the first of the events; smoke drifted up from the food stall; passers-by stopped to stare and then to join in. The few clouds that had been in the sky cleared, as if dispelling on the orders of the Chieftain of the Games. Angus, wearing his steward's badge, a Glengarry on his head, girt with his faded kilt, moved amongst the lined-up competitors, instructing one, exhorting another, pointing out on the programme where individual events would take place.

Near the judges' tent, the place from which the Games would be ring-mastered, Domenica sat with a small group of friends, enjoying the spectacle. To Dilly Emslie, one of her longest-standing friends, she pointed out Fat Bob, singing his praises as she did so.

"I've never seen Big Lou so happy," she confided. "And she certainly deserves it."

Dilly agreed that Fat Bob seemed to be just the right man for Big Lou. "It wouldn't seem right for her to marry a mousey man," she said. "And there are one or two of those around these days."

They surveyed the crowd, hoping to identify an example, but there was none that stood out, which was not surprising, perhaps, as that was what mousey men, by definition, tended not to do.

"I have a feeling," Domenica said, "that these Games are somehow *right*. It's odd. I don't quite know how to put it, but I feel that the *energy* here is just as it should be." She paused. "I know that sounds a bit New Agey, but . . ."

Dilly smiled. "I know what you mean. But I think you're right. There are moments when it seems that the world is at peace with itself. It's curious. But you know them when they happen."

"And we have had rather a difficult time, haven't we?" Domenica continued. "It seems to me that there's been so much confrontation and conflict. Where does one look for something positive?"

"Perhaps over there," said Dilly. She pointed towards a corner of the Garden where Elspeth and Matthew were standing with their triplets, holding the hands of the boys who, although overwhelmed by the noise and the movement, were looking at the scene with expressions of wonder.

"Look at them in their little kilts," said Domenica. "Oh, my goodness, I'm welling up inside . . ." She pointed at Bertie and Ranald Braveheart Macpherson, both of whom had been given a role as runners, carrying results from the judges of individual events to the tent where they were recorded. They, too, were in their kilts.

The caber tossing was about to begin, and their conversation paused as they watched five extremely muscular men, clad only in kilts, singlets, and rough working boots, take their place beside a couple of heavy poles. The first competitor, a red-haired mesomorph with impossibly bulging biceps, struggled to lift the pole, managed to get it vertical, and then, with a few staggering steps, tossed it across the grass. The judges ran after it, tape measures at the ready, to record the length of the throw. A cheer arose from Domenica's student neighbours. "Epic!" shouted one.

More cabers were tossed, and a winner was identified. This was one Rab Macreadie, from Fife, who waved a hand to his cheering supporters when his name was announced as winner. Then Billy Gilmore, from Ayrshire, won the men's long jump, and received his two-pound prize with dignity and modesty. Cookie Dunbar, from Kirkintilloch, won most of the women's running events, but generously declined to take home more than one first prize, donating it instead to the competitor who finished last. "It's not just coming first that's important," she said. "Coming last is important too."

Now it was time for the hammer throwing, and silence descended as the first of the entrants, Rab Macreadie, who had distinguished himself in the caber tossing, took to the field. Round and round he twirled before, with a grunt that could be heard throughout the Garden, he let slip the hammer shaft and sent the implement on its journey: a mighty throw that stretched the judges' tape measures to their limits.

The next to step forward was Bruce. In the past he would have done so with braggadocio, savouring the attention, preening himself as he prepared to throw. Not so now; he was a picture of self-effacement as if he had been pressed to compete only in order to keep numbers up.

He picked up the hammer and began to twirl. Round and round he went, until, after he lost his grip at a critical moment, the hammer prematurely left his hand, sailing off in entirely the wrong direction. Although not as burly as Fat Bob and his friends, Bruce was powerfully built, and the hammer had considerable velocity. It crossed the road and made landfall through the window of a house on the south side of Drummond Place, landing in a shower of glass. Nobody was hurt – not even the man at whose feet it came to rest. He was playing the harpsichord at the time, and barely missed a note.

"Caroline," he called to his wife. "A Turner Prize event has occurred in the drawing room."

And with that he continued his prelude by Bach.

63

A Hammer Hurled

The Games drew to a triumphant conclusion. The major events – the caber tossing and the hammer throwing – were dominated, as Fat Bob had expected they would be, by the professional entrants. The results of the tug of war, though, in which sixteen sides competed, were more difficult to predict. A team of Watsonians emerged victorious in the final heats, beating a side composed of Hearts supporters; the Fettesian team came last, not even managing to beat the Scottish Arts Club team, which was two members short.

The children's relay race, although supervised by Big Lou herself, was marked by blatant cheating. That was won by Olive's team, in which she, Pansy, and their friend, Arabella, elbowed, tripped up, and generally disrupted the efforts of Bertie, Ranald Braveheart Macpherson, and an unknown boy with spectacles. At the end of the race, the boy with spectacles complained vociferously to Big Lou, who unfortunately had seen none of the foul play.

"They cheated, miss," said the boy. "Those girls cheated like mad. They tripped me up twice and that one . . ." He pointed an accusing finger at Olive, "That one tried to tie my laces together."

Ranald Braveheart Macpherson nodded. "He's right," he protested. "They're the biggest cheats in Scotland. Ask anyone."

Olive bristled with indignation. "Oh, listen to the poor losers. Sad. Tragic. Listen to them. They can't bear the thought that the girls have won. They can't bear it."

"Male privilege," spat out Pansy. "It's always the same. They think they should win everything."

Bertie put an arm around Ranald's shoulder. "Don't worry, Ranald. We know we would have won. That's the important thing."

"But it's so unfair," sniffed Ranald Braveheart Macpherson.

Bertie sighed. "Lots of things are unfair, Ranald," he said.

Big Lou felt unable to disturb the result, although she had her suspicions, and the first prize was awarded to Olive's team.

"See," said Olive. "That's going to give you something to think about, Bertie Pollock. The days of boys winning anything are over."

"Finished," said Pansy.

Olive was ready to rub it in. "Yes, finished. Past tense, Bertie. You and Ranald and that stupid boy with glasses are *soo* past tense."

At the end of the Games, after the pipe band had played its last tune and the spectators had left the Garden, Domenica went back to her flat in Scotland Street to prepare for the dinner that she and Angus were hosting to mark the occasion. The menu was to be the same as it always was, as nobody really wanted anything new to happen. Why should they, when what they were used to was so perfect?

It was a slightly larger gathering than usual, though, as the students from down below came up, and Fat Bob and Big Lou had been invited too. While they were waiting for dinner to be served, Roger Collins and Judith McClure jointly proposed a toast to the newly engaged couple. "To Big Lou and Fat Bob," said Roger, raising his glass. "May your happiness be complete," added Judith.

There was a murmur of assent, but this was soon followed by spontaneous applause, led by the students. They knew neither Big Lou nor Fat Bob, of course, but they were still at that stage of life where they liked everybody – because they thought everybody was the same. And as the evening progressed, that liking became firmer and more real as they talked to the newly engaged couple. Torquil spent a good hour in conversation with Domenica and Big Lou, discussing the essays he had been writing at university. He had finished Nero and had embarked on an examination of the persistence of myth.

"Nothing is original, you know," he said airily.

"Including that statement," Domenica said wryly, but added, immediately, "Sorry, I didn't mean to sound dismissive."

Torquil laughed. "Oh, I don't mind. I have a tutor who sits there and winces whenever any of us say anything. Now *that's* dismissive."

"But what you say is true," said Big Lou. "When did you last hear anybody say anything new?"

Domenica looked thoughtful. "Occasionally somebody questions the consensus. But it's rare: there's immense pressure to conform."

This chimed with Big Lou. "Aye, you're right. People are becoming afraid to think for themselves. They're definitely afraid to express their views in case they offend somebody."

"The classics are pretty offensive," said Torquil. "Did you see that piece in the papers recently about removing texts that might offend students because of violence and so on?"

"Which would leave very little," said Domenica.

"Exactly," said Torquil. "Nothing, in fact. Take the *Odyssey*. Look at the way Odysseus behaves when he gets home. Where's the forgiveness? Not there. Instead, there's a bloodbath. Odysseus goes and . . ."

"Goes and behaves exactly like an ancient Greek?" interjected Domenica.

Big Lou laughed. "That's the way they were. And we were too. Scotland was red in tooth and claw until . . . well, yesterday, I suppose."

Domenica was not sure that she would go quite that far. "There must have been peaceful corners, surely. And relatively peaceful times, too. Isn't it thought that Macbeth's rule was benevolent and relatively untroubled? And yet he got such a bad press."

"Shakespeare's fault," said Torquil.

"Mind you," said Domenica, returning to the *Odyssey*. "I was thinking only the other day of the Cyclops. I forget why he crossed my mind, but he did." She paused. She remembered now: it had been his strength, and she had been thinking of the strong men at the Games.

Torquil became animated. "But there you are, you see. Polyphemos is completely pertinent to what we're talking about."

"What are we talking about?" asked Big Lou, and laughed.

"That whole encounter," Torquil continued, "can be read in a way that's sympathetic to the Cyclops. There are whole papers on the issue, you know. I've been wading through them. And a fantastic book, *The Return of Ulysses*. It's by a classics professor called Edith Hall. It's about how Homer has penetrated every corner of our culture – and still does. There are films . . . every year there are films that are replays of the story of Odysseus. Again and again. Computer games. Comic strips. Fan fiction. The lot. It goes on and on. It's *the* big story."

Domenica listened carefully. Torquil was right. "It's because we're all yearning for home," she said. "*Heimat*, as the Germans put it. We want to find the place we've lost. We remember it, but when we look out of our window, it's not always there. So we look for it."

"And do we find it?" asked Torquil.

"Sometimes," said Domenica, and then added, "Almost." She paused. "Scotland," she said simply.

Big Lou was silent. Then she said. "Is that what you're looking for, Domenica?"

Domenica looked into the eyes of her two friends, suddenly aware, with great clarity, of their humanity.

64

Love, Simpliciter

"The only reason I can be here," Elspeth said to Stuart, "is because James – you know him, I think, our au pair – has taken the boys back to Nine Mile Burn. He has his driving licence now, and it takes all the pressure off."

"I know what you mean," said Stuart. "The only reason I can be out is because of my mother. She looks after Bertie and Ulysses. She does the shopping. She does everything. I do my best to help, of course . . ."

Elspeth assured him that she knew that he did. "I've always known you were hands-on," she said. "With Irene being so . . ." She stopped herself.

"Don't worry," said Stuart. "You can say what you like. I made a mistake. I know that."

Elspeth waited. Then, very cautiously, she said, "In marrying her in the first place?"

Stuart looked down at the floor. He had been loyal. For years he had said nothing, but now he felt that he could be honest. He nodded.

Elspeth reached out and touched his forearm gently. He looked up. She did not say anything.

"Yes," Stuart continued. "We weren't suited. She never thought much of me."

"I don't know," said Elspeth. "I'm sure she appreciated you – in her way."

Stuart smiled. "You're being kind."

"No, I mean it."

"Perhaps she did," Stuart conceded. "Anyway, it's over now.

We had a long conversation yesterday. We've agreed to go our separate ways properly now. She told me she wants to marry Dr Fairbairn."

Elspeth hesitated. But did Dr Fairbairn want to marry Irene?

"Apparently he does," said Stuart. "And that makes me happy for her. I know that may sound corny, but I don't want her to be unhappy."

"Of course you don't." Elspeth paused. "Will you . . . Will you find somebody now?"

Stuart nodded. "I'm going to be serious about it. I'm ready."

"Good."

"And you?" Stuart asked. "How are you feeling . . . about everything?"

Elspeth shrugged. "I'm all right. I felt a bit low, I suppose, being stuck out of town with the boys, but I've thought long and hard about it, and I'm all right with that. I realised that it's going to get better. They're growing up, and I don't want to miss their being little anyway. I've reminded myself to value what I have."

"Which is a lot," said Stuart. "Matthew. And the boys. And that house of yours. And the view of the hills."

Elspeth smiled. "I suppose we should all remind ourselves of our view. Things may get bad, and then we say to ourselves, *Remember your view.*"

"And everything looks better," said Stuart.

Elspeth leant forward to whisper something to him. "Over there. Bruce. Have you heard?"

Stuart followed her gaze to the other side of the room where Bruce was sitting next to Sister Maria-Fiore dei Fiori di Montagna, deep in conversation. "I find it hard to believe," he said.

"Yes, it's true. He's going up to Pluscarden Abbey next week."

"All from being struck by lightning?" Stuart looked across the room again. "Will one of the monks shave his hair off, do you think? What about that hair gel of his?"

Elspeth laughed. "I read a book by Iris Murdoch in which one by one she made her characters better. At the end there was only one – a real psychopath – whom she had to work out how to redeem. So you know what she did?"

"No."

"She had him see a UFO. He was changed completely."

Stuart rolled his eyes. "Novels should be credible. That sounds a bit unlikely."

"Maybe it's life that's unlikely," said Elspeth. "Who would have thought that Big Lou would meet somebody called Fat Bob? And that he would toss the caber? And that they'd be blissfully happy?"

Stuart shook his head. "I always believed that," he said. "Always."

From a corner of the room, James Holloway tapped a glass for silence. "Every year," he said, "Angus writes a poem for us. This has not been an easy year for many, but perhaps that makes his poem all the more important."

"It does," agreed Dilly.

Angus rose to his feet. "I thought I might say something about love," he said. "Because love, as well all know, is at the heart of the lives of all of us – whether we know it or not." He paused. He closed his eyes. "So this is about love."

"Love," he began, "is as often about what does not happen
As it is about what actually occurs;
Love is to be found in things unsaid
When it would be easy, or tempting,
To say something harsh or unkind;
Love is a matter of silences,
Just as much as it is of open declaration;

Love is never concealed nor disguised,
Its face and position are always familiar,
Which means that it is only rarely
Mistaken for what it is not;
Love is not diminished by use –
That is its particular miracle; love fills
The entire space it is offered,
Never denies those who approach it,
Turns none away who mean what they say;
Love merely warns: 'Make sure you choose
That form of my expression that is true to you.'
Love remains on duty constantly,
Is never dimmed by night, nor too faint
To assume the demands of the day;
If you would say anything about love
To one about to embark on life's journey,
It might be this: There is only one guide
To which you should pay attention,
And that guide is love; only one voice
Whose whispers should be heeded,
And that voice is love; remember that, my dear,
I ask you to remember that."

Angus sat down. There was silence. But after a moment or
two, they heard, from outside, the sound of one of the pipers
who had entertained them at the Games playing a final tune
before he went home. They waited until the last notes had
drifted away. There is a particular silence at the end of a piece
of pipe music. It is very moving.

THE END
(for the time being, at least)